THE
SILLINGHAM ROBINS

THE

SILLINGHAM ROBINS

For Margaret

Enjoy the read!

Peter Watson

BY

Peter Watson

© Peter Watson, 2024

Published by Sillingham Press

www.thesillinghamrobins.com

A CIP catalogue record for this book is available from the British Library.

ISBN 978-1-0687984-0-5

Book layout and cover design by Clare Brayshaw

Cover images © www.dreamstime.com

Prepared and printed by:

York Publishing Services Ltd
64 Hallfield Road
Layerthorpe
York YO31 7ZQ

Tel: 01904 431213

Website: www.yps-publishing.co.uk

For Ruth
Without your endless support and patience during the
production of this epic, it would never have happened.

About the Author

Peter Watson was born in North Norfolk. Melton Constable to be exact. Most of his working life was spent in the IT industry where, as a technician, he was considered marginally better than useless. When it came to creative writing within marketing and management roles however, things improved. Once retirement dawned, the thought of producing legitimate fiction took root. He was urged to write about his experiences of being 'old' and, if he could remember, what life was like when he was young. So he eventually developed a plot, wrote 170,000 words, was advised to edit half of them out, and ended up with The Sillingham Robins. Hoping to prove that age is no barrier, his second novel is on the way.

What readers are saying about
The Sillingham Robins

Congratulations on a very readable book. I thoroughly enjoyed it. I look forward to novel number two!

I liked the main protagonists being from my age group. We have very few books of this ilk.

An excellent first novel written with compassion and empathy.

A good read for a long flight!

What a great bunch of characters. I feel I now know them well.

It started with excellent scene setting then gathered pace, and what a good ending!

As I got into it, I found it hard to put down.

Acknowledgements

Thanks go to Janice Rees, Elspeth Davidson, Joyce Horsefall, Peter Dodman, Alison Lobban and Amy Pebworth for critiquing and proofreading this novel before publication. Thanks also to Stephanie Vernier for putting me on the right editing pathway, Arton Baleci for his advice on self-publishing and Ming Ho for her suggestions on structure and flow. Special thanks to Hattie and Romilly Pebworth for inspiration on the front cover design. And to Steve Waters of ITSECPC for designing and producing The Sillingham Robins website.

I'd like to thank Frances Lawrence, CEO of Dementia Carers Count, for her support. If you are a carer or family member affected by dementia, visit the Dementia Carers Count website. https://dementiacarers.org.uk Thanks also to the Young Dementia Network who do so much to highlight the special needs of people of working age diagnosed with dementia. https://www.youngdementianetwork.org

And I must thank Bob Lawrence and Sandy Adair. Not only did they lend me their first names, but their tolerance of the ear-bending they received about this book's progress at the Ploughman's on many a Friday night was exemplary.

The poem recited in Chapter 22 is *Crossing the Bar* by Alfred, Lord Tennyson.

CHAPTER 1

The Cat's Unexpected Journey

It was a lovely day, as they so often are during late Spring in Sheringham. Tuppence's balcony was south-facing, so it got the sun and was protected from the cooling breezes that tended to blow in off the sea as the day wore on. She enjoyed lounging on her recliner reading one of her celebrity magazines. If the inclination took her, as it so often did, she would accompany her reading with a small gin and tonic. Or two. But she had a rule. There would be no gin and tonic until the sun was over the yardarm. In her view, that meant lunchtime. Well, lunchtime-ish.

Today was one of those restful occasions. At least it was until Tuppence was alerted by what she thought was an approaching siren. It was immediately followed by a dark shape sinking into her parasol and then springing away from the apartment block. This happened just as she had raised the glass towards her lips. Peace turned to shock. The glass missed her mouth and emptied its contents down her front. The liquid soon reached her waist leaving ice cubes lodged in her bikini top. She saw the shape heading in an arc towards the top of the Scots Pine that dominated the garden behind the apartment building. Her brain instantly recognised the shape as being a small tabby cat.

Tuppence was in no way built for speed but she scrambled up in time to watch the cat's progress. The hapless animal, visibly using up one of its nine lives, bounced from branch to branch on its downward journey, just like a ball in a pinball machine. It desperately tried but failed to get its claws to catch onto something that would slow its progress. Eventually, it reached the bottommost branch, almost managed to cling on, but then, exhausted, dropped the next ten feet towards the ground.

It was spared a hard landing though as the paddling pool belonging to the five-year-old son of the Payne family, who lived in a ground-floor apartment, had been placed in the shade under the tree and was full of lukewarm water. Generally, cats are not too keen on water, but the trauma of the journey had left it stunned, disoriented, and frankly amazed it was still breathing. So, for now, it stayed where it was.

The cat wasn't the only one in the pool. The five-year-old was there too. He took one look at the cat, slapped it on the head and started screaming. The cat, unsurprisingly, was not happy with this turn of events. After its painful journey, it felt that this smack was an indignity too far. So, turning its head towards the howling infant as he was scrambling out of the paddling pool, it sank its teeth into his receding backside.

The cat decided it was time to move and find somewhere safe to hide. It clambered over the side of the pool, shook itself and started to make its way towards a large shrub. Unfortunately, most of the muscles it needed to run efficiently hurt, so it didn't make very fast progress. The next thing it knew was being grabbed by the scruff of the neck by a man who shouted a lot. It was quickly deposited into a large bag which was then fastened at the top. Everything went dark.

Tuppence, watching the scene unfold from her high vantage point, decided to intervene in the cat's defence. She didn't know Harry Payne at all well, but he came with a bit of a reputation. "Mr Payne" Tuppence called from the balcony, "that's the cat from the penthouse. It belongs to the man who moved in a short while ago. I'll tell him you've got it, shall I?" Harry Payne looked around, trying to locate the voice. "I'm up here" shouted Tuppence peeling off a slice of lime that had stuck to her stomach. Harry Payne looked up. She had taken him unawares just as he was trying to decide how best to dispose of the miserable animal.

"This damned cat keeps crapping in my garden and now it's bitten my son. We're going to have to take him to A&E. Cat bites are dangerous. I've buried lots of people who've been bitten by cats!" He hadn't of course, but the truth was never something that seemed to particularly concern Harry Payne.

"I'll take a look at it if you like, I used to be a nurse." If Payne can lie so can I, thought Tuppence. "Anyway you don't need to go all the way to Norwich, the Minor Injuries Unit at Cromer Hospital deals with bites." Tuppence kept staring at him and he realised he now had to return the cat to the guy upstairs. He determined to give him a piece of his mind though. "I'll take the cat up once my son has calmed down". And he stomped off into his apartment.

I think I'd better go and warn the chap upstairs that Payne is on the warpath and tell him what's happened to his cat, thought Tuppence. An opportunity to meet him too! Now she had to make herself presentable, something she always insisted upon when out in public. So, she cleaned off the sticky residue from her front and undertook just a moderate amount of cosmetic application. She then sought out her best sarong and put it on over her shorts and bikini top. She had bought it from the shop at that lovely resort in Malaysia. It was hard to find one that fitted and, in the end, got the largest they stocked. These Malaysian women are so undernourished she thought at the time.

Tuppence headed for the lift. She pressed 6 and it whirred upwards. When she got out there was a very short corridor with an entry pad by the door. She pressed the bell. A low warble came from the small loudspeaker. Nothing happened for a while. Then there was a click and she heard what she felt was a slightly harassed "Hello."

She leaned down towards the bell push and shouted "I'm Tuppence from number 41 and I've got some news about your cat."

"My cat? What sort of news? He's in here asleep."

"I don't think he is I'm afraid. He seems to have fallen off your balcony."

"Pardon? Hold on." There was a crackle as the intercom phone was replaced on its hook. She could hear footsteps on a wooden floor and the door swung open. Tuppence was practised at taking in an image, assessing the person's taste, social and economic status, and something of the character within a couple of seconds of meeting them. She didn't always get it right, but she was pretty good. She saw Loake brogue boots, blue tailored Levi's, what looked like a white Vivienne Westwood fitted shirt and a classic oatmeal Harris Tweed jacket. The man inside was tallish, slimmish, going grey but not quite there yet, a square face that had been looked after, decorated with designer spectacles. His smooth hands hadn't seen much hard work. So, she immediately decided, he was well off. Not unreasonable, as he lived in the penthouse. The demeanour and his attire spelt well-bred British. The only slight question – why was he wearing a Tweed jacket on such a warm day?

As she had thought earlier he was harassed and to that was now added concern. "Hello, I'm Tony," and he reached out to shake Tuppence's hand. "Are you sure it's my cat? I thought he was in here asleep. Is he ......?"

"He seems fine" Tuppence butted in quickly. "He bounced off a few things and landed in a paddling pool. Harry Payne from downstairs has him and said he would bring him up to you after he'd checked on his son."

"Checked on his son? Look, come in, don't stand on the doorstep." Tony stepped aside to let Tuppence into the flat. "Go through to the sitting room, straight ahead."

Tuppence added well-spoken and polite to her character profile, and British became English as she recognised a little bit of a west country burr. She loved looking at people's houses, so was delighted to be invited in. Arty proved to be correct and while she didn't feel she could stop to look, she noticed what seemed to be old railway advertising posters covering the walls of the large hall. She reached the sitting room. It was beautifully decorated with lots of mainly watercolours on the walls, photographs of presumably family on shelves and sideboards and tables. What looked like sumptuous sofas and chairs were arranged in a large square. An array of table and standard lamps would provide subtle, warm lighting. It was all very cool and hygge she thought. The double sliding doors onto the balcony (she had a feeling Tony might call it a terrace) were open.

Tony followed Tuppence into the sitting room. "I'm sorry it's a bit untidy but my granddaughters have been here. They have a habit of hiding things and I've been desperately searching for my car keys. Have a seat. So please tell me about my cat and the boy. What happened?" he said as Tuppence's ample frame sank into a sofa. Fleetingly she wondered how she was going to get up again while retaining some semblance of elegance.

"Well, I live two floors down from you and was sitting on my balcony when I heard this shriek and your cat bounced off my parasol. He ricocheted down through the tree and landed in the paddling pool of the young lad on the ground floor. The boy was a bit frightened I suppose and screamed. He then cuffed your cat across the head. As he was jumping out, your cat sunk his teeth into the boy's bottom. Your cat was caught and dumped into a bag by the father, Harry Payne, who shouted that he would bring the cat up to you after he had checked if the lad was OK. Why would your cat have fallen off the balcony? They're usually so sure-footed, aren't they?"

"He's usually happy going up and down in the lift, I don't think he would have jumped." Tony looked puzzled, then aghast. "Oh, my goodness," he said, "I think I may have thrown him out of the window."

"What?" cried a startled Tuppence.

"Not intentionally! The kids tidy things up, as they would call it. They'd obviously tidied up my car keys and I found them in a toy kettle at the bottom of that bag." He pointed to a large fabric container with pictures of Peppa Pig on the outside, now lying empty. "It was full of toys and I pulled them out and flung them backwards looking for my keys. There are lots of fluffy animals as you can see, reds, yellows, blues. And there are a variety of cats. Willie, that's my cat, often burrows down into them and snoozes. I have a horrible feeling I might have hurled him backwards too. What a stupid thing to do. Thank heavens he's OK. Anyway, what about the child?"

"Don't know. I'm sure his father will tell you. Do you know Harry Payne?"

"No, wouldn't know him if I saw him I'm afraid. I only moved in about six weeks ago and have spent half of that time away and the rest in here trying to make the place liveable-in."

You've achieved that all right thought Tuppence. "Well I don't know him either, but Harry has a bit of a bad reputation. He's apparently quite unpleasant and I'm told you shouldn't trust him an inch. I told him I was a nurse and said I'd look at the wound. But he didn't take me up on the offer."

"Oh, so you're a nurse, are you? Maybe I should go down and apologise."

"No, I'm not a nurse. But he doesn't know that. I just wanted to check. You see I wouldn't put it past him to tell you the child was hurt more than he really is." Tuppence couldn't stand cheats and bullies, she had known so many of them during her acting career. Just then the doorbell warbled.

"Mm, that could be him now," said Tony. He leapt up, "You stay here, and I'll go and talk to him." He headed for the door. Tuppence listened carefully, fascinated to know what was going to happen.

Tony opened the door and was faced by a short, stout man in shorts and a tee-shirt carrying a hessian bag. "Hello," said Tony pleasantly but with a concerned look on his face, "I guess you must be Mr Payne. Tuppence has just told me what happened. How is your son?"

"Not very good thanks to your cat," said Harry. "Animals that attack children should be put down. I've a good mind to report it to the authorities."

"Oh dear, I'm sorry about that. He's normally very docile. He plays with my two grandchildren and he's never harmed either of them. Something must have provoked him. Is it a bad bite? Have you taken him to get it looked at?"

"No, he's too upset for that. He's just clinging to his mother. He's frightened to go out unless he's attacked again."

Ah, thought Tony, sounds as if the kid was more frightened than hurt and the bite isn't bad otherwise they are the sort of people to take him straight to the doctor. "If a cat bite breaks the skin you really should get it looked at. Why don't you let Tuppence have a look, she used to be a nurse I believe?"

"I'm not having some alcoholic floozy play around with my boy's bottom thank you very much. Your cat's in here." And with that, he began to unzip the hessian bag.

Tuppence, listening from the comfort of her seat in the sitting room, snorted with contempt. Snivelling little oik she thought. Alcoholic floozy indeed! Meanwhile at the door, "I think my cat may be a bit upset himself and could scratch if either of us puts our hand in there to get him out. Here, give it to me and I'll open it up on the floor so he can get out himself." Tony took the proffered bag, gently placed it on the floor and pulled the zip across. Out came a rather bemused-looking cat. He would have liked to speed quickly to a place of safety in the apartment but his limbs ached after his ordeal and he limped as fast as he could towards the sitting room. Halfway along the hall he paused, looked back, and fixed his eyes on the squat figure of Harry standing in the doorway. I'll remember you, he thought. He turned and limped into the sitting room, passed the reclining figure of Tuppence and headed for the upturned toy bag.

Tony picked up the hessian bag and handed it to Harry. "And another thing," said Harry, "Your cat, or kitten more like, keeps crapping in my garden."

"No, he's not a kitten," said Tony, "he's a year old. His name's Willie."

"It's very small."

"A family trait I'm afraid."

"What? Well you need to stop him soiling my garden. It's unhealthy for my son. Goodness knows what he could catch from it."

"I haven't come across your garden, where is that? I only know the communal gardens downstairs," said Tony knowing full well that there were no private gardens.

"It's outside my apartment. We have doors straight out onto it from our lounge. I don't want people sitting around looking into our windows."

"Are you sure it's Willie? He has a cat flap from the utility room onto the terrace and I've set up a little toilet for him out there in a small dog kennel. He's very good at using it. He doesn't come downstairs often."

"Well, I've seen him in my garden and he goes under one of the bushes."

"I'm so pleased he's that thoughtful. I tell you what I'll do," said Tony, "I'll pop down every morning with my pooper scooper and have a look to see if there are any deposits. I promise not to look in your windows. That's always the problem with ground-floor apartments, isn't it? A lack of privacy."

"Well we can't all afford penthouses," said Harry, and he turned on his heel and strode towards the lift. "You'll be hearing from me again if my son becomes ill!" The lift was still at that level, he stepped in and left the scene. That told him, Harry thought to himself.

Tony closed the door and returned to the sitting room. Tuppence was seething. "Well," she said, "I've been insulted before, but I've never been called an alcoholic floozy! And by a short, miserable little toe rag of an undertaker. Do you know what they call him in the town? Payne in the 'earse, that's what! Anyway, I'm sure the boy is OK. You won't be

9

hearing from him on that score. And as for his garden, it's all communal and you could sit right outside his window if you liked."

Tony smiled, "I tried not to upset him too much. Thank you for giving me the heads up though, it really helped." He looked at his watch, "I've missed the meeting I was going to, with all my key searching. I'll have to ring up to apologise." Tuppence sensed that it was time to go. She also sensed that getting up from the sofa would be a bit of a damage-limitation exercise. Seeing her beginning to struggle Tony offered Tuppence his hand. "Here," he said, "that's a ridiculous sofa. Far too low and squashy."

"Thank you," she said. "It's been nice meeting you and I hope Willie is all right." She walked into the hall.

"I like your pictures," she said stopping in front of the middle one depicting a large green steam locomotive hurtling towards Cornwall, Devon, Somerset or Wales if the description was anything to go by.

"Thank you," said Tony, "most people don't. They ask why I've got old posters on the wall."

"Oh, I do like them," said Tuppence. Then after a pause, "Why have you got old posters on the wall?"

"Because to me, they're not just old posters. I lived close to the railway, and my father worked on the railway when I was young, and I've always loved steam trains; the smell, the noise, the drama. I managed to pick them up at a specialist auction."

"Auction? You mean you had to pay for them?"

Tony chuckled, "I'm afraid so. Rather a lot actually. They're originals." He opened the door.

She stopped and turned before she reached the lift, "I'm planning a little drinks party soon for some friends. Maybe you would like to join us? It would be a good way of meeting a few nice people from the building. Harry Payne won't be there!"

"That's very kind of you, thanks. I do spend a bit of time in London but I hope I'll be here." He smiled as Tuppence called the lift.

"I haven't quite settled on a date yet, but I'll let you know. Bye!" She waved and disappeared into the lift. Tuppence had invented the party on the spur of the moment so now she needed to get something organised. Well at least it will give me something to do she mused as the doors closed and the lift whirred its way back to her floor.

CHAPTER 2

The Bench

Outside the front of the apartment building were a bench and two chairs. They were solid constructions built out of Norfolk Cedar rescued from the devastation of one of the so-called 'Great Storms' of a few years back. Arranged on a paved terrace they caught the afternoon sun and were surrounded by a tidy garden of lawns and shrubs that gave some shelter from any breeze coming up over the cliffs. The day after Willie's downhill adventure, they were occupied by Henry, Ken and Margaret, all in their early 70's.

Henry, like Tuppence, was fairly recently retired and found he now had all the time in the world to do whatever he wanted. But just like her, he couldn't come up with things he wanted to do in which to fill all the time in the world he now had. So mostly he was at a loose end. A tiny part of the solution was to sit on the bench with his friends, which often included Tuppence and his grandson Wayne, and put the world to rights. They also had their 'grumpy old men and women' days where they railed about social attitudes, politicians, bankers, the media and anything else that took their fancy.

Ken, on the other hand, didn't have a care in the world most of the time. Sadly, for the rest of the time, he was either angry, frustrated or upset, which is why Margaret, his wife, encouraged him to join Henry as often as he could. Margaret did have a care in the world. For most of the last several years, that was Ken. He'd become ill, and her job was to care for him. Ken on the bench gave both of them, in different ways, some space. She'd stayed for a while and now she was about to leave to get some respite.

"You'll look after him won't you."

"Of course. You just take an hour or so to yourself. We'll chat about the old times." By that, Henry meant he'd chat about the old times. Ken might respond. He might not. Margaret kissed Ken on the cheek and told him she wouldn't be long. Henry watched as she crossed the grass towards the steps down to the promenade. Her grey hair was lank. She was pale, wearing no make-up. She wore well-used clothes. The smile she gave Henry as she left was forced through a cloak of depression.

Henry decided to reminisce about good times he and Ken had as pupils at Paston Grammar School. He talked about football and cricket, then got on to the rock group they formed. "Can you remember The Travellers?" Ken continued to stare out to sea but a smile lit his face. "You played lead didn't you and I sang," said Henry. "Snot was on rhythm, Abel on bass." Ken nodded as Henry said, "Remember Fat Alex? He played drums so he could sit down for the whole session! His drum kit was rubbish and the hi-hat decidedly dicky. Got it all in a Jumble sale I seem to remember." He talked about dances they played at, what their favourite numbers were and their fan base which was that extensive he named and counted them all on the fingers of one hand.

"Can you remember when Fat Alex's hi-hat exploded?" Ken turned to him and giggled as Henry retold the story. The problem with the hi-hat was the spring that pushed the two cymbals apart after he'd crashed them together. It was knackered and took its time to expand, so if Fat Alex wanted a series of clashes, however hard he stamped on the pedal, all he'd get was a muffled clap. His dad repaired it with a much heavier-duty spring he found in his workshop. Unfortunately, the nut that held the whole thing together kept coming loose. It finally came off when the Travellers were playing at a youth centre. Henry was halfway through a very passable impression of Jerry Lee Lewis doing *Great Balls of Fire* when Fat Alex gave the pedal a particularly vicious thump. The expanding spring took over and the nut, like a bullet, shot straight up and shattered a fluorescent light fitting, showering Fat Alex and Abel, who was playing nearest him, with shards of white plastic light shade.

The top cymbal followed suit, arced forward missing Ken by inches and crashed loudly onto the front of the stage. Meanwhile the light fitting, having had its fixings at one end destroyed, swung down and struck Snot on the back of his head. It knocked him forward and he slithered off the stage into the welcoming arms of three of their biggest fans. As the light fitting swung down it exerted so much tension on the flimsy ceiling panel that it split away from the roof beams, disintegrated and crashed down onto the stage. The members of the band were peppered with bits of fibreboard and fifty years' worth of dust, splinters and bat droppings. It marked the premature end of their performance and a request from the caretaker never to darken the door of his youth centre again.

Throughout Henry's highly embroidered rendition, Ken smiled and laughed. There is still something deep in that damaged brain thought Henry. It was then that Tuppence, about to take a small amount of exercise, stopped to join them. Larger than life in more senses than one, she filled one of the chairs opposite the bench, so much so that Henry was mildly concerned about its ability to survive the experience. "I met the new arrival from the penthouse yesterday and had a little bit of a contretemps with that chap Payne who runs the undertakers. I'll tell you about it." In her usual rip-roaring fashion, she went on to explain what had happened.

Then, switching into Grumpy-Old-Woman mode, she set about the mobile phone signal in her apartment. She'd eventually managed to get through to a human being at the service provider, who blamed it on the fact that she lived in a building held up by steel girders. Tuppence explained that the signal worked perfectly well in office buildings which were also built with steel girders but that was as far as she got. On the same subject, Henry said he couldn't understand all these people who seemed to be permanently glued to the damn things. "Mobile phones are destroying the art of conversation," he said. "The number of people we get in our restaurant who sit down, plonk their mobiles in front of them, and then proceed to ignore each other. Christ," he said, "they don't need to pay our prices, they could ignore one another at home."

The restaurant he was talking about specialised in seafood of all sorts and its reputation extended throughout Norfolk. It had developed from what was originally a small café opened by Henry with his wife Elsie. That and a stall in town selling fresh crabs and other local fish were to supplement family income beyond the April to October crab season. Elsie originally ran the café while Henry concentrated on the family crabbing business. He'd now handed that and the stall over to his eldest son Paul while their daughter Michelle was in charge of the restaurant with Elsie still heavily involved. Henry added a bit of what he considered customer-side bonhomie to the enterprise, which wasn't often. He was usually considered surplus to requirements. A bit too old Michelle told him.

Henry didn't subscribe to this 'old' label. At 72 he still considered himself to be in late middle age. One thing he'd noticed about this aging process though was that people kept pestering him about his health. His response was always the same, "I'm absolutely fine on the outside, no idea what's happening on the inside." Mind you, his knees needed replacing, but then what do you expect when you spend your life leaning on the edge of a boat pulling heavy crab pots over the side?

He didn't have an apartment in Sillingham House. Instead, he and Elsie lived in a flint cottage a few steps from the Sheringham seafront. They'd moved there from Cromer six years previously after Henry had retired. Since then he'd spent much of his time being bored. He started taking a newspaper because he liked doing the crossword. But then he began to read what was in it and disagreed with almost everything he saw. So then he was not only bored but became angry too. His respite was joining the others on the bench.

Tuppence, not unlike Henry, and for the first time in her life, spent much of her time being bored too. As an actress she'd spent plenty of time 'resting' but that didn't mean doing nothing. There were auditions to undertake, scripts to be read, friends to catch up with after long tours away. As a result of yesterday's little escapade she at least had a short-term remedy. "Now," she said." I have something to tell you. I have decided to have a party."

"Lovely. Who's going to be invited?" asked Henry.

"You, if you behave yourself. And Ken and Margaret of course."

"I'm up for that," said Henry, "When?"

"Not sure. Soon though."

That sounds like fun, thought Henry, while Ken continued to gaze into the distance.

"Hello you three, putting the world to rights again?" Margaret had come back to collect Ken. "Have you been joining in today, Ken?" He turned towards Margaret and smiled but didn't say anything. "Come on, let's get you up to the apartment and we'll have a cup of tea."

"If you're not in a rush I'll pop him over to the cliff for a few minutes, he likes a quick look at the beach and sea," said Henry. Margaret smiled and nodded. "Come on old boy," and Henry helped him up and they walked slowly over the grass.

As Margaret took her place on the bench, Tuppence observed a woman who looked as if she had all the troubles in the world piled on her shoulders. "How are things?" she asked more brightly than she intended.

Margaret sighed, "They're not getting any better. His TIA's are getting more frequent." She looked at Tuppence and shook her head, "he can't speak now." Tuppence thought she was close to tears but wasn't quite sure what to do. Margaret was silent for some time. "Washing, dressing, going to the toilet. They're all a bit hit or miss, especially the toilet." She grimaced. "He just doesn't want me to help him with that kind of thing. He gets angry. Frustration I suppose. He's taken to emptying stuff down the pan. All his aftershave has gone. Luckily I managed to save most of my perfume." Tuppence nodded. "It's just so sad. I feel such a failure."

"No, of course you're not," said Tuppence.

There was more silence and then Henry returned with Ken. Margaret took his arm and they unhurriedly walked towards the main door of Sillingham House. When

Tuppence had first joined the others on the bench, Ken was much more engaged. He could be caustic, funny, rude and wise. He talked about his working life, his love affair with the violin, his family and particularly Margaret. A year ago it all changed. He had another TIA, what Margaret described as a mini-stroke, and it took away a lot of his cognitive ability.

From those earlier conversations, Tuppence had learned something of Ken's life. He and Henry had been close friends for sixty years or more. Unlike Henry, he left Norfolk once he left school, joining a computer company called ICT and hadn't come back to live until a few years ago. With his mathematical ability and logical mind he was a natural at these 'new computer things' as he described them. Ken became involved in some pioneering development and over time became a respected and in-demand expert in his field. Then he set up a consultancy with some colleagues to advise corporations and governments on the strategic application of IT. He was awarded an OBE for services to technology fifteen years ago.

After Ken and Margaret had gone, the two sat quietly for a time, deep in their own thoughts, saddened by Ken's deterioration. Henry felt he'd lost his best friend. He was in the same body, but it wasn't the Ken he knew. Whatever his thoughts though, he vowed to do as much for Ken as he could while he was still around. Tuppence broke the silence. "Right, I'm going for a short walk to think about my party, so I'll bid you farewell." They both got up, Tuppence squeezing herself uneasily out of the chair. While Henry headed for the promenade and home, Tuppence made her way slowly towards the boating pool where she would rest in the shelter for a few minutes before returning to Sillingham House and some party planning.

CHAPTER 3

A Dastardly Plot

The whole audience was hushed in expectation. The tragic figure of Fantine falteringly moved downstage. Softly, the strings and then the oboe began their melancholy journey, tugging at the heartstrings of everyone in the theatre. Tuppence prepared herself for another emotional delivery of the song that had become synonymous with her rise to stardom. A deep breath so that the all-important first line would sound like a whisper but be heard in the furthest corners of the auditorium. And then came the delicate soprano, *There was a time when men were kind.*

Except that there wasn't. Not a sound came from Tuppence's lips. Inside she was singing but outside there was nothing. Zilch. She carried on. *When their voices were soft and their words inviting.* Still nothing. Staring out through the Spot she could hardly see the audience, but she could smell the disbelief. The music tailed off. Then out in front of her someone's phone started to ring. "Turn that bloody phone off!" she shouted, but it just kept ringing. Everything went dark except for a pulsating green light just to her left. She turned her head, and slowly into focus came her phone ringing and angrily vibrating on her bedside cabinet. She grabbed it, touched the screen and, half asleep, shouted "What?"

"Christ Almighty! You get out of bed the wrong side this morning?" It was her friend Poppy.

"Eh? Oh, it's you. Not out of bed! Having a bad dream." She blinked her eyes. It was still dark. "What time is it?"

"Just after six."

"What?" yelled Tuppence, "why are you calling me at just after six?"

"I just wondered whether you'd fancy lunch in Norwich today?"

"Lunch? I haven't had breakfast yet!"

"It's just that Trevor announced last night he had a production meeting at the Theatre Royal in the morning and it struck me I could come with him. He's got to leave about eight and I don't want to go to all the bother of getting ready if you're galivanting somewhere else."

"Hold on a sec." Tuppence switched on the bedside light and looked at her calendar. "Yes, looks like I can."

"Wonderful," said Poppy "let's meet in the Maids Head at say, one-ish. Maybe you will have calmed down by then. Toodle-oo!" And she was gone. Tuppence swung her legs out of bed, shuffled over to the window, peered through the curtains and was greeted by dark clouds and drizzle. She felt guilty about snapping at Poppy so sent her a text, 'Sorry, bad dream, will smile later'. By return, she received happy face and thumbs-up emojis.

Just for a moment, she envied Poppy, always upbeat and optimistic, energetic, never taking offence. Whereas lately she was inclined to mope about rather. Why? she wondered. She loved where she lived, particularly the slower pace of life, her comfortable modern apartment, walking along the prom, breathing in air that didn't smell of traffic fumes. She did though miss the buzz of London and didn't have a wide circle of friends on her doorstep. And she did sit on her balcony drinking on her own far too often. "Maybe I need something to spice up my life," she said out loud.

What she needed she realised, was a project. Her whole working life had been one project after another. She needed something to get her teeth into. Find that and she would be back to her old self. The party could be the first. That little decision made, she began to cheer up. And in the meantime, she thought, there were plenty of shops in Norwich. A couple of hours of retail therapy might give her a few ideas. She'd catch an early train!

A leisurely breakfast later she popped out onto her balcony. The rain had stopped, the sky was clearing and it was getting warm. She decided to wear her yellow cotton dress with a design of climbing roses over it, a navy bolero jacket she had picked up at the John Lewis sale and her new Karen Millen sandals. And she'd put on her beautiful sapphire drop earrings Poppy and Trevor had given her for her last big birthday.

"To walk to the station or not to walk? That is the question," she orated. Then a flash of inspiration shot through her mind. Poppy had been bugging her to lose weight for months. That would be her next project. Lose weight! Walking to the station would be a start. It wasn't long before she set off at, for her at least, a brisk pace. The train to Norwich then took an hour. The newly invigorated Tuppence even walked into the city from Thorpe station, where she hit the shops. Soon after one o'clock, she arrived in the bar of the Maid's Head Hotel to see Poppy sitting on a large leather sofa, waiting for her.

The two had met at Drama School back in the late 60's. Poppy's real name was Georgiana Antoinette Beresford-Pease. She came from a family in the Cotswolds with enthusiastic aristocratic pretensions. Her mother 'had horses' and her father was the ubiquitous 'something big in the city'. Georgiana never knew exactly what he was big at, but the family was never short of money.

At school, she showed an exceptional talent for acting and dance and her mother decided she would have ballet as a career. Georgiana preferred the likes of Jive and Twist however so when it came to auditions for The Royal Ballet she made sure she wasn't quite up to standard. Then, without her mother's knowledge, she applied for a place at the Royal Central School of Speech and Drama. She was accepted. Her mother, who had made a career out of being appalled at anything she couldn't control, was duly appalled. Her father though managed to calm things down explaining that he could introduce Georgiana to plenty of suitable young men in London, after which she would settle down and deliver the requisite number of grandchildren.

Their fellow students, being students, made fun of both the girls' names. Tuppence then was Dora Nobbs. Named after her maternal grandmother, her parents didn't seem to recognise the consequences of mixing that and her father's surname. Dora defused the taunting by laughing about it herself. On the odd occasion when that didn't work, she used a devastating right hook picked up from an amateur boxing uncle.

The two girls became great friends. While Dora had dark hair and was well-built, Georgiana was a redhead, tall and slim. However, as she told Dora, when chests were handed out she received more than her fair share. She'd often used this as an excuse for not doing ballet as all the ballerinas she knew were like drainpipes. As the attempted bullying subsided, the two became an integral part of student society. They were rather affectionately known as 'Nobbs and Knockers'.

"Feeling better?" smiled Poppy as Tuppence sat next to her. "My goodness, you were an old grump this morning. Mind you I suppose it was rather early. I've just ordered a nice bottle of Taittinger for us to get on with. Trevor will be here about three, so we've got lots of time to catch up." Not a pause for breath as usual thought Tuppence as Poppy meandered into a tale of what she'd been up to at the old Drama School. How could anyone ever be miserable with Poppy around? She just sparkled and was as effervescent as the bubbly they were about to consume.

A young man, snake-hipped, with black hair, an attempt at designer stubble and looking very smart in his waiter's outfit, with a badge on his chest that read 'Leon', brought the bottle in an ice bucket along with two glasses. With a little bit of difficulty, he managed to remove the foil cap and untwist the wire, putting both in his pocket. He then grasped the neck of the bottle in his left hand and started to twist the cork with his right. It didn't move. The two ladies gave him an encouraging look. His eyes held Poppy's as his smile morphed into a grimace. His brow furrowed.

As Tuppence and Poppy smiled encouragingly, Leon's face began to turn pink. The cork refused to budge. "Young man," said Tuppence, "turn the bottle, not the cork. Look, pass it here." She took the bottle from him, grasped the cork with her left hand and the base of the bottle in her right and twisted it firmly away from her. The cork soon popped gently out of the neck and she directed the stream of champagne into first one glass and then the other. She then handed the bottle back to Leon who placed it in the ice bucket, inclined his head slightly, and then left still forcing a smile.

The two friends never had a problem finding things to talk about and spent the rest of their time catching up on one another's news. This included Tuppence's new weight loss plan and her forthcoming party for which they settled on two potential dates. They decided not to go into the restaurant for a meal and instead stayed for something light in the bar. In no time at all they found that they'd emptied their bottle and debated, but only for a few seconds, about getting another. Leon delivered the replacement and opened it expertly. The ladies clapped, Leon bowed and he walked away with a broad smile on his face.

They'd just ordered a coffee when Poppy's husband Trevor walked in. He gazed at them, then at the empty bottle upside down in the ice bucket, and then back to them. "Pissed again I see," he sighed with a resigned look on his face. "Well you'd better pop to the loo, we've got a long journey."

"Yes sir," said Poppy giving him a mock salute. She giggled and nipped off, rather unsteadily, to the toilet.

Trevor and Tuppence had been friends almost since the day he and Poppy had met. Tuppence had been delegated to give him the once-over at a party they were attending. At the time he was a jobbing pianist working the clubs in London and doing rather well for himself. This led to a short, intense courtship and a long and happy marriage. That was despite the initial antagonism of Poppy's mother. Her label of 'some sort of bordello entertainer' endured until Trevor collected his gong at Buckingham Palace with an adoring wife and daughter on his arm.

Tuppence said her goodbyes to Poppy and Trevor. She stayed on to finish her coffee. Then the time came to get up, which would have proved a bit of a challenge even before she'd consumed a bottle of wine. She decided it needed a few more minutes thinking about it and fluffed up her hair instead. As she pushed her hands through her hair, she felt something solid followed by a little tinkling sound behind her. When she checked she discovered one of her lovely earrings was missing.

She looked around her, on the sofa and floor, but could see nothing. With some difficulty, she shuffled round and noticed there was a gap between the back of the sofa and the wall. With even more difficulty she managed to turn and kneel on the cushions. Peering down behind the sofa she could just make out her missing earring, lying at the very end where a screen jutted out from the wall. She grunted, turned back, and with a monumental effort, manoeuvred herself up from the sofa. While she got her breath back, she quickly texted Poppy to thank her for lunch, then set about the job of working out how to recover her earring.

The bar had been reasonably busy during lunch but was now empty. No staff were in sight either. Tuppence decided to move the sofa away from the wall so she could reach her jewellery. She grabbed one end and pulled. It didn't budge. Then she heaved with all her might but even with her not inconsiderable beef behind it, there was still no movement. She crossed to the bar and called to see if anyone was near. No response. Fuelled with Champagne her confidence was high, so she decided to crawl into the gap behind the sofa to retrieve the earring herself.

She left her bag, jacket and shopping beside the sofa and with some effort got down onto her knees. Crawling wasn't in Tuppence's skillset. There were bits of her anatomy front, back and sideways that were going to take up all the space in the gap behind the sofa. But she was not about to be thwarted, and in she squeezed. It was a tight fit but with much effort, she set off. She didn't so much crawl as wriggle. After a couple of stops for breath, she reached her goal, picked up her earring, managed to put it back on and prepared to go into reverse.

It was then she heard the voices. People, at least two of them, were coming into the bar. Now what was she to do? Tuppence was in a dilemma. She could start edging out backwards, or she could call out for them to move the sofa, or she could just wait until they had gone. She heard a voice say, "This won't take long. We'll sit here. Michael, pull up a chair." In that case, she thought, I'll stay where I am. It will be less embarrassing. She felt the back of the sofa press into her side as two people sat down.

"Now, you need to know, I am not a happy bunny. And if I'm not a happy bunny, you're not going to be a happy bunny. Is that not right Michael?" Tuppence's antennae homed in. What's going on, she thought.

"That's right boss," said a voice coming from a bit further away, presumably the person sitting on a chair. "I've told him that many times, but he won't listen." Tuppence's ear for accents switched on. He had spoken in a nasal drawl from somewhere near Birmingham.

"Now, I said I was not a happy bunny and I'm not a happy bunny for two reasons. One, I was just getting ready to go out to the first tee when Michael phoned and asked me to come up to this God-forsaken place and beat some sense into you. I have just driven one hundred and twelve miles to get here, and I know that because satnavs on Bentley's don't lie!" Jesus, thought Tuppence, what's going on here? Is it some sort of family feud? Is it a business problem? Maybe it's something criminal.

"The other reason is, it has been explained to you what you have to do and why, but you refuse. Why is that?" This voice, calm but with a definite edge to it, registered in Tuppence's mind as coming from the East End of London but over the years had been worked on to become more rounded. Maybe that was to fit in with people who drove posh cars. He sounded quite a bit older than the Birmingham man. "Michael, get me a coffee. And bring it in yourself, I don't want any nosey waiters hanging around." There was a long pause. "Well? I'm waiting," said the older man.

A deep and distinctly Norfolk accent replied, "You're trying to blackmail me and I'm not having any of it. I've done nothing wrong."

Tuppence heard a door open and then close and the Birmingham voice saying, "Your coffee boss," followed by the sound of a cup and saucer being placed on the table.

"I wouldn't have come here at all, but your ape became very threatening. I decided to tell the boss to his face."

"Did you really," said the older man, "well that wasn't such a good idea. I'm afraid the price has now gone up to cover my costs and disruption."

Just at that moment, there was a 'ping' from Tuppence's phone. In the silence, it sounded like Big Ben. She realised she still had her mobile in her hand after texting Poppy. Her heart stopped. She held her breath.

"What was that?" came the East End voice, "was that a phone?

"Not mine boss", from the Birmingham man. "What about you?"

"Don't know," said the man with the Norfolk accent. "Maybe. It makes that noise when I get a WhatsApp."

"Check it." The voice was now much harsher. "Michael check if there's anyone around?"

Tuppence could hear some shuffling and the door opening and closing again. Hardly breathing, she was petrified. What if they found her? What would she do? More to the point, what would they do? After a few seconds that seemed like minutes, she heard, "Nobody about Boss. Just us three."

"Well?"

"I've got a couple of unread WhatsApp's so it could have been me."

"Switch it off. I don't want any more interruptions."

Struth, thought Tuppence breathing again, that was close. She quickly and carefully turned the sound on her phone to silent. Then, with what subsequently she told people was incredible presence of mind, she thought, I'll record what's going on. If it's as criminal as it sounds, I'll give it to the police. She clicked on her Recorder App.

"Now let's stop messing around. Michael, have you shown him the photographs?"

"Yes Boss. I said once he's paid up, he could keep them."

"Well done. You don't think that's a bit dodgy then? Old man like you, arm round a pretty young thing, leering at her?"

"I'd had a few after the rugby. All of us were a bit plastered. Just putting your arm around someone when you're singing isn't a crime."

"It didn't stop there though, did it? You went off with her." There was an accusing air to the older man's voice.

"Come off it. She said she didn't feel well and needed some fresh air. I just helped her outside. She was in as bad a state as the rest of us."

"And?"

"And nothing!" said the Norfolk man, obviously getting very annoyed. "She almost collapsed, I held her up, and after a few minutes she said she felt better, and I took her back inside".

"Well, that's what you say. We know better than that though, do we not Michael? Let me show you a couple of other photographs we have."

Tuppence heard the rustling sound of paper being withdrawn from an envelope. "There you go".

There was a gasp. "What the hell are these? I didn't do any of that!"

The older man spoke again, his East End accent coming through his acquired urbanity, "Well, everyone knows the camera doesn't lie. We may have done a little bit of photographic manipulation but only an expert would know that. Add these to the video we have of the party in the pub where you were being 'very friendly' shall we say and I think people would quickly come to the conclusion that you weren't the upstanding pillar of the community you have made yourself out to be. What do you think your wife would make of these? Or the rest of your family? And the vicar? I hear you're a churchwarden."

There was nothing coherent coming from the Norfolk man's mouth, just "What? This is …. I didn't …"

"Now, we've asked you for a small payment, after which you can have all of these to do with as you please and you will hear no more from us. However, as I mentioned, you've caused me to miss an important game at my golf club today, so the price has gone up. It's now £150,000!"

"What! I can't afford that."

"You should've thought of that before you upset me."

"And how the hell can I trust you to give me all the photos."

"Michael will tell you, my word is my bond and I promise you, you will get everything and never hear from us again. You've got exactly a week to deliver your payment. Michael has explained the arrangements for this."

There was a long silence. Tuppence was desperately trying to breathe quietly. She was shaking, frightened to think what would happen if they discovered her.

Finally, the now resigned man from Norfolk said quietly, "I suppose I don't have a choice, do I?"

"No. You don't."

"You might get it in two or three chunks. It's not easy coming up with that sort of money."

"Come off it," said the Eastender, "We know you are a wealthy man or we wouldn't have wasted our time on you. We do our research! The money can come in as many chunks as you like as long as it's all with us in a week's time." There was a pause. "We've got you by the Orchestras me old China. Michael will be in touch by phone. I have to go. Michael, a word."

Tuppence felt someone get up from the sofa and shortly afterwards a door open and close. All was then silent apart from her breathing. She kept that as quiet as possible and heard a couple of faint groans. No doubt Norfolk Man was still there. She wondered whether she should call out to him or just stay hidden. Before she could decide, she felt him getting off the sofa and heard the door open and close again.

Oh my goodness thought Tuppence, that chap is being blackmailed! I'm a witness! I'll have to do something about it. Call the police, that's what I'll do. She turned her voice recorder off and thought about dialling 999. Then she realised she would have to tell them where she was. It would probably be best to wait. The birds had flown the nest anyway so there was no chance of them being caught. Now she just had to get out from behind the sofa.

That turned out to be easier said than done. Sliding in forwards on her stomach was difficult enough but going backwards was an entirely different proposition. She pushed back to try to get up onto her knees, but her bum wedged itself between the wall and the back of the sofa. She tried again, with the same result. After a few attempts, she began to panic. How on earth am I going to get out of here? she thought. The embarrassment of calling for help and being dragged out by her ankles was beyond the pale.

She tried another method by pushing with her hands and wriggling her thighs. It worked and she moved a couple of inches. She rested and then did it again. It was hard work and she had to stop to get her breath back after each push. She was concentrating so much on the task at hand, she didn't hear the door to the bar open. It was Leon, who had been told by the Norfolk man as he went out that someone seemed to have left some shopping and a jacket behind. He soon found them beside the sofa. The sofa, from behind which were slowly emerging a pair of legs with bright yellow sandals attached to the ends. Leon was transfixed.

It didn't take him long to work out who was at the other end of the legs. It was the larger of the two old dears who had lunch and drank an awful lot of booze. Out the legs came, a little bit at a time accompanied by grunts from the body pushing them. Soon Leon saw that these legs were attached to a large white bottom. The dress Tuppence was wearing was now gathered about her waist. Luckily, whenever she wore dresses Tuppence abandoned skimpy underwear, so today she had on a pair of her very best passion-killers.

Leon, for all his attempts at worldliness, had never experienced the likes of this before. It was way beyond his job description. In his imagination, it was like a larva emerging from a cocoon. On one of its frequent halts, he fleetingly wondered whether he should grasp it and give it a pull, but sensibly decided against it. Eventually Tuppence in her entirety emerged from her hiding place. She was met by a wide-eyed, open-mouthed Leon her bag and jacket in one hand, shopping in the other.

"Hello," she said. "Don't just stand there give me a hand. And for goodness sake shut that mouth. Have you never seen anybody emerging from behind a sofa before?" Between them, they managed to get her vertical and she brushed herself down. "It's far too long a story to explain," she said. "Did you see three men leave the bar a few minutes ago?"

"Did they shove you behind there?" he asked.

"No, I just happened to be behind the sofa when they came in."

Leon just stared at her, even wider-eyed. "So did you see anybody?"

"I saw one man. He told me someone had left things behind."

"Did he speak with a Norfolk accent?"

"He just spoke normal."

"Not London or Birmingham?"

"No, just normal."

"Norfolk then. So what did he look like?"

"He just looked normal" said a confused Leon. This is not going to be easy, just be patient girl, Tuppence thought. She got her little notebook out of her bag.

"Alright. How old do you think he was."

"Pretty old." She stared at Leon, willing him to be a bit more useful. It worked. "Older than my dad."

"How old is he?"

"My dad? He's fifty-five."

"Probably in his sixties then?" Leon nodded. "How tall? Well built?"

"Shorter than me. I'm one hundred and seventy-five centimetres."

"Jesus! What's that in real money? Don't worry I'll work it out later. What about his hair?"

"He had quite a lot of hair. And it was grey. He had a bit of a beer belly too. And a red face. Been outside a lot. Had light brown corduroy trousers on and brown shoes." Leon was getting into his stride. "Checked shirt, cream with brown lines. A hairy brown jacket with patches on the elbows. Looked like a farmer."

"Anything else?"

"I only saw him for a second or two, then he was off. Has he done something wrong?"

"Don't think so," said Tuppence, "I just want to trace him if I can. Anyway, thank you, Leon, you're very kind to have retrieved my belongings. Could you get me a taxi? I need to get to Thorpe."

"Sure," said Leon and quite happily trotted off. Wait 'til I tell the lads about this, he thought.

Fifteen minutes later Tuppence was at the station and was able to get a train ten minutes after that. She wondered what on earth she should do. She decided on nothing until she was able to talk to someone about the whole episode. The boys on the bench were her best bet she thought. Maybe they would be there when she got back home. During the whole episode behind the sofa, adrenaline must have counteracted the effects of the champagne. Now it resumed its influence and as the train jogged along and the sun shone in through the windows, she nodded off and only woke up as it pulled into Sheringham station.

CHAPTER 4

Tony Joins The Gang

While Tuppence was supping a little too much champagne in Norwich, Tony was drinking too much coffee on his balcony. He was suffering a bout of uncertainty over his pending retirement. What would he do? After all, retirement was akin to unemployment and he'd never been unemployed in his life. It was still not too late to change his mind, his successor hadn't accepted the job yet. Come on, he said to himself, you are Chairman of Brodie Vellum, one of the country's biggest advertising agencies, you should be more decisive.

He gazed out over the golf course now resplendent in Spring sunshine, listened to the waves gently lapping on the beach and the gulls cawing overhead, then looked down at Willie who was purring as he cleaned his paws. All was peace. "No!" he said and banged his hand on the table causing Willie to jump and scamper away. "You're not changing your mind. Let's get the timetable settled and you can get out completely." He looked over towards the cat who now sat staring at him quizzically, "Get yourself sorted Willie, we'll go down to the garden."

If he'd been asked, Willie would have certainly backed Tony's retirement. He had a near-perfect life. A warm comfortable bed, food appearing twice a day, his own cosy khasi with plenty of grey granules to scrape over his poo. From his high vantage point, there were so many exciting sights and smells. The sea, the pine trees, the often-new mown grass in the garden, the occasional exhaust fumes drifting upwards on their way to the ozone layer, they were all part of his daily experience. The only danger came when large white birds bigger than him would swoop over his territory prompting him to dive noisily through his little door.

After telling Harry that he would clear up any of Willie's deposits from the garden, Tony thought he ought to keep to his word, so he had bought a long-handled pooper scooper and some poo bags. Out he went to the lift with Willie trotting along behind. They went down to the ground floor and Tony opened the door to the garden. Willie shot out, running towards the first of the big bushes. Tony searched but only came across one suspicious item which didn't look quite like cat's poo. It was also slightly squashy which eliminated Willie from the suspects as any of his would have become hard by now. Tony had an idea. He got down on his knees, leaned over and started pulling the offending object apart.

"What the hell are you up to?" barked a gruff voice from behind him. Tony turned to see where it was coming from and found he was looking up at Harry Payne.

"Ah ha! I was just looking to collect any of my cat's poos as promised," said Tony getting to his feet and brushing grass cuttings from his jeans.

"Oh, it's you. Have you got some sort of fetish then? People don't normally play with crap before they collect it."

"Indeed no, and nor do I. It's just that this is the only piece I can find. And it doesn't belong to my cat!" said Tony.

"How the hell do you know that?" from a genuinely incredulous Harry Payne.

"First of all, it's too fresh and secondly, it's not cat's poo. It's from a fox! Have a look and you'll see it's got some feathers and seeds in it." Payne turned up his nose.

"No thank you!" he said crinkling his face. "I haven't seen any foxes around here."

"They'll be around mainly at night."

"They're dangerous. They'll attack kids. We should report it and get it disposed of."

"They don't as it happens. Foxes won't hurt anyone unless they're cornered or protecting cubs. They're far less dangerous than a lot of dogs."

"How do you know so much about foxes? I thought you came from London."

"There are lots of foxes in London as it happens, they're just good at hiding. No, I was brought up in the country. Knowing about wildlife was just part of growing up."

"Even inspecting their," Payne hesitated and pulled a face, "crap?"

"Absolutely! If you look at it, pull it apart to see what the animal has been eating, it's a great way of telling what's around when you can't actually see it."

Tony thought it was about time to move on, so changed the subject, "We haven't really met. I'm Tony Goodman. I moved up a couple of months ago."

"Yes, there's quite a few of you Incomers in this place," said Payne.

"Really? I've only met one other person and that's Tuppence. I've been so busy tying up loose ends in London that I haven't had a chance to meet anyone else." He thought maybe he should defuse any second-home issues.

"I've sold my house in Richmond, well almost, and I'm looking forward to settling down here. My daughter and family live near Norwich."

"So, have you retired then?" A bit of a breakthrough maybe.

"Near enough, yes. I'll end up doing a couple of days a month until I can get out completely. What about you? You look too young to retire." Tony was trying hard and he heard a quiet groan from Harry Payne. A realisation that he was going to have to engage in some sort of conversation.

"I run Payne's Funeral Services."

"Really? Go on."

"Oh, Payne's has been a family business in Cromer for over a hundred years. My great, great, grandfather set it up in 1881. It was Smith's then, J. Smith & Sons, Undertaker. It became Payne's when my grandfather on the other side took it over in 1961."

"Goodness me, that's amazing! Did you inherit it from your father then?" said Tony, who gazed at Harry in a 'well tell me more' sort of way. Harry could see he was not going to get away easily.

"Inherit's the wrong word. It was foisted on me."

"You didn't want the business?"

"No, I didn't. I told my father I had no intention of touching dead bodies, dropping them in holes or pushing them into furnaces. And I certainly didn't want anything to do with negotiating prices for dispatching said bodies with grieving relatives, or wearing a top hat and marching in front of a hearse."

"Mm, I suppose it could be a bit depressing."

"Depressing's not the word. I had to work in the business while I was still at school. The smell of formaldehyde just stuck around on my clothes. I used to get the piss taken out of me something rotten. Then I got the grades for University but was soon put right on that score. I had to go straight into the business. Family bloody pressure!"

Goodness me what an angry man, thought Tony, "What would you rather have done?"

"Well, that doesn't matter does it? It didn't happen," said Harry Payne in what was clearly the end of the conversation. "Anyway, I've got to go," and he started to walk away. Then he turned round "It's Harry, by the way." And off he went.

Well Harry Payne doesn't seem to be that bad, thought Tony, just angry, disappointed, bitter maybe. I could imagine me being like that if I had been bullied into following a career I was not interested in. No wonder he is a bit touchy and grumpy. I wonder what he truly wanted to do mused Tony as he cast his eyes around for Willie. He spotted the little cat peering out from beneath a shrub not too far away. "Come on Willie, let's get back upstairs" he called and walked off towards the door with Willie dutifully trotting along behind.

Ten minutes later, having decided to take a walk along the cliff path for some exercise, he left Sillingham House just as Margaret was entering with Ken. Not knowing her but faintly recognising him, he held the door for them. He saw two men sitting on the bench at the front. One looked familiar but the younger one was new. They turned to look at him as he walked past, so he smiled, nodded and said, "Good afternoon".

"Good afternoon," said Henry.

"Hi", said Wayne.

"You're pretty new here aren't you?" said Henry, "I think Tuppence has mentioned you."

Tony paused and said "yes I've been in the process of moving in for a couple of months now. I'm just about there."

"We should introduce ourselves. I'm Henry. My old friends Ken and Margaret live here and I often visit them. I live in the middle of town. And this young lad," he said gesturing towards the 29-year-old sitting next to him, "is my grandson Wayne." Wayne smiled and nodded.

"Well, it's good to meet you. I'm Tony and I live right up there," he glanced up to the top of the building, "with an almost permanent lodger."

"Lodger?" questioned Wayne.

"A feline one!" answered Tony. "He's my daughter's but seems to be permanently fostered here. I'm not sure why she got him in the first place. She already had an older Tom who took great exception to a new model arriving. So, I suppose he's mine now."

"Why don't you join us," said Henry pointing to one of the chairs opposite.

"Why not?" said Tony thinking it was a good opportunity to meet some locals. He sat down facing the other two.

"Talking about your cat," said Henry, "Tuppence said it had a bit of an accident".

"Yes, I took him to the vet and amazingly he wasn't badly hurt. He's fine now."

"You threw him out of the window I hear."

"He did what?" squealed Wayne.

"Well not on purpose! Did Tuppence tell you the boy's father came up and complained?"

She did. So you've met Harry Payne?" said Henry, chuckling. "He has a bit of a reputation for being a misery-guts. Payne by name, pain by nature I hear. Ken and I went to school with his father. He did well turning the funeral business around, although I hear Harry has grown it even more since."

"He did seem a bit grumpy, let's say. Funnily enough, I was talking to him earlier. He's not a happy man. There's probably more to him than meets the eye."

"So, what about you," said Henry. "What made you move up here?"

"I've been working in London for many years and I'm just about retired. I wanted to get away from the hustle and bustle, back to the country. And away from my old company being able to get hold of me too easily!"

"So why Norfolk?"

"Oh, I've been coming up to North Norfolk since I was tiny," said Tony. "We lived in Berkshire. My father worked on the railways and we used to get cheap travel, so it was pretty easy for holidays. We came to Cromer, Sheringham. Great Yarmouth. Wells sometimes."

"So why settle in Sheringham?" asked Henry.

"It was mostly my daughter being sensible. I thought I would like a nice old cottage in the middle of the countryside with a big garden. She said, Dad, you're getting old. Old houses take lots of upkeep. You need to be close to shops, medical facilities, and a pub. And it won't be long before you have to stop driving. You need to live in a small town. Also, get a bungalow or a flat with a lift, so everything is on one floor. It will be better as you get decrepit."

"That's nice," said Wayne.

"She lives in Aylsham," Tony added in explanation. "Works part-time at UEA. She said I'd like it up here. Be near the twins too. She's got eight-year-old girls."

"What line of business are you in?" asked Henry.

"Give him a chance Grandad. You sound like you're conducting an interview," said Wayne pulling a face. "Sorry about that, but he always wants to know everything about everybody."

"That's alright," said Tony, smiling. "A bit like me! I'm about to leave the world of advertising."

"How did you get into that?"

"Long story." Tony paused thoughtfully. "I'll give you the short version. I was brought up in Hungerford. I didn't do that well at school so went on to technical college and came out as a draughtsman. Worked in a factory for a while doing technical drawing, then joined a surveyor's practice. I found myself drawing building plans but then also sketching what the outcome would look like. Did well at that and then for various reasons moved to London and joined an advertising agency. Did graphic work and then somehow got into the copywriting side which also seemed to go well. Eventually, I ended up in management."

Tony thought he'd done a pretty good job of giving a bit of background without going into the nitty-gritty. He omitted to say that he'd been married twice, had a colourful life mixing with lots of well-known people you see on TV, and had earned a fortune through share options. So much so that he had been able to buy the penthouse before he even thought of selling his large house in Richmond. "So what about you chaps," he said looking from Henry to Wayne.

Henry jumped in first, "I was a crab fisherman all my life," he said. "I worked out of Cromer. Like lots of fishermen, I was also a lifeboatman, just like my father. There are nowhere near as many fishermen now as there used to be of course. Not that there's a shortage of crabs or a shortage in demand. EU regulations reduced our profits and the kids today don't like the hard work and difficult hours. During the season you have to work probably 70 or 80 hours a week. My son Paul, Wayne's dad, took over my business. He's a hard worker and he's doing pretty well. Wayne chose not to keep up the family tradition."

"Grandad!" said Wayne, folding his arms and staring at Henry, "How many gay crab fishermen do you know? Anyway, fishing is much more up Kevin's street than mine." He glanced at Tony, "Kevin is my younger brother. I work hard and do long hours, it's just that I do them in front of a screen. If you are interested I'll tell you what I do before Grandad monopolises the whole conversation." Tony smiled and nodded.

"I'm a cyber-security consultant. I spend my time working for big organisations trying to hack into their systems. When I do, I tell them how to make improvements to stop people who do it illegally. Of course, the illegals keep getting better and better, so organisations keep asking me to make their security even tighter. No shortage of work. And I can do it within reason when I want to and from wherever I happen to be."

"How often do you manage to break into people's systems?" asked Tony.

"Too regularly!" said Wayne. "People just don't give it the attention it deserves."

"So how did you get into a job like that?" Asked Tony.

Henry interrupted the flow, "I'll tell you how he got the job." He turned towards Wayne. "Let me introduce you to Wayne, super-hacker, and one-time guest of our government at, what was then, Her Majesty's pleasure."

"Only for a couple of months grandad," said Wayne with a mock hurt look on his face.

"Wayne has always been a bit of a geek. Always messing about with computers. Don't ask me what he sees in them. Well, ten years ago, he hacked into somebody's computer and stole some money."

Wayne butted in, "Grandad, there were extenuating circumstances as you well know, which is why it was only two months! I'll explain Tony." He shifted himself in his seat and Henry leaned back grinning. "My cousin Elizabeth worked for this dodgy outfit in Holt. She was on the admin side. They were into import and export, and quite a lot of it seemed to be fairly shady. One day Liz noticed that there were some discrepancies in numbers between some import documentation and VAT reports and went to see her boss. He told her to keep her nose out of such things and when she said it might be illegal, he fired her on the spot. She was marched out of the office."

"The next day she got a letter saying that her employment had been terminated through gross misconduct and she would receive no further salary. It also said that if she wished to take the matter any further, they would report her to the police for perpetrating a fraud. You could imagine, she was out of her wits, sacked for no fault of her own, no income and not even paid for work that she had done." All of Wayne's little speech was delivered in dramatic fashion.

Tony was wide-eyed. "That's terrible, what happened?"

"Well!" said Wayne, "Uncle John rang the company to complain but was threatened with all sorts of legalese. They refused to pay her any money. So poor old Liz had to look for another job without any references. Liz is my favourite cousin and I couldn't see her treated like that without doing something to help. I'd become very interested in IT and how it functioned online. I had found that it was really easy to get into people's systems if you knew what you were doing. I spent many a happy hour looking around these systems, particularly Norfolk County Council. I'm sure I could have changed the course of many council decisions if I'd so wished."

"Anyway, I decided to hack into Liz's company to see if I could find out what was going on. It was a piece of cake! I don't know too much about finance, but even I could see there were differences between what companies were paying them and what was reported to HMG. I also discovered I could get into their payroll system. So, over a glass or two of Prosecco, Liz and I hatched a plot. I accessed all the documentation for the last three months and sat it on my PC and Liz went through it to see how much they had failed to declare. We found nearly £50,000 and there was probably a lot more. She wrote a little report with all the details for us to send to the police. In the meantime, we worked out how much she should've been paid, and I put it into their payroll a day before the payroll run. We thought that was absolutely justified. The money appeared in her account a few days later."

Tony, now with a rather startled look on his face, but a knowing smile on his lips said, "I have a sneaking suspicion, something must've gone wrong though."

"Yes, unfortunately," said Wayne. "Liz had the money she was due, and one evening we were at her house trying to work out who best within the police force to send the incriminating information to, when there was a knock at her door. And, what a coincidence we thought, two very nice boys-in-blue were standing on her doorstep. Unfortunately, they had come to question her about how money from the company had been illegally transferred to her bank account."

We tried to explain, but they didn't seem particularly interested, and we were both marched down to the police station. Sadly it appeared that what I had done was illegal. I told them about what the company had been doing, but they said it had nothing to do with this investigation, so I was arrested and charged. I was eventually tried, pleaded guilty and was given a six-month sentence and a record. Liz had to pay all the money back. I tried to use the information about the company at the trial but they had a pretty smart QC who managed to get that disallowed as evidence."

"They got away with it then did they?" asked Tony.

"Well, let me . . . ." started Wayne, but his story was halted by a concerned Henry.

"Hold on a minute Wayne, isn't that Tuppence? She looks in a bit of a state." He had seen Tuppence approaching Sillingham House looking rather dishevelled, waving one of her arms in the air. It was not a fast approach, but then it never was with Tuppence. And it wasn't in a particularly straight line. He got up and went over quickly to meet her. He took her arm, led her over to the group and asked her what had happened.

"Let me just sit down and get my breath back." She plonked herself down on the spare chair. "Now," she said still puffing, "you just listen to what I've got to tell you!"

Wayne's story would have to wait.

CHAPTER 5

Tuppence Tells Her Tale

Tuppence paused long enough to regain her breath and recover some composure. Henry knew what was coming. Something had happened which required a dramatic re-enactment. It would likely be an oration accompanied by verbatim speeches, dramatic asides, and even the equivalent of stage directions. When Tuppence was in this mode, she was at home with a captive audience she could entertain. She'd worked hard to hone her trade and liked to use her skills whenever possible.

Tuppence was brought up in Leeds where her father was a market trader who, from a tax perspective, had a low income. Her mother, when not helping out on the stall, cleaned the houses of some of the more well-off members of the community. For this, she received no income at all as far as the tax man was concerned. Despite an apparent shortage of money they owned outright a three-bedroomed semi-detached house in Headingly. Her father ran two 'vans' to support the business, one of which was an estate car, or shooting brake as it was called in those days. It was big enough to cart the family around and take them on holidays to Whitby or Scarborough.

In her youth, Tuppence was friendly, scatty, funny, loved dressing up, was great at imitating accents and was an accomplished impersonator. She was attractive but not pretty, curvy in a well-built sort of way, and taller than most. People described her as flighty and a bit of a show-off. They said she wouldn't come to much but might make someone a good wife if only she'd learn to cook and clean the house. Tuppence had other ideas. From an early age, she decided she wanted to become an actress. She loved singing and dancing and was always in the school plays.

While at school she worked part-time on the market stall but also got a Saturday and occasional evening job at the City Varieties doing anything from cleaning to usheretting to selling programmes. She progressed to working backstage and on to part-time assistant stage manager roles. She learned the ropes. She appeared in amateur productions at the Civic Theatre and had small parts in a couple of pantomimes at the Alhambra in Bradford. Then came time to leave school.

Her mother was very much against any sort of theatrical employment. She felt her daughter should work at the market or cleaning. She tried to persuade her to join the local Young Conservatives where she believed she would find a 'nice young man' and settle down. Tuppence baulked at the very thought. Luckily her father was a great fan of the stage and gave her the support she needed. She applied and was accepted to join the Royal Central School of Speech and Drama in London. The deal was, that her father would pay the fees and accommodation but she would have to find casual work to earn enough money to live on.

Tuppence left home and moved into a rented attic flat in Kilburn. She became a part-time barmaid. Her experience of working at the market enabled her to add up complicated orders in pounds, shillings and pence in her head without difficulty. She was also well able to look after herself in the dubious pubs she often worked in. She said later that she based several of her characters on the people she met at the spit-and-sawdust end of the catering trade.

She did well at drama school taking several walk-on roles in London productions. During this time however, it dawned on her that acting was a perilous profession and there were not that many graduates from the drama school who became household names. So she was happy to take on board ideas from tutors and other actors she met, and her dad proved a tower of strength when she got disillusioned. It was he who suggested she didn't go for the big, starring, glamorous roles but concentrated on character parts. That turned out to be a good move. She had a long career on stage, radio and television, and in film. Now she was retired and like the others, wondering what to do with herself.

"You may notice that I'm a bit bedraggled. I will explain that. And I will openly admit I may be slightly befuddled too. I've had a bit of a liquid lunch. Now you are going to find this difficult to believe. Prepare yourselves." The assembled company were desperately suppressing grins. "This afternoon I was witness to a major piece of criminal activity, perpetrated by mobsters on a helpless old man!" A theatrical gasp from Henry went undetected by Tuppence. "I need your advice."

Tuppence looked around and noticed that Tony was there in addition to the regulars. She smiled and said "Hello. We meet again. Believe me, I don't always come with bad news!"

"I'm sure you don't," he answered. "Carry on, I'm intrigued."

Henry leant back on the bench, "Tell us what happened, right from the beginning Tuppence old girl."

"That's enough of the old girl if you don't mind Henry Bennett, I've got a few more years before I catch up with you." She took a deep breath, prepared herself, and started her story.

"Today I met my friend Poppy for lunch at the Maids Head."

"Poppy? That's a weird name", said Wayne.

"Stage name!" said Tuppence. "We'd finished our lunch and Trevor had come to pick her up."

"Who's Trevor?" asked Wayne.

"Poppy's husband. Well, after they left I found myself behind the sofa when into the bar came …"

"Behind the sofa? What on earth were you doing behind a sofa?" said Henry incredulously.

"Stop interrupting! The reasons are neither here nor there."

"I think you'd just better explain Tuppence. Why didn't you just walk behind the sofa?" asked Tony.

Tuppence sighed. "Because it was up against the wall and I had dropped something behind it which I needed to retrieve."

"You managed that then?" asked Henry raising his eyebrows.

"With a great deal of difficulty. But anyway, into the bar came three people. One was a Mafia boss, another was his sidekick, and the third was an old man they were blackmailing." Tuppence paused looking at her audience.

"How much did you have to drink with your lunch Tuppence?" asked Henry, grinning from ear to ear.

"Enough to have been stupid enough to crawl behind a sofa but not enough to make this up, so just listen will you. The Mafia boss had driven up from somewhere near London because the man being blackmailed had refused to pay the sidekick. He said because of that he was increasing the ransom to £150,000!" This revelation was accompanied by a few raised eyebrows. "It seems that the old man had been to a rugby match and they had some photos which they had doctored to make it look like he'd been doing some naughty things to a young lady!"

"That sounds dreadful Tuppence," said Tony, "are you sure about that? You were stuck behind a sofa after all."

"Yes, I am absolutely certain," she said, getting a little shirty.

"Did you manage to get a look at any of them?" asked Henry.

"Henry, I have many skills as well you know, but one of them isn't being able to see through solid furniture. All I can say is the sidekick was called Michael. He referred to the other criminal as 'Boss'. Michael had a Birmingham accent and the boss was from East London or maybe Essex. The victim was from Norfolk. Now, what shall I do?"

The men looked around at one another. "I don't think there's anything you can do Tuppence. The only evidence you have is your word on the matter," said Wayne. "I'm sure we all believe you but from my experience of the police, you might have a problem getting them on board. Only one name, no faces, nothing that could tie this to anybody at all. And they're going to ask you how much you had to drink and what you were doing behind the sofa. Sorry." Tuppence was deflated.

"What happened in the end Tuppence?" asked Tony.

"The Norfolk man realised he had no choice but to pay the money. They said he'd have to pay everything within a week."

"Well I think the whole thing is terrible," said Tony. "This poor fellow is being conned out of an awful lot of money. There must be something we can do."

"With no evidence, the police would laugh us out of

court," said Wayne. "Well actually, we wouldn't even get to court." There was silence amongst the gathering.

"Hold on a minute," exclaimed Tuppence, "I do have some evidence. I switched on my voice recorder app part way through their conversation. Shall I find it?" She dug her phone out of her handbag and started swiping and tapping. Eventually, she found what she was after and said, "Have a listen to this." She clicked on her phone again. Very muffled voices could be heard but they were too indistinct to pick up what was being said.

"Can you make it louder Tuppence?" asked Wayne. She fiddled with the volume button and the sound increased a bit. "Wind it back and start again." She did as asked, Wayne got up and moved nearer to where she was sitting, and the others leaned in. While louder, the recording was still hard to hear and there was an irregular hissing noise. Wayne said, "I think what we can hear mostly is you breathing. Could you just stop it for a minute."

"What breathing?"

"No, the recording. How much of that could you hear guys?"

"Sod all," said Henry.

"Same here," agreed Tony.

"I guess my ears are a bit better than yours. If I tried hard, I might be able to pick out half of it. Look, I've got some kit at home that should make the whole recording a bit clearer. Would you like me to have a go at that?"

"Yes please Wayne," said Tuppence, brightening up. "When can you do it?"

"I've got nothing on this evening, so I could do it then. I'll need your phone for a couple of hours though. And you're going to have to trust me with your passcode!"

"I'd trust you with my body young man."

"No danger there then," quipped Henry earning a black look from Tuppence.

She fished around in her handbag and found her small notebook, wrote her phone number and passcode on a sheet, tore it out and gave it to Wayne. "You say you'll be a couple of hours?"

"I can drop it back later this evening. Hopefully, I can make the recording more audible. When will everyone be around?"

"Are you up for this?" Henry asked Tony.

"Certainly, If you don't mind."

They agreed early afternoon the next day.

"OK all, I'll see you tomorrow," said Wayne getting up to leave.

He was halted by Tuppence shouting "Hold on a minute! there's something else, look." She was waving her notebook in the air. "Before I left I asked the waiter whether he had seen any men leaving the bar. He said he had only seen one and he spoke to him. I asked what his voice was like, and it turned out that he spoke with a Norfolk accent."

"What did he look like? Did he say?" asked Wayne.

Tuppence looked at her notes. "Right, it would appear he was in his mid to late sixties, under a hundred and seventy-five centimetres. What's that in feet and inches?"

The men stared at each other, "No idea" said Tony, "I'll check on my phone".

Tuppence read out the man's description. "Leon, he was the waiter, said he looked like a farmer."

"One hundred and seventy-five centimetres is about five feet nine," announced Tony.

"Well, that gives us a bit more to go on doesn't it?" said Tuppence in triumph.

"If we ever get to the stage of providing the police with evidence it should be very useful," said Wayne.

With that, the group broke up. Wayne set off to walk back to his cottage in Upper Sheringham and Henry to his in town. Tuppence felt she needed to have a little lie-down, although she managed to check Tony's party availability before doing so. Tony for his part decided to restart his walk and headed up the cliff path. You can't stroll beside a stunning golf course and a sparkling seascape in Richmond he thought. With renewed vigour, he strode out happy that he'd made the right decision about the future.

CHAPTER 6

The Victim Identified

The next morning Tuppence woke later than usual, somewhat under the weather. This was caused less by the Champagne with Poppy, more the several nightcaps she consumed to settle her nerves before bed. However, years of after-show parties had spawned an infallible solution. Andrew's Liver Salts. She'd bought up packs of the stuff when the company stopped making it. So she rolled out of bed, headed to the kitchen and stirred a large teaspoonful into a glass of water. She then swallowed it as quickly as the wind coming in the other direction would allow.

After another 30 minutes dozing followed by a shower Tuppence felt ready to face the world. She made herself a cup of tea and almost prepared some thick slices of toast with butter and marmalade but managed to stop herself. No, she needed to start as she meant to go on. She dug out the sensible-eating book Poppy had bought her some time back, scanned through the breakfast section, and decided she needed to do some sensible-eating shopping. She prepared a list. After some soul searching she added bathroom scales, equipment she had previously excluded from her life as being superfluous to requirements.

Mid-morning she called Poppy. "Hello old thing," said Poppy as soon as the ringing tone stopped, "how are you? I had a bit of a headache this morning."

"Bit jaded but not too bad. Right, first things first, I've fixed the party date and will do the invitations later. Secondly, my reducing weight campaign starts in earnest today. I will be out shopping appropriately later. However, the most important thing to tell you is what happened after you left yesterday." Tuppence paused, "just listen to this. I witnessed a gang of blackmailers in operation!"

"What? You're pulling my leg!"

"I certainly am not." Tuppence relayed the story just as she had with her friends on the bench. Poppy was concerned that she had put herself in danger. Tuppence explained that her key concern regarding danger was less about the villains and more about not being able to get out from behind the sofa.

"So what are you going to do? Have you spoken to the police?"

Tuppence told her about the difficulties with that, and also what Wayne was doing.

"The villains came into the bar soon after you left. I don't suppose you happened to see anybody looking suspicious did you?"

"Don't know. What does suspicious look like?"

"Not sure. Shifty, shady maybe. What about in the car park? The boss of the baddies said he was driving a Bentley. Did you see anybody in a Bentley?"

"No, can't say I did. I wasn't exactly with it I'm afraid. Trevor might have. I'll ask him when he gets home."

Without very much more ado Tuppence left on her shopping expedition during which she would deliver two party invitations to friends at Cromer Pier Theatre. For somebody so sedate in other forms of movement, Tuppence was nippy when it came to driving. In ten minutes she was parking at Meadow Road car park. The walk from here to the top of the cliffs was to her a challenge in itself. Then she had to go down the ramp to the promenade, walk along the pier and into the theatre to meet her friends Sangeetha and Deborah. They were both delighted to receive the invites. On her return, at the base of the ramp, she stared upwards and steeled herself to get to the top with a minimum of stops. Once up, and out of breath, she paused for a while and congratulated herself. "I can do this!" she said out loud.

After she had completed her shopping expedition, Tuppence made her way to the terrace at the front of the building. Tony and Henry were already there. As she approached the bench she heard an animated Henry declare, "They're bloody mongrels. That's all."

"What's this all about?" asked Tuppence sitting on one of the chairs.

"My son Paul. He's just bought a Labradoodle. Stupid name."

"There are plenty of them now," said Tony. "Cockapoos. I think they're a cross between a Cocker Spaniel and a Poodle. And I think there's also one called a Schnoodle,' he added. "A bit of Schnauzer in there with the Poodle I should imagine."

"Well, seems to me there's one lucky poodle out there having a great time," said Henry. "So what happens if this Labradoodle of Paul's gets its leg over with another poodle? What would that make? A Labradoodledo?" The others chuckled. "Anyway, I think it's all bullshit. Or maybe that's a Bulldog crossed with a Shih Tzu!"

Just then Margaret came past with Ken on her arm having had a walk around the block. "What sort of mischief are you lot up to then?" Everyone said hello and Henry gave her and Ken a very short explanation.

"Why don't you join us Ken?" he said, and to Margaret, "Is that OK with you?"

"No problem at all, I've got plenty to do. Good luck with the detective work!" Tony moved over to the other chair and she manoeuvered Ken onto the bench next to Henry. "Will you bring him up when you're ready Henry?"

"Course I will. See you soon." She gave Ken a kiss on the cheek and off she went.

There was no reaction from Ken to Henry's explanation and having sat down, he stared out to sea, just as he usually did.

A moment later Wayne arrived. He told the others that he had managed to improve the sound quality of the recording. He said he had played around with the bits that were very muffled and that now you could understand just about everything that was said. All this, he said, had been transferred onto a laptop. He fished this out of his rucksack. "Have a listen," he said and played the whole of the recording. The others listened transfixed, captivated by what they were hearing.

"You're right about the blackmail Tuppence," said Henry, "that poor sod is being swindled out of a hundred and fifty thousand."

"If it were me, I'd like to think I'd call their bluff," chipped in Tony.

"The old chap is not going to do that though, is he? You can tell he's worried his reputation won't survive an onslaught of nasty pictures being sent to people he knows. They've done their homework. They know his weak points and they've worked out that he can come up with the money."

"We must do something," said Tuppence. "Can't we give the recording to the police?"

"I don't want to be a killjoy," replied Tony, "but there's still very little to go on. Just a random recording of three anonymous men. And no description of the villains."

Wayne butted in. He said he'd also extracted a few clear bits of the recording of each participant into separate files to give a better feel for their voices. "Would you like to hear them?" he got a positive response. "Hold on." He fiddled with his laptop. "I'll play an extract of the guy who is obviously the boss first." It lasted ten seconds or so and Wayne played it a couple of times.

Tuppence gave her opinion. "I think he's most likely East London, not Essex."

"How can you tell?" asked Wayne.

"There's lots of Cockney in there." She gave some examples of East End vernacular. "He uses rhyming slang too. Did you hear him say 'me old China'? Well, that's short for China Plate, meaning mate."

"He said something else didn't he" Tony interjected. "We've got you by the orchestras or something."

"That's right, short for Orchestra Stalls. I'll leave you to work out what that means! Essex is a bit different," and she went on to demonstrate.

Wayne said, "I'll play the other villain now." This was a shorter extract, but very clear.

"Birmingham definitely," said Tuppence, mimicking the accent perfectly. "Sounds much younger too." Everyone agreed.

"I suppose it brings these guys to life a bit," said Tony, "but is it going to help us?"

"Possibly," replied Wayne. "If somehow or another we get to the stage where we know much more about them, someone in the police force might recognise the voices if they are criminals already known to them."

"What about the victim?" chimed in Henry. "Let's hear him."

Wayne pressed a few more keys and said "here we go."

He had extracted two sections of the Norfolk man's dialogue and played both of them a couple of times each.

"Definitely Norfolk," said Henry." Many years ago I could have probably worked out where in Norfolk he came from."

"Sounds to me exactly like you Henry, so maybe he comes from Cromer," said Tony. "Different voice obviously, but the accent seems the same. What do you think Tuppence?"

"Wouldn't disagree."

There was silence for a second or two, everyone thinking about what they'd heard, not knowing quite where to go from here. Then out of nowhere came "Hay." It took a moment before they realised it was Ken. He was still staring out towards the horizon. He said "Hay" again. It was the first sound anyone had heard him utter in weeks.

"Hay Ken? What do you mean hay?"

"Hay." He turned his head and looked at Henry, "Hay!"

"Sorry Ken, not quite sure what you're trying to say."

"Hay! Hay!" Repeated Ken getting agitated and nodding towards Wayne.

"He doesn't recognise the voice does he?" said Wayne to Henry.

"Dunno. Are you talking about the voice Wayne played, Ken?" Ken nodded.

"Hay! Hay!" said Ken raising his voice.

"So you recognise it?" Ken nodded vigorously this time.

"Hay!" And then slower, "Hay-ee! Hay-ee!"

Henry thought for a moment. "Christ! That would be a turn-up for the book. Where do you know him from?" Ken just stared at Henry.

Of course he's not going to be able to say is he, Henry realised. "Is he from here?" He turned and waved towards the apartment building beside them.

There was a shake of the head from Ken, "nah, nah."

"OK. Have you met him since coming up here?"

More shaking of the head, "nah, nah, nah!"

"So you know him from London? Another Norfolk person. Did you work with him?" To both of these, a shake of the head and "nah!".

Henry thought for a while. I know, "did you know him from when you lived here before you went to London? Maybe from school?"

This was followed by a vigorous nodding of the head, "mmm, mmm" from Ken.

The others were spellbound by this exchange. Tuppence was getting excited.

"Bloody 'ell Ken so, is hay-ee his name?"

A blank stare from Ken. "Maybe it's Harry?" Said Wayne.

"Nah, nah. Har-ee!" said Ken.

"Right," said Henry to the assembled onlookers, "it's going to be something that begins with an H and maybe starts hay or har. Hayworth? Haydon? Harvey?".

The others came up with a few names that could fit, but Ken dismissed them all. Wayne asked his grandad to think about who he went to school with and who might have a name like that. Henry thought for a minute. "Hold on." He then looked at Ken and said "Ken, do you mean Harley?"

Very aggressive nodding from Ken, "mmm, mmm, mmm," and a broad smile filled his whole face. Satisfied, he turned his head away.

"Gord struth," said Henry looking at Wayne, "you know who that is don't you?" Wayne didn't. "It's Harley Payne".

"Who?" asked Wayne.

"Harland Payne funeral services!" Said Henry. "We always knew him as Harley because we thought Harland was such a stupid name.

"Harry Payne's father?" asked Tony.

"The very one. Play the recording again Wayne."

They all listened again to the Norfolk voice coming from Wayne's laptop. "You know, I think he's right. I haven't seen Harley for a while now but it does really sound like him."

Tony felt that there could be hundreds of people sounding like the man in the recording so he put his being-sensible hat on. "If it is Harry Payne's father, that's astonishing. Look I don't want to put a dampener on this again but we need to be sure before we do anything else. We need some corroborative evidence. What about other things mentioned in the main recording? The church was spoken about for example. What's this Harley like? Who are his friends? Is he a pillar of the community? Does he go to rugby internationals?"

"If it is Harley, that puts a completely different complexion on the whole thing," said Henry. "It's personal. Well almost. I wonder if Harry knows anything about it. No, that would be my guess. But I do agree, we need to be sure. I can probably check a lot of this out. I know several people who are friends of his or the wider family. I'll get some discrete questions asked. I can assure you now though, he is definitely thought of as a pillar of the community. Picture often in the paper, mainly to do with the Rotary Club. Long-term church-goer as well I think."

"Well, whatever happens, we need to thank Ken for pointing us in that direction," said Wayne.

"Ken! Well done. You've done a good job there mate." Ken turned his head towards Henry, face beaming. Everybody thought it was a good idea for Henry to do a bit more investigation in the short term. Wayne wondered whether his grandad should talk to Harley himself. Henry suggested not. He guessed Harley gave in to the blackmailers precisely because he didn't want anyone else to know.

Wayne moved the conversation on somewhat. "It looks as if we may know who the victim is, and that the boss drives a Bentley. Beyond that, the only positive we have, if we are going to try to find this guy, is that he plays golf." He told the others he'd spent yesterday evening looking for potential golf courses he had driven from. "The ones I looked at are all to the east of London, around the right distance from the Maids Head. I'm not a golfer but I looked at their websites and picked what I thought were good quality courses, possibly the sorts of places a person like him would play." He produced a list he'd printed off. "You're a golfer aren't you Tony? Could you have a look at these to see what you think."

At that moment Tuppence's mobile rang. "Oh, I need to answer this." She pressed green. "Hello dear, I'm in a meeting. Have you any news?" She listened, producing a few 'umms' and 'ahhs', and finally, "that might be really important. Thank Trevor for us. I'll call you later." She looked around the group. "Now, this might just help. That was Poppy. As she and Trevor left the Maids Head they were nearly hit by a car that was just arriving. It was a Bentley according to Trevor. He should know, he's got one. It was light green and the driver was oldish with light grey hair. And, get this, Trevor thinks his name was Lee."

"How on earth would he know that?" Asked Henry.

"He noticed the letters on the numberplate spelt LEE. They were followed by two digits." Tuppence looked around, her face tinged with triumph.

"So, we are looking for someone who may be called Lee, who drives a Bentley and could play golf somewhere east of London. And in his spare time he's blackmailing Harry Payne's dad," said Tony. The others stared at him. "Once again, I don't want to put a dampener on this but how is that going to help us find this rogue? I suppose we could go to all the golf courses to see if we can spot this Bentley in the car park. Bit like looking for a needle in a haystack, I'd say. I have a feeling if we ring up the courses and ask if someone called Lee plays at their course, we'd get short shrift too. Data Protection." Henry frowned and Tuppence looked particularly dejected.

Wayne looked far chirpier, "I think I can help there. I'll use some of the techniques I employ to test peoples' security systems. I may be able to access membership lists if there are such things." Henry told him not to do anything illegal. Wayne smiled, "Of course I won't grandad!" He said he needed to know a bit more about golf, so Tony said he would email him some information. He said he would also look at the websites of the courses Wayne had listed and give him some feedback. "Right," said Wayne now fired up and ready to go, "I've nothing on tonight so I'll get started. I'll be in touch. Bye!"

Henry said that if Harley was the victim, it would be a good idea to let Harry know. Everyone agreed that Tony should have that conversation. The meeting broke up and Tony left saying he'd send golf details off to Wayne. Henry said to Ken, "Come on old boy, let's get you back up to Margaret." Ken turned his head away from the sea and smiled. Henry took his arm and gently eased him off the bench.

"I'll come with you," said Tuppence, and the three of them walked slowly towards Sillingham House.

Having dropped Ken at his apartment, Tuppence invited Henry in for a coffee. "It would be something stronger but I've decided to go on the wagon during the week," she explained. They sat on her balcony, each clutching a mug of coffee. She said to Henry, "I have to ask you something. I've known Ken for some time but I've never been sure what's wrong with him. Is it Alzheimer's?"

"Nearly, Vascular Dementia. Different cause, same outcome." Henry saw that Tuppence looked confused. "With Alzheimer's, there's a steady decline but with Vascular, it goes down in steps. It started in his early 60's. They call that 'young onset'. He had to leave work, so no income till his pension clicked in. Plans for retirement blown out of the water. Can you imagine how that affects your mind? Since Ken became ill I've studied it a lot, I'll give you a lecture on it sometime. Just recently there seems to have been lots of changes. You'll notice he can't speak properly now."

"Yes, it looked painful for him earlier. I believe it's difficult for Margaret too?"

"You're not joking, she goes through hell. You wouldn't think it, but he's become very difficult to deal with. He even hits her sometimes. That's not Ken. He would never do anything to hurt Margaret. He's becoming a danger to himself and she can't leave him for any length of time. Luckily their son John can help out fairly frequently. I try to do my bit by taking him for a walk every week. It gives Margaret a bit of time to herself. She's becoming frazzled though."

"I can tell you through a woman's eye, she's right on the edge. Do you think it would help if I spent some time with her?"

"I'm sure it would, but she's very independent. And private. You might get the brush off."

"I've got a bit of time now so why don't you give me your lecture so at least I know a bit about the subject." So Henry gave Tuppence a rundown on everything he'd learnt on the subject from Margaret, John and Dr Google. She vowed to find an opportunity to at least give Margaret someone to talk to. Maybe even a shoulder to cry on.

CHAPTER 7

Wayne Investigates

Wayne made his way home, keen to get started on investigating who Lee, or even Mr Lee, might be. The most straightforward way would be to hack into the DVLC website to find out who owned a Bentley with the LEE number plate. He could do that easily, they had used his services in the past and he knew his way around their system. However, it would be abusing their trust as well as breaking the law. Get found out and all his business would disappear. He might end up languishing in a rancid gaol somewhere too.

He had to take the golf club route. To do that he needed the information Tony was sending him. He looked at his email inbox. Nothing yet. His stomach was telling him it was time for dinner so he decided to throw something together while he was waiting. Wayne was a good cook and a prawn and chilli linguine along with a glass of chilled Sauvignon Blanc was soon in front of him. While he was cooking, Tony's e-mail arrived so he read and ate at the same time.

It was fulsome in its content so he had to separate out the important bits. He discovered a game of golf was called a round. Up to four people play together. Each group process around the golf course one after the other. The starting time of each round is called a tee time. Tee times are typically 7 to

10 minutes apart. You pay to be a member of most clubs in the UK. Members can invite and pay for guests, and visitors can book to play at a one-off cost. Clubs record the name of every member playing a round.

By the time he'd finished his meal, Tony's analysis of the golf clubs arrived. He'd eliminated any public courses and two that only had nine holes. He'd then put the rest into likely and less likely groups. This left 27 courses in total, all of which had websites that Wayne could use as starting points for his investigation. While he was wary of going anywhere near the DVLC, he felt the minor misdeed of breaking into golf club systems in the cause of pursuing criminals was acceptable. Well, just about.

He thought the best starting point was to pick a club and peer inside their computer system. It didn't take him long to penetrate security. He soon found membership details including amongst other things name, gender, date of birth, address and contact phone number. He then found the tee-time booking data. Members' names within a slot were recorded, guests were referred to as such and a visitor who booked and paid for a game was named although other visitors were referred to simply as visitors. He assumed the same would apply at other clubs.

This put something of a dampener on his planned investigation. He realised Lee's name wouldn't be recorded if he was a guest or a visitor who didn't make the booking. But then in the far reaches of his mind, he remembered the boss referring to his missed game. What was that? He clicked on the recording and let it play. Almost at the end, he heard ". . . . caused me to miss an important game at my golf club today. . . ." His club! Bingo! He must be a member, no need to worry about un-named visitors or guests. He decided the best approach would be to create a database on his laptop into which he could extract relevant membership and booking data from all the golf clubs. He could then analyse the database looking for the name Lee.

Wayne was not short of sophisticated software. It didn't take him long to design his database and download information on all male members and tee-time bookings from the club he was looking at. This done, all he had to do was to break into the other 26 Golf Club systems and download the same data from them. Wayne was an expert in his field but even so, it still took a long time. He was helped by the fact that several clubs used the same bespoke Golf Club Management Software, which meant that both hacking and data manipulation were replicated. He finished the task at half past midnight.

Many would have given up for the night at this stage, but not Wayne. He got his software to search for tee bookings with Lee as a first name or surname. It only took a few seconds. He came up with members from seven different clubs, most of them appearing several times. Now he needed to work out when the villain would have been playing if he hadn't had to drive to Norwich. It was two days ago, but at what time? He went into his phone's GPS and picked Brentwood as being about the right distance away in the right general area. It showed two hours and ten minutes to The Maid's Head at the moment, so probably would be two and a half hours or more at the time he travelled. Trevor picked up Poppy at about 3.00 pm which was when the villain arrived. So, with a bit of leeway, his tee time would have been somewhere between 12.00 am and 1.00 pm. Now came the crunch. When were the seven Lees playing? Wayne's heart missed a beat, three of them had tees booked between those times on Wednesday. Which one was the baddy?

He needed to find out more about each of them. Wayne being Wayne, he turned to social media. He soon dismissed Lee Duggan whose Facebook profile featured him as a 35-year-old GP with a penchant for baking and Porche cars. Adrian Lee was 60 and his Facebook pages were packed with pictures of people and parties. Criminals presumably partied just like other people thought Wayne. Could be interesting. He checked out his address on Google Street View. In the drive of his semi-detached house was an old BMW and a red van advertising Adrian Lee, Master Plumber. Probably not the man but Wayne decided to keep him in mind anyway. Then it didn't take long for him to drop George Lee from consideration. He turned out to be a Professor of Economics at UCL. Lots of online mentions, research contributions, membership of professional and government advisory bodies. Definitely not him.

Wayne realised he had only one possibility and an unlikely one at that. So what now? He was dispirited but too tired to do anything more. He would carry on in the morning. A short time later he sank into the sumptuous mattress in his tastefully decorated bedroom and was soon in the land of nod. After his parents suggested he fly the nest five years ago he had searched for many months before he found the house he wanted. It was a run-down old flint cottage with an overgrown garden. He was able to use his design and project management skills to turn it into a beautiful and cosy home. The smallest bedroom he converted into his office which was now full of hi-tech gear. The kitchen and bathroom had been ripped out and were now bang up to date, packed with the latest gadgets. His father and Henry had helped turn the small garden into an easy-to-maintain sanctuary of peace. Despite having to learn to look after himself, Wayne was very content.

He woke with a start at 4.45 am during a dream about the number plate on his old car. the numbers and letters had kept moving around. Oddly, he was not perturbed about the moving characters, it was the fact that it was a personalised plate which concerned him. He didn't have one. The only person in the family who did was his uncle Stephen with the letters SAM followed by some digits. SAM stood for Stephen and Marie, his wife. Wayne sat bolt upright, suddenly wide awake. "Maybe our blackmailer's name isn't Lee." He said out loud. "Maybe his initials are L.E.E." Wayne thought about going back to sleep, but he needed to solve the LEE problem. So he got up, made a strong cup of coffee, then went into his office and sat down in front of his computer.

Wayne searched his tee-bookings database for all surnames beginning with an E that had a first name beginning with L. He ended up with 53 members spread across the 27 clubs. He narrowed them down by finding two with tee bookings at the appropriate time. The first was Lawrence Enrici aged 57. He had no online presence at all that Wayne could dig up. He decided to look at where he lived. It was in a complex of apartments with a security gate at the front. Satellite View showed there were only a few cars parked but as he homed in on them, two were light coloured and the larger one seemed to be greenish. Difficult to be sure though because there were small trees throwing shade onto them. Wayne decided he would put him on the list.

Secondly, there was Lionel Edgar. He looked interesting too. He was not on Facebook or X or Instagram but he did have a website. He seemed to be a sculptor who repurposed old agricultural machinery. In his photograph, he looked younger than the 59 declared to the golf club and sported a long, dark-haired pigtail. Could be an old photo thought

Wayne and maybe he'd discovered a good way of laundering money. So that was two, maybe three possibilities in total.

Light was beginning to filter in through the pulled curtains of his office. Wayne could have put his head down for a couple of hours but decided he was far too awake to sleep. He wanted to tell the others what he had discovered but realised he didn't have all their numbers. So he texted his grandad to get him to fix a meeting. Within minutes his phone rang. It was Henry. "What on earth are you doing up so early?" Wayne gave him a quick rundown. "Leave it to me," said Henry and it wasn't long before a meeting was set up for 11.00.

Henry, Tony and Tuppence were waiting for him when Wayne arrived. They were all mightily impressed with his nocturnal activity and eager to hear the outcome. Wayne talked them through his analysis. Tony said, "As long as your collection of golf clubs is right, then there's a good chance one of these three could be our man. Can you get their club websites up on your laptop?" He needn't have asked. The artistic scrap merchant's was first. Tony looked over Wayne's shoulder and spent a couple of minutes looking mainly at the gallery. "Looks a decent course but not exceptional. What about the plumber?"

A few more clicks and up came another web page. "This is more like it," said Tony. Wayne clicked through gallery photos, "nice course, smart. Much better."

"Hold on a minute," cried Wayne as a shot of three golfers came into view, "that's him! The plumber." He clicked on Adrian Lee's Facebook page. "See. There he is, same man."

Metaphorically jumping up and down, Tuppence shouted, "Have we found him?"

"There's some text below the photo", said Tony. "Can you enlarge it?" Wayne did. "Ah!" said Tony in a rather resigned way. "He's Club Captain. He'll be tied up at the club and playing several days a week. If he's also a working plumber I doubt he'd have time to be a criminal too."

Henry, looking over Tony's shoulder, pointed out a lush growth of ginger hair.

"Maybe not him then," said Wayne

"Can we have a look at the other one?" asked Tony. Wayne tapped a few keys and up popped the home page of Lawrence Enrici's course. After Wayne scrolled through several pages Tony said, "This is better. Elegant website, expensive visitor rates, lovely course. Lots of smart cars in the car park."

"Where does he live?" asked Tony. Wayne had captured shots of the apartment complex and the parked cars. They discussed the three alternatives and concluded that if any, Lawrence Enrici was the most likely candidate. "We should check him out," said Tony to a murmur of agreement.

"How are we going to do that?" asked Tuppence.

"I don't suppose you are able to look at their tee-time bookings now are you?" asked Tony.

"No problem." Wayne had already allocated himself a membership number and password and was soon looking at today's reservations. It didn't take him long to scroll through the bookings. "Here we go, Enrici has a tee-time booked for Wednesday week at 11.50 for himself, another member called Graham Ford, and two guests."

"That's encouraging. Yesterday was a Wednesday of course. People often get into the habit of playing on the same day of the week." He asked Wayne whether there were any tee times available near Enrici's. "There's one a couple of slots after him."

"Right, I'll book as a visitor. I don't suppose either of you play golf do you?" looking at Henry and Tuppence.

"Yes of course! And I pole vault and run marathons too," she said, wide-eyed. Henry just shook his head.

"Ah, guessed as much. I'll see whether I can get one of my buddies to join me. Can I book online Wayne?"

"Let's have a look. No, I'm afraid not. You have to ring the pro shop."

"Ok, I'll give them a call." Tony rang up straightaway and booked his slot.

He turned to the assembled company. "I'll have a look at this guy then."

"You'll have to be careful," said Tuppence, "he's not a nice person remember."

Wayne added, "I'll set up a WhatsApp Group to make communication between us a bit easier."

"What about Ken?" asked Tuppence.

Henry answered. "Why not? He got this whole investigation going, so he's part of it. Which reminds me, I'd better get moving on my Harley investigations, hadn't I?"

There were lots of nods and beaming faces. This was getting very interesting.

CHAPTER 8

How To Find The Villain

On Sunday morning Tony was sitting at the breakfast bar clutching his first coffee of the day. Staring up at him from the middle of the kitchen was Willie. He wasn't just sitting there idly, he appeared to be glaring with a purpose. "What's the matter?" Tony said, meeting Willie's stare full-on. The cat didn't react beyond a slight twitch of his mouth and a faint, foreshortened meow. "I've given you your breakfast." The cat didn't take his eyes off Tony and there was another twitch. "I know it's not your favourite but it's perfectly edible!"

Tony had a feeling he was going to lose this contest. For some reason Willie had recently decided to go pescatarian, turning his nose up at his usual food. Not wishing to waste the boxes he'd already bought Tony kept trying but to no avail. His daughter had given him a hint. "Just sprinkle some Dried Sprat Treats over the top and that might do the trick." So Tony gave in and that's what he did. Willie then greedily tucked into his breakfast, ate all the fish, turned his nose up at the rest and left through his little door. Bloody animals, thought Tony.

He went back to his coffee. He decided to bite the bullet and talk to Harry Payne today. Waiting until mid-morning he went down to the ground floor and worked out which apartment the Payne's lived in. He paused, then rang the bell. Harry Payne came to the door. Looking surprised and slightly aggressive he said, "Hello, what can I do for you?"

Tony came straight to the point, "I'm afraid your father is in a bit of trouble. I wanted to tell you about it in case you weren't aware."

"Trouble?" Harry looked a tad worried. "You'd better come in." He held the door open, "straight ahead." Tony walked into the lounge. "Have a seat. So what's going on?"

"Well, something extremely unpleasant has happened and we think your father is very embarrassed and significantly out of pocket."

"Oh Gord, he's been at a loose end ever since he retired. What on earth has he been up to? He hasn't talked to me about anything."

"Well, not wishing to beat about the bush, he's being blackmailed!"

"What!?" Harry was clearly shocked. "Who by? What's he done?"

"Your dad was photographed in a compromising position with a young lady after a rugby international earlier this year. He was set up by blackmailers. They've threatened to release these photographs if your father doesn't pay them a substantial sum of money."

Harry stared at Tony aghast, mouth wide open. Then he burst out laughing. "If he's been a bit naughty, he's gone up in my estimation. He's such a straight-laced old bugger, it's about time he let his hair down."

"Ah, I'm sorry if it's going to disappoint you but he was just helping the girl and the photos were tampered with to make them look compromising."

Harry became rather more serious. "No, it's me that should be sorry. How the hell do you know all this?"

Tony told him the tale. "So, either he pays them £150,000 or they distribute the photographs."

"£150,000? Jesus that's a lot of dosh. I can tell you now, he'd rather pay than have those photos coming out."

"We'd assumed that. He's got until Wednesday."

Harry, obviously taken aback, paced around his lounge. "This is terrible. He's not hard up so I'm sure he can find £150,000 if he needs to. He's a miserable old git at times but he doesn't deserve this. Have you spoken to the police?"

"No, we haven't. We're not experts but we don't think we have enough evidence. So, we've decided to do more investigation ourselves before we hand everything over to them."

"You're investigating? Why on earth are you doing that?"

"Initially it was Tuppence who wanted justice. Henry knows your father and jumped on board. It turned out that one of Tuppence's friends saw who we think is the villain at the Maids Head. She got his car number and with all manner of online jiggery-pokery Wayne turned up a name. We're going to check him out."

"You're doing that for my father? That's amazing. I feel terrible. I've not been very polite to this Tuppence person in the past. When you see her could you offer my apologies? And appreciation. You need to let me do something to help."

Tony thought for a second. "Maybe there's a couple of things. Why don't you listen to the voice recording to confirm it's your dad?" Harry said that was no problem. "Secondly, I don't suppose you play golf do you?"

Just then the door to the apartment opened and into the lounge rushed a small boy holding a toy car aloft, "Look Daddy, what granny gave me!" Trailing behind was a tall, very attractive woman.

"Oh hello, I'm Sofia." She spoke English with an East European accent. "All times he goes to see grandparents they buy him something!"

"This is Tony. From the penthouse," interrupted Harry. There was an uncomfortable pause. The Willie incident was no doubt still in her mind.

"Good to meet you. I'm a grandparent too. I know how irresponsible we can be!"

"How were they today?" asked Harry quickly.

"OK. Your dad very quiet. He seem worried about something. Your Mother probably. I tell them she should have her hip done privately. Your dad normally agree with me but he don't say anything today."

Harry glanced at Tony and raised his eyebrows.

Tony got up and said, "I must be going Harry." He headed for the door and Harry followed. "Thanks for what you're doing. What was the second thing you said I could do to help?"

"I wondered whether you played golf?"

"Badly. Why?"

"We think we know who the villain is and I'm going to check him out Wednesday week at his golf club. I need a partner."

Harry looked at the diary on his phone, "I can do that. I'll listen to that recording too. Give me your mobile number and I can contact you directly." Then Harry wrote 'Harry and Sofia' on a business card and gave it to Tony. "I'll get in touch. Bye!"

* * *

While Tony was talking to Harry, Tuppence was pondering whether to make a phone call. One of her old friends in the business was from Aberdeen. Her son spent his formative years there but had forged a career in the Metropolitan Police. Tuppence had taken him under her wing early on and they had remained close. He was one of only a few friends who went back pre-fame. She thought he might be able to give her and the team some advice. They hadn't spoken for maybe six months, so this could be a good excuse. Yes, I'll give Bob a ring she thought.

"Well if it isn't Auntie Dora," came a cheery voice at the other end of the phone. "Where have you been while I've been slaving away paying for your pension?"

"Becoming a bit rusty on the north Norfolk coast, Chief Superintendent Henderson. Or is it still? You move so fast I can never be sure."

"Near enough." They chatted for a few minutes about family and who'd been doing what. "Anyway, to what do I owe this pleasure?"

"Well I've got a bit of a conundrum and I need your advice," said Tuppence.

"Me give you advice? That's a bit of a turnaround."

"I'm sure you'll manage. Look, this is a bit delicate. It involves a crime."

"You're not in trouble are you?"

"Not as far as I'm aware. I'll give you a bit of background." Tuppence gave Bob a succinct précis of the case, omitting Wayne's hacking involvement. "So, should we continue or just hand over to the local constabulary?"

There was momentary silence at the other end. "You still there?"

"Yes, sorry. I was just picturing you behind a sofa. Right, I have to advise you to hand over everything you have to the local police. However, I can tell you now it hasn't a snowball's chance in hell of getting anywhere. If you did involve them they'd also want to interview the victim."

"I guessed that."

"So what are you going to do?"

"We'll do some more investigation ourselves. We have a stab at two names. One is the victim and the other the boss of the blackmailers."

There was a chuckle at the other end of the line. "How on earth have you come up with them?"

"Probably best not talked about over the phone. I'm coming down to see Poppy soon, we could meet over a glass of something and talk then."

"Suits me. How is Poppy? I haven't seen her for ages."

"She's doing well. So is Trevor. I don't suppose in advance of that, you could do something for me could you?"

"If I can."

"Well, we believe the villain is a career criminal. Could you check his name out for us?"

"Auntie Dora. You know I can't do that. Totally against the rules."

"Well, it was worth an ask!"

"I suppose so. Anyway, purely as a matter of interest, what name have you got?"

"We think he is Lawrence Enrici, probably East-End or Essex."

Just then Tuppence heard a phone ringing at the other end of the line.

"Oh, that's my other phone, I need to take it. Text me the dates you're coming down and we'll arrange to meet. Got to go. Oh, and be careful! Bye!"

* * *

Tony had rung Harry later on Sunday and they'd arranged to meet on Monday lunchtime at the Robin Hood to plan their expedition to Lawrence Enrici's Golf Club. Harry didn't seem to be the sociable sort but Tony thought a quiet beer and a sandwich might break the ice nicely. He hadn't been in the pub more than a minute when Harry joined him at the bar. They ordered beer and toasted sandwiches and found a table. "I've just been to see my new GP for a check-up," said Tony. "Luckily, no life-threatening issues. Most importantly she didn't tell me to cut this out," he said holding up his pint. Harry responded, "Good news, cheers!" He seems relaxed enough thought Tony.

"You'd better tell me what we're going to do about this Enrici chap?" said Harry.

"All we have for certain is a voice, so we have to at least identify that. His car would corroborate things. It's a long shot but if we could record him speaking, that would be real evidence."

"I've got a digital meeting recorder if that would help," offered Harry. "It's small enough for me to conceal. We just need to get close enough to him,"

"That would have to be in the clubhouse I guess," said Tony.

"What about photos?"

"The car would be easy. Photos of him would have to be out on the course."

"I've got a good telephoto lens I use when I'm birdwatching."

"Excellent. I'll book a buggy. Easier to carry it around."

Just then their toasted sandwiches arrived. They set about them with gusto.

"Do you think that would be enough for the police to become interested?" asked Harry.

"Hopefully. If we're sure he's our man it wouldn't do any harm making some discrete enquiries at the golf club as well."

"Where is this club exactly?"

Tony explained then got his phone out, clicked on maps and found the route. "It says about three hours door to door. Why don't we give ourselves another hour leeway and then we can get set up and spot our man before we start?"

They finished their sandwiches. "Time for another jar I think. Same again?" asked Harry.

Tony was enjoying Harry's unexpected sociability. "Absolutely," he replied.

Harry came back with two more pints. Tony expected to have to drive the conversation from now on but Harry surprised him. "It's a pleasure coming out for a lunchtime drink, I don't do it very often. Tell me, what did you do before you came up here? Living in a penthouse and driving that limousine of yours, it must have been pretty lucrative." This was said with an interested, not envious, emphasis.

"Yes, I downsized the house, I suppose I should downsize the car too. I was in the advertising business."

"How did you get into that?"

Tony gave him the same spiel he'd given to Henry and Wayne a few days ago adding the elevation to Chairman of Brodie Vellum into the mix. "Have you been married? I haven't seen anyone around."

"Several times."

"Sounds interesting. Go on." Harry evidently didn't beat about the bush.

"My first wife was Dawn. She worked at the surveyor's practice I mentioned. She was very nice, homely, thoughtful. Lived with her parents in Newbury. We got married and rented a minuscule house in Thatcham. Dawn was happy working in the practice, seeing a lot of her parents, watching television in the evenings and occasionally trying for babies. The trouble was, she put me under constant pressure to spend all evenings and weekends in with her. Didn't see much of my friends. Playing squash was limited to once a week. Golf was completely banned. I got fed up. I wasn't suited to all this settling down stuff."

"So it didn't last."

"No. Without telling her, I got a job as a graphic designer with an advertising agency in London. The proverbial hit the fan and that was the beginning of the end. After a couple of months travelling up and down, I was told I had to get a job back in Newbury. I disagreed, divorce proceedings were initiated and 9 months later at the age of 24, I was single again. I found a small flat and moved up to London."

"So footloose and fancy-free living in London. I should imagine you had a good time."

"Yes, I liked working in advertising. Began earning a decent income and put down a deposit on a house in Ealing. It was very sociable. We had some stonking parties! Had a few flings including an on/off relationship with a bit of a bombshell called Geraldine. I certainly burned the candle at both ends. More hangovers than I care to remember, occasionally waking up in a bed wondering who I was sleeping next to. Anyway, I decided I needed to get a grip. One of my golfing partners was a solicitor from Twickenham and at a function, I met his daughter. Susan her name. A doctor at Chelsea & Westminster Hospital. Keen on sport, loved good food and seemingly happy to chat to me all evening. It was the beginning of a beautiful relationship." He paused just a second. "I feel another pint coming on. Yes?" Harry handed him his empty glass.

When he returned with full glasses Harry said, "I assume this Susan became another of your wives?"

"Indeed she did. Eventually, we had three kids. Jessica the youngest lives in Aylsham. We had a lovely life, nice house, good jobs, lots of holidays. She ticked every single box."

Harry heard the release of a big sigh. "You're using the past tense. What happened?"

"Almost every year we went skiing somewhere, usually in Europe but sometimes in North America. In March 2015 Susan and I went with two friends to the Portes du Soleil area in France. On a fast run through Morzine, Susan was leading the group when the binding on her left ski snapped. She crashed off the piste into a wooded area and hit a tree. When we got to her she was unconscious." Tony took a large swallow of beer. "She never came round. She died later that day in hospital. Broken neck and other head injuries. That was the worst day of my life."

Even reluctant undertaker Harry was touched. "Sorry to hear that. It must have been awful."

"Yes. Life was great. Then in an instant, it wasn't. The children were devastated. Everyone was devastated. It was made worse by all the red tape and shenanigans needed to get her home. My friends packed her case. Unpacking it when I got back was hard. In one of the pockets was an envelope with my name on. It was a wedding anniversary card. Looking forward to the next 32 years it said." Tony took a deep breath. "Sorry, will you just excuse me? Got to go to the gents. All this beer." And with an excuse registered, he left the table.

Harry was nowhere near his comfort zone and sat uncomfortably blaming himself for unsettling Tony. But he needn't have worried. A minute later Tony returned, a weary smile on his face. "Sorry about that. It just catches me out every now and then. We all got over it eventually. The kids have been great. Wherever we are on her birthday we coordinate a time and make a toast to the best mum and wife in the world. The old adage is true, life has to go on." Just then his mobile phone pinged. It was a WhatsApp from Henry calling a meeting tomorrow on the bench. He had an update. It was an excuse to call it a day. "I need to get back," he said. "I'll get in touch about arrangements for Wednesday." And with that, they both strolled back to Sillingham House.

* * *

By the following afternoon, the sun had burnt through early clouds and the group, with the exception of Ken, were gathered for their meeting. Before they got down to business though, Tuppence said she wanted to say something. Because she didn't seem her usual upbeat self, the group were somewhat mystified. "I've learnt something today," she said. "I met Margaret for coffee earlier while her son John was looking after Ken. I now realise Margaret is affected by Ken's dementia just as much as he is. Differently, of course. It's his brain that's damaged after all. He's the one who can't speak, can't do things, who's becoming a danger to himself. And he's the one who will likely die as a result of his illness." She paused to allow everyone to reflect.

"The effect on Margaret's health is huge too. She has to be on duty the whole time Ken's awake. It's relentless. She feels helpless. Guilty she can't make him better. Desperately sad. She's grieving for him while he's still alive. Her Ken has gone, yet she spends each day caring for him. She does her best to make him content and comfortable and safe. She said it's a Godsend that you take him out for a walk each week Henry. And John has put her in touch with a charity. Dementia Carers Count I think it's called. She's getting some one-to-one support through them, and they have a website with loads of good stuff on difficult behaviour, emotions, you name it. She's joined an online support group through them too where she can talk to people in the same situation as herself. It's helped a lot apparently."

"Despite that, she's exhausted. I don't think she's looking after herself either which she needs to, otherwise she'll have a breakdown. I think the big problem is she gets almost no company. She's lonely. So I'm going to try to chat to her regularly. If anyone else can talk, even on the phone, that might help." She sighed deeply. "Sorry. Didn't mean to go on but I thought you ought to know."

"Anyway," she said, "we'd better get on with what we're here for. What have you found out about Harley, Henry?"

"OK. Well Harley is both a churchwarden and on the Parochial Church Council."

"What does that involve?" Asked Wayne.

"The PCC runs the church. Churchwardens look after the day-to-day operation along with the vicar. They're prestigious roles occupied by upright members of the community. He's also about to be made President of the Rotary Club and he's a trustee of a local wildlife trust. People in those positions need to be squeaky clean." Everybody nodded in understanding. "And because he used to run probably the biggest undertakers in the area he is well known and respected. So he has a high profile in the area as an honest, trustworthy and honourable person."

"I can see where you're heading here," said Tony.

"Absolutely! I also chatted to a few people who know him well. They confirmed he is a proud man and very conscious of his respectability. They all said he seemed to have retreated into his shell recently. One of them put it down to the fact that his wife is not well. Oh, and by the way, he is very into cricket and rugby. So what do we make of all that?"

"It sounds as if he's not the sort of person who would want incriminating photographs or dubious stories circulating, even if they were eventually proved to be false," stated Tuppence. Everybody agreed.

"I've got some feedback as well," said Tony. "I've spoken to Harry Payne and told him what was going on. He said his dad wouldn't be able to handle any nasties from the blackmail threat. Also, he mentioned his mother needed a hip operation. His father has gone cold on her having it done privately. Maybe he's worried about the money. Harry's also not heard anything from the blackmailers. He also said he was happy to listen to the recording. If anyone can confirm the voice it should be him."

Tony carried on, "While we are on the subject of Harry, another couple of things. Firstly he is amazed by what we are doing and very appreciative. He wants to help as much as he can. He's probably in a good position to do that. I suggest we invite him onto the team." All agreed, with the exception of Tuppence.

"I'm not sure about that. He's a miserable scumbag!"

"Now come on, don't mince your words Tuppence," said Henry.

"That's where a second thing comes in. He would like to apologise to you for being rude and unpleasant," said Tony

"You mean for calling me an alcoholic floozy?" The others laughed.

"He seemed very genuine to me."

"Come on, I think we should give him a chance," said Wayne. Begrudgingly Tuppence gave her approval. "I'll add him to the WhatsApp and arrange to meet him with the recording."

"Then there's a third thing," said Tony. "I need a golf partner for when I spy on Mr Enrici. I was going to ask a friend from London but I discovered Harry golfs. He has agreed to do it instead." Everyone, including Tuppence, nodded their approval to that.

"I have something to report too," said Tuppence, "An old family friend is pretty senior in the Metropolitan Police. I thought I'd give him a ring about what we are up to. He said it's unlikely the local Bobbies would have enough to go on unless they spoke to the victim. So that puts the kibosh on that. He also said he would be happy to chat through where we are up to if we get any more information. So I'm going to arrange to see him when I next go down to see Poppy."

And with that the meeting ended with everybody going their separate ways, all fascinated by what Tony and Harry would uncover next week."

CHAPTER 9

The Villain Identified

Just over a week later, the two golfers left Sheringham at 8.00 in the morning. A Fret had rolled in overnight and the journey through the fog was slow until they got beyond Holt. Harry had made himself comfortable in the big leather seat and they listened to the Today programme on Radio 4. Soon after 9.00 Tony's phone rang. "Hi Sandy," he answered using hands-free. There were a few pleasantries, then Sandy said, "The Board are concerned that your life is going to get tedious and that will affect your health. We're wondering whether you would stay on as a non-exec."

"That's kind but I'm afraid not. In fact, life up here at the moment is anything but tedious."

"I suspected that might be your answer. Worth a try though. Anyway, I've got another idea up my sleeve. I'll put some meat on the bones and get back to you."

Tony laughed. "OK, talk to you later."

Tony said to Harry by way of explanation, "Sandy is one of the agency directors. We've worked together for years. Really good guy. I'm not going back!"

They made good progress down the M11, turned east onto the M25 and it wasn't long before the satnav told them they were just five minutes from the golf course. The approach to the club was along a tree-lined drive between fairways. A very smart clubhouse appeared with a large car park to the left. No Bentley with the L.E.E. number plate though. They parked and headed for the pro shop.

They checked in and discovered that there was a cancellation for the slot between them and Enrici. Taking that would give Harry a better opportunity for photos. The young lad behind the counter gave them the key to their buggy and told them where to pick it up.

They drove back to the car and loaded their golf bags. They were about to go to the clubhouse when a green Bentley drove past them, parking a few spaces away. The letters L.E.E stood out like a sore thumb. With heart rates rising noticeably Tony drove the buggy towards the clubhouse. Harry glanced back and saw three people getting out of the Bentley, one of them with almost white hair.

There were still 30 minutes before Enrici's tee time, so they were pretty sure he would go into the bar. They waited outside in the buggy until he and the other two parked their trolleys and went into the clubhouse. Tony and Harry followed quickly. Enrici and one of the others were sitting at a table while the third was at the bar. Tony went to the bar too, while Harry chose a table hopefully close enough to be able to pick up some sound. Enrici's man ordered three coffees, paid and joined the others.

The barman turned to Tony who said, "I'll have two coffees and two bacon rolls, please. Looks like a tough course, I think we might need the sustenance."

"You'll like it, it's hard but not punishing."

Inspiration sparked. He lowered his voice. "Tell me," he said, "that chap over there with the white hair. He looks familiar somehow. I feel I should know him but his name escapes me."

"Ah. That's Mr Enrici," said the barman without any obvious sign of pleasure.

"Enrici?" Tony's brow furrowed. "No. Must be mistaken. Thanks anyway."

"You're probably better off not knowing him," muttered the barman as Tony turned to join Harry.

Enrici's group was deep in conversation as Tony sat down with his back to them. "Definitely Enrici," he whispered. "Confirmed by the barman."

"Recorder is under my hat." Harry pointed to his baseball cap lying on the table. "Hope it'll pick something up."

As he was speaking a waiter delivered the order to Enrici's table. "Ta muchly, I'm needing this," from the man who was first to sit down with Enrici.

"That was a Birmingham accent," said Tony. "How old do you reckon he is?"

"Difficult to say with that receding hairline. Early thirty's? The other guy's older. They're both brutes. The one who was at the bar has a nose that looks as if it's been in a punch-up or two. I guess they would be called 'The Muscle'."

Just as the waiter delivered their coffee and bacon rolls, Enrici's raised voice could be heard. "Get on to it Joe. You can't let them delay. Pressure. You know what to do." A few moments later, a fourth man approached Enrici's table and sat down. "Hello, Doc." He gestured to the other two, "Michael, Joe."

"Good to meet you," said Doc. "Must be just about time to go."

"We'll go when I say so," said Enrici. "I need a quiet word with you. Have you got the stuff?" Doc handed Enrici what looked like the sort of bag pharmacy prescriptions come in. "Michael go put this in the car," he handed him the package. "Joe, scarper. I'll be out in a couple of minutes."

The two men left and Enrici began talking to Doc very quietly. They then both got up and left the bar.

Harry took the recorder from under his hat and turned it off. "I reckon we might have got some of that," he said. "Not a very nice man is he? Shall we get going so we're close behind them? I just need to get my camera from the car and take a photo of the Bentley."

"Good thinking!" said Tony.

By the time they approached the tee, Enrici and Doc had already teed off. Joe took his drive followed quickly by Michael. The four then marched off down the first fairway.

"Well we might as well enjoy our round," said Tony.

So off they went. Tony teed off first. He was a single-digit handicapper and his ball soared straight down the centre of the fairway. Harry had a much larger handicap but he could at least usually get round a course without making a fool of himself. His drive was a pale imitation of Tony's, but at least it went straight.

Because they were in a buggy, they were able to go faster than the group in front. It meant they could also get close enough for Harry to duck down behind it and take photos. He took lots of them. Golf etiquette is such that if you are going faster than the group in front you should be 'called through' to overtake them. Harry and Tony decided to invoke this so they could take a close look at Enrici's group as they passed them. Eventually, the hint was taken and Doc beckoned them through. Tony was effusive with his thanks.

When they got back, the clubhouse bar was busy. Tony took a table, strategically placed so that wherever Enrici's group sat they would be close, while Harry went to the bar.

"Did you enjoy your game? asked the barman.

"Certainly did. Lovely course."

"How did you do?"

"I came second!"

The barman chuckled. "What can I get you?"

"I think we'll have a couple of pints of that," said Harry pointing at a hand pump advertising a local draft beer, "and a nice big bowl of chips please."

The barman served the beer. "I'll get the chips over to you."

Harry placed the two glasses on the table saying, "It's only 3.8%, so you'll be OK driving," Enrici's group, minus Doc, came in and sat at a nearby table. Tony and Harry sat quietly, ear-wigging.

The other group showed no signs of having enjoyed their round. Enrici particularly complained about bad luck. Happy souls thought Tony. What slightly worried him though was that Enrici kept glancing at them. Their chips arrived and then they overheard Enrici saying, "We can't stay long. I've got to visit the old lady in the nursing home. I'll drop you at the hotel."

"How is she," asked Michael.

"What do you care how she is?" There was a pause. "She's beginning to lose it, but not fast enough. That's where the Doc comes in. I need to get her to sign some documents before she goes completely doolally. Right, come on, we're off." He got up and he and the other two marched out of the bar.

"What do you make of that?" asked Tony.

"Sounds to me as if he's trying to swindle someone."

The barman came over to collect the empties from Enrici's table. "Do you guys want anything more?"

"No thanks. We'll be heading off pretty soon." Harry thought it might be worth pressing him for a bit more information. "Can I just ask you something? We couldn't help overhearing Mr Enrici's conversation just now, something about diddling an old lady."

The barman looked around to make sure nobody overheard, "Look, you didn't get this from me, but I have a feeling he's a crook. I guess he is talking about Grace. Grace Fielding. She's a member here but I haven't seen her for ages. Lovely lady. She's a widow and I think Enrici sees her as a cash cow, excuse the expression. He can be pleasant when he wants to and I think he charmed the socks off her. He moved in with her several months ago. She's very wealthy. He's running around in her late husband's Bentley. Had his own personal number plate put on it. I heard she'd gone into Burns Croft. I couldn't believe it, she seemed as fit as a fiddle."

"Burns Croft?"

"Yes, a care home not far from here. Very smart. Watch Enrici, most people stay clear of him."

"We will, thank you."

Harry picked up his baseball cap with the recorder underneath still operating. They left the clubhouse.

When they sat down in the car they were delighted to discover that despite a lot of background noise almost everything they wanted had been recorded. "Hopefully Wayne can download it," said Tony. "How do you think your photos came out?"

Harry looked at the small screen on his camera. "Some look OK. I'll download them when I get home."

Tony started the car, clicked 'Home' into the satnav and began to move down the long drive, initially deep in thought. Then he asked Harry "Are you in a hurry to get back?"

"Not particularly, why?"

"I'm convinced we've found our man but there was no specific evidence pointing towards your dad's blackmail. However, it looks like he is trying to defraud this lady called

Grace. I'm thinking if we can uncover a bit more about that it will add to the reasons why the police should get involved."

"Sounds sensible to me. How do we go about it?"

Tony suggested they visit the care home. He could say he was from the CQC and that he was looking into a case of elder abuse. Harry thought it worth a try but said they'd want evidence. "We'll face that hurdle when it comes. Can you look up the number and I'll call the manager," said Tony. She was initially reticent but mellowed when Enrici's name was mentioned. They agreed to meet after Enrici's visit. At Burns Croft, they parked as far from the Bentley as they could. It wasn't long before Enrici returned and drove away. Harry and Tony were shown directly into Bernadette Dixon's office. She was the tall, smartly dressed, black-haired, stern-faced and surprisingly young manager.

Her office was tidy, furniture was good quality, some art on the walls along with a framed certificate of some sort. She said she was unaware of abuse taking place but took any report very seriously. She was patently switched on and wanted evidence they were bone-fide inspectors, so Tony had to come clean. "I have absolutely no authority at all. However, I do have some evidence of wrongdoing."

"This is most unconventional. I can't have any old Tom, Dick or Harry coming in off the streets and demanding information about one of my residents," said a glowering manager.

Tony could also be assertive. "I appreciate that. We don't want information about Mrs Fielding. On the contrary, we are trying to protect her by warning you about a possible problem. Let me explain." He told her about their investigations and particularly what they'd heard at the golf club. She still seemed reticent.

Harry realised they were in a bit of a stand-off. "I appreciate the difficult position we're putting you in. Would it help if we played you the recording of Enrici we made?"

There was a pause, "OK. Go ahead."

He dug the recorder out of his pocket and rewound to where Enrici was talking at the table. Bernadette listened, looking more and more shocked as she did so. Tony then fast-forwarded to the to the point where the barman came over and spoke to them. He started the playback again. "What do you think?"

"That's dreadful. It's definitely Enrici. Who is the other voice giving his opinion?"

"Please keep it to yourself," said Tony, "it's the barman from the clubhouse."

"Right. I'm not aware of any suspicious activity concerning Enrici. However, the circumstances around Grace coming here were unusual. They may need further investigation. Now, you need to keep what I tell you to yourselves."

Bernadette called the senior carer on Grace's floor and asked her to pop down. She then explained that Grace had been admitted about two months ago for respite and observation. Enrici appeared to be the instigator. He said he couldn't manage her difficult behaviour. Grace seemed fully compliant with the plan. He provided a letter from her GP explaining she had a diagnosis of Alzheimer's and provided a package of drugs he said her GP insisted she take. When she came in she seemed to be depressed, was very unresponsive and complained of pains. It turned out that she had a UTI and after a few days, she perked up.

The carer, Dorota, joined them. She explained that the care home used a local GP practice which conducted a 'ward round' every Tuesday. The GP reported that Grace displayed symptoms of depression but she could find no evidence of dementia. Most of her drugs were fine but they included an antipsychotic which is for serious psychological conditions and not appropriate for Grace. Bernadette added, "they can dull the senses and potentially make someone vulnerable!" Bernadette thanked Dorota and she left.

Within seconds of her leaving, they heard a kerfuffle and a raised voice in reception, "if you don't get her now, I know where her office is."

"That's Enrici," said Tony, looking and feeling alarmed.

Bernadette leapt up and locked her door. "I guess you don't want to come face-to-face with him do you?"

"Certainly not. Where does that go?" He pointed to a door behind Bernadette's desk.

"It's my filing cupboard." She opened the door to reveal a small space lined with shelves stacked with files and other paraphernalia. "You could squeeze in," she said.

As more shouting came from Enrici, Tony said "we'll try."

Smiling, Bernadette closed the door on them saying, "good job you're friends!" It was pitch black. As they tried to get comfortable, Harry's elbow dislodged what they later discovered was a mug. It smashed noisily to pieces as it hit the floor.

"Bugger," he whispered. They hardly dare breathe. Tony heaved a silent sigh of relief as he heard Bernadette unlock her office door.

"What's going on?" Staring at Enrici, she spoke forcefully, "There's no need to shout!".

"I need a word with you. Now!" bellowed Enrici.

"You're not getting a word or anything else until you stop shouting."

A male carer appeared, "do you need any help, Miss Dixon?"

"No, it's alright thank you Patrick, Mr Enrici just needs to calm down and then we'll have a chat." A red-faced, fuming Enrici, clearly unused to people facing him down, was silent for a moment. "Good. Come into my office and we'll have a civilised conversation." She turned on her heel, went into her office and sat behind her desk. Enrici followed. "Shut the door." He did so. "Now what's the problem?"

"These!" He said waving a plastic binder containing papers in the air. "I took my wife's notes home to read."

"Grace is not your wife and those notes are confidential. They're used all the time and must not leave the premises. Give them to me please." She held out her hand.

"She's my partner, I can do what I like with them. Why have you changed her medication?"

"Some of it was not appropriate. Now please give me the notes."

"She needed her sleeping tablets and you've taken her off them."

"They were not sleeping tablets, they were antipsychotics. She has no illness that requires antipsychotics. Now, give me those notes."

"You have no right to change her medication without my approval. They were prescribed by her GP."

"Mr Enrici, Grace has a different GP while she is under my care. She has full mental capacity and agreed to the withdrawal of that medication. Hand over those notes to me. Now!"

"The old biddy is going doolally. She doesn't know what she's talking about." He stared at Bernadette for a moment then threw the file onto her desk. "This is a crap care home and it's costing me a fortune. I'll move her somewhere else."

"You do not pay Grace's bill, she does. You have no power to move her anywhere without her agreement. Now

I'd rather you leave. Immediately!" She pointed her finger, "There's the door."

Enrici stood up glaring at her, venom dripping from his eyes. "You won't get away with this you bitch, people do what I say. Watch your back!" And with that, he turned on his heel and strode out of the office.

During this whole episode, Tony and Harry stood very quietly, shoulder to shoulder, in the darkness. There was now no sound from the office so Harry knocked gently on the door. It was opened quickly by Bernadette. "Sorry, I was just trying to compose myself. That was fun," she said.

"We heard everything," said Tony. "You handled that very well. What are you going to do about the threats?"

"I'll have to file an incident report but I don't suppose I'll take it any further. He's a horrible little man but I doubt he'll do anything nasty."

"Be very careful, he does do nasty things," said Harry. "I hope you don't mind but I clicked my recorder on. We've got his threat for posterity."

"We do seem to have a bit of a problem. I can only thank you for your interest and warning. I'm not sure how it will help with your investigation though."

Tony said, "we're building up a case against him and this may prove significant. Would you mind if we keep in touch?"

"Of course, no problem." They exchanged phone numbers.

As they left, Tony said, "Did you notice the certificate on the wall?"

"I did but couldn't read it. I assume it was a management qualification or something."

"That was my guess. It turns out she was British Muay Thai Ladies Amateur Champion."

"What's Muay Thai?"

"No idea."

They started their journey and Harry located a pub where they could stop for a meal. He also Googled Muay Thai and discovered it was a form of Kickboxing. No wonder she wasn't intimidated by Enrici.

Over their meal, they mulled over the day. They'd made a big step forward but there was now a lot to think about. Tony texted Wayne to check that he could download Harry's recordings and received a thumbs-up emoji in reply. He also sent a WhatsApp to the group saying, '*We've found our man and uncovered yet more dirty deeds! Full story when we meet next. When can you make?*' Lots of excited responses but the first time everyone could make a meeting was the following Monday morning. It had been a long, eventful and bizarre sort of day and both men were mentally exhausted. It was a quiet drive home.

CHAPTER 10

A Busy Thursday

The following morning it was back to normal for Harry. He was very busy running the business. In the early days, he hated working at the undertaker's although he did day release courses in Norwich on Bookkeeping, Accountancy and Business Administration which kept him sane. Somehow he managed to minimise involvement with the front end of the business and much to his surprise, he rather enjoyed the back end. Over time he was able to improve some of the old-fashioned practices his father employed. Once Harland retired Harry set about changing the organisation. It became more modern, efficient and profitable. The company grew significantly, acquiring undertakers in Norwich, Great Yarmouth and Kings Lynn. Harry had his eye on others. This morning he held a strategy meeting over Zoom with the four directors. In the afternoon he intended to do something completely different.

That something was to find out, if he could, whether his father really had been blackmailed, whether he had paid the money, and if so where he'd got it from. Despite his ambivalence towards his father he wanted to make sure that both he and his mother were not suffering as a result. Harry drove to Cromer to see them. Harland always asked about the business and inevitably took issue with something or another. Today though he was very subdued. This was definitely not normal.

His mother was in the kitchen, baking. She said she was worried about his father. Just recently he'd lost interest in everything. He was a member of Norfolk County Cricket Club but hadn't been to a single match so far. He did his church duties and went to Rotary every week, but that was about it. She tried, but he wouldn't talk about it. This, along with everything else he'd heard, including the recording Wayne had played him, was confirmation to Harry that it was his father being blackmailed. So where did the money come from? He knew his father had a good pension and plenty of savings but didn't imagine he could magic up £150,000 just like that. Maybe he took out a short-term loan from the bank.

Harry knew his father regularly popped into the Cromer office to chat to a couple of long-term employees he was pally with. Maybe he could pick up some sort of pointer there. He could also have a chat with Anthony, the director. Harland was initially adamant that Anthony was the wrong person for the job after Harry had installed him a few years ago. However, having seen how he ran the Cromer business, he had changed his mind. Indeed, they got on very well.

Anthony Christian was tall, elegant and from Barbados. As a Royal Marine, he had seen action in often secret operations abroad. He left the forces as a Warrant Officer Class 1. His commanding officer introduced him to a friend who ran a funeral company and was looking for someone to manage a small branch. Associating with dead bodies was no problem for Anthony. He had dealt with, indeed caused, many of these in his time. He rapidly made his mark and soon wanted a bigger challenge. Through the National Association, he met Harry who was looking for somebody to direct the Cromer Head-Office operation. They gelled, and Harry took him on.

They were complete opposites. Harry was short, slightly tubby, very white and introverted. Anthony was tall, muscular, black and very outgoing. Anthony took care of all those things Harry hated. In particular, he cut a dramatic figure marching slowly in front of the hearse in full morning suit, with top hat and a magnificent Silver topped cane. He was warm, caring, kind, conscientious and ran a fair, well-disciplined, tight ship. Much to Harry's surprise, Anthony had become one of his very few friends.

Harry spoke to Harland's two pals. They were both concerned about him. One thought he might be depressed, the other that maybe he didn't like retirement. He then spent some time with Anthony who said Harland had been in a few times recently and didn't seem too bad on the whole. He didn't elaborate. Anthony was usually far more chatty about people so this surprised Harry. He sat back, looked Anthony in the eye and asked whether he was telling the full story. After a bit of verbal batting backwards and forwards, Anthony said he had to tell Harry something very embarrassing. Goodness me, thought Harry, he knows about the blackmail. Harry asked him to go on.

Anthony took a deep breath and came straight out with it. Harland had borrowed £100,000 from the business for about 10 days but had paid it back in full two days ago. He had told Anthony that as a board member, he was allowed to take out loans but not to tell anybody about it. Anthony accepted he should've spoken to Harry but Harland put him under a lot of pressure not to. Harry agreed he should have told him, but he knew what his father could be like. When asked, Anthony said he didn't know what the money was for. Harry wondered where the other £50,000 had come from, presumably savings he could get at quickly. At least he had his answer. His father had been blackmailed and paid up.

* * *

Tuppence wasn't particularly busy, but she was troubled. She was unhappy that Harry Payne was joining the team. But then his father was being blackmailed, so didn't he have the right to help bring the transgressors to account? On the other hand, they had a jolly little group who had begun to develop a real closeness. The worthless little wretch could disrupt that. Although Tony, whose opinion she wanted to believe, seemed to think there was more to him than his reputation afforded. Well, he should grow up and stop being rude. But then he had said he wanted to apologise. What a conundrum.

To take her mind off that problem, she decided to fix the meeting with Bob from the Met. She called Poppy and arranged to stay with her for a couple of days. "Any time," she said, "we're not planning on going anywhere." So she texted Bob to see whether they could meet the weekend after next. It wasn't long before a reply arrived saying he could manage the Sunday evening. He said he would find somewhere traditional but respectable enough for a lady of her vintage. That didn't pass without a robust response.

Having got that out of the way, she took her now daily walk and had a nice light soup for lunch. Her mind flipped back to Harry Payne. Tuppence asked herself what it was that was irking her. She had to admit it was because he had called her an alcoholic floozy. Come on girl, you've had worse insults in the past. Ignore it and get a life! So she sat back, decided to be sensible and make fun of it. She texted Tony to ask if he knew Harry's wife's name. By return, her phone pinged 'Sofia. Why?' She responded, 'I'll tell you Monday'. She took a party invitation, wrote on it 'Harry and Sofia', and at the bottom wrote 'From Tuppence, aka The Alcoholic Floozy'. She put it in an envelope and sealed it before she could change her mind, wrote their names on the front and posted it through their door. Back in her apartment she switched the kettle on, heaved a big sigh, and felt much better about herself.

* * *

Henry and Elsie had gone to Norwich to buy new outfits for Tuppence's party. They didn't tend to frequent social occasions with television stars, so Elsie was adamant they were going for it, damn the cost. This expedition was not up Henry's street. It meant traipsing around half a dozen shops before eventually settling on what was acceptable to Elsie. And that was just for his clothes. There would be another dozen or more shops on top of that until she found something for herself. Sartorial elegance was not something that rested well on Henry's shoulders. Jeans, open-necked shirts and floppy cardigans were more his bag. Choosing something smart was quite beyond him. That was Elsie's job.

It took a couple of hours and lots of grumbling from Henry for her to settle on his outfit. Navy trousers, a light blue shirt with a patterned red tie, a very nice and not too creased linen jacket, and even some blue suede shoes. He'd never had shoes that were not black or brown so this was a real adventure. Secretly he rather liked it. The trousers and jacket had to be left behind for the legs and arms to be shortened, a perennial problem for Henry, but they'd be ready for pickup in a few days.

Elsie said it would be at least another two hours before she had her outfit so told Henry to buzz off and do something useful but not spend too much time in a pub. She'd call him when she was ready. That markedly improved Henry's mood. So he decided to wander around the market, walk down Elm Hill and then stroll through the Cathedral. He lasted an hour before thinking about a pub. On the way back into the city centre he passed the Maids Head. Thinking how opportune, he decided to pop in for a beer and see for himself the scene of the misdemeanour.

He ordered a pint and sat by the bar, then went over to what must have been the sofa Tuppence had spent time behind. He chuckled as he imagined her attempting to extricate herself. A voice from the bar asked him whether he was alright. He explained that a friend had got stuck behind the sofa. The voice belonged to a young man who laughed and said he had helped pull her out. He was quite taken aback when Henry said, "You must be Leon."

Henry enjoyed Leon's description of the event. "Maybe you could give her something for me," said Leon. "She asked me if I'd seen anybody other than the old farmer. I hadn't, but remembered a man bought coffee with a card. I wrote his name down, hold on." He disappeared, then came back with a piece of paper on which was written 'Michael Bradley'. "There you go." Henry felt he hadn't contributed much to the investigation so far, but now he had the name of Enrici's accomplice. He celebrated with another pint.

* * *

Tony woke that morning to thoughts of capturing the robbers but with no idea how to go about it. He was sure they had identified the villain and didn't want his misdeeds going unpunished, but every time he thought about how they could prove his guilt, he hit a brick wall. Was there a way to get Harley involved? Could their experience at the care home help in some way? "What do you think?" he asked Willie who was licking his paws and washing his face after a breakfast of new fishy cat food with added sprat sprinkles on top. Willie paused, looked at Tony in a disinterested fashion, then unhelpfully continued his ablutions.

Over more coffee, he considered several ways of confronting or tricking the scoundrels. He dismissed them all because they were either most unlikely to succeed, illegal, or downright dangerous. He needed to put his creative hat on. In the old days coming up with ideas was easy. He would storyboard, bounce thoughts off others and slowly build up a plan. This was altogether new territory. He needed to redirect his train of thought. Some sea air would help. It was breezy so he put a jacket on and went out for a walk along the promenade and then over the cliffs towards West Runton.

He was still running ideas around in his head when he received a call from Bernadette Dixon. Apparently, raised voices had been heard in Grace's room during Enrici's visits. Then this morning Grace had asked Dorota to contact her daughter Susan. It seemed Enrici had taken her mobile phone away. Bernadette found Rhona's number in Grace's care plan and rang her. She had been away for three weeks on holiday and was shocked that her mother was anywhere near a care home. She told Bernadette she held Grace's Power of Attorney. An idea sprang into Tony's mind and he said he would call Bernadette back.

If they could catch Enrici in the act of defrauding Grace, maybe that would help their case in some way. He called technical guru Wayne and gave him the complete story. He asked whether he thought security cameras in Grace's room would be possible. Wayne did and said he would look into it. Ten minutes later he called Tony back. "We would need a two camera system, small so they could be hidden, linked wirelessly to a laptop as a recorder. The cost is about £2,000 plus a laptop." There was a sharp intake of breath at Tony's end of the line. "However," said Wayne, "I have a friend in the business and as long as we can guarantee we're using it legally, he has a system he can lend us for a while. I can install it."

"Excellent," said a relieved Tony. "I'll tell Bernadette."

He phoned and put the idea to her. She said that was not something she would normally countenance, "but then these are exceptional circumstances. Let me think about it and I'll get back to you." It didn't take her long. "The company has a protocol for such a thing," she told him. I've spoken to Grace's daughter who was all for it. I've also discussed it with Grace. She was a bit nervous but will agree to go ahead. So if you can fix it and teach us what to do, we're all systems go."

By now Tony had turned back towards Sheringham and was putting his mind to a way forward in their quest for justice. For quite some time he got nowhere until inspiration struck as he was heading past the caravan park at Beeston. "Willie, you're a genius!" he shouted out loud, attracting curious looks from a group of holidaymakers. "A sprat to catch a mackerel! That's what we need." The thought of blackmail had been bouncing around in his mind when the idea struck. He wondered whether they could catch them at their own game. Set up some sort of sting whereby the team pretended they were blackmailing somebody else, get the villains to join them as 'the muscle', and from there, shop them to the police.

By the time he got home, his ideas had crystallised. It would depend on working with his company, Brodie Vellum. He was retiring soon but still had a lot of clout and he reckoned he could persuade the board to play ball. He needed to go to London to film his retirement speech the following Tuesday, so arranged to have dinner on Monday night with two key directors who would need to sanction his plans. Tony felt very pleased with himself and told Willie as much. Willie studiously ignored him.

CHAPTER 11

The Bones Of A Plan

Next Monday morning, the team rose from their beds and each pulled back their curtains to survey the new day. They were confronted with grey skies and steady rain falling over Sheringham. The bad weather looked set in, so there was no way they could meet on the bench. Henry sent a WhatsApp suggesting they move inside to one of the pubs. Tony responded quickly. Concerned about privacy he suggested instead they all assemble in his apartment. One by one the team replied in the affirmative and by mid-morning they had all gathered. Tony had laid on coffee, tea and biscuits. The latter was a temptation for Tuppence she would have to bravely overcome.

Once he had been introduced to everybody by Tony, Harry said how much he appreciated what they were doing to help his father. He told them he could confirm that it was definitely him being blackmailed, where most of the money had come from and that his father seemed understandably depressed.

Tony and Harry between them gave a rundown of the action at the golf club. Wayne had transferred the recordings onto his laptop, which he played along with the original Maids Head recordings for comparison. They all agreed that Enrici and Michael's voices were the same on both. "So we've found our man and his henchman then," said Tuppence. "And there seems to be two more of them."

"The one called Joe is for sure another villain," said Tony. "I don't think Doc is part of the blackmail group but he does seem to be implicated in another matter we have to tell you about."

"We can put faces to the names too," said Harry opening up his iPad. He turned it for everybody to see and scrolled through several shots he'd taken.

Henry joined in, "I've found out what Michael's surname is by the way. It's Bradley."

"How did you do that?" Tuppence's face registered complete disbelief.

"From Leon in the Maids Head. I was in there last Thursday. He remembered your little episode and said he'd found the name of the person who had paid for coffee and kept it in case you went back in. Very nice of him I thought."

"Leon is going up in my estimation," said Tuppence, "which reminds me, I don't think I've told you that I have a friend in the Metropolitan Police. I told him a week or so ago what we were doing and he said there was absolutely not enough to go on for them to get involved. There might be now though. I'm meeting him in London at the weekend so I'll ask him shall I?"

"Sounds good to me. Be a bit careful though, we don't want them to go off half cock."

"Not a problem, he knows I'd flatten him if he did."

"You said there was something else you wanted to talk about," said Tuppence.

"Yes," said Tony. "You heard Enrici mention an old lady and a care home. We think he is trying to cheat this lady out of something or another, probably money." He and Harry took the group through what happened on their visit to the care home and Wayne played a cut-down and improved version of the recording.

The others thought hiding in a cupboard much more comical than the participants, "I hope you two behaved yourselves in there," quipped Henry. They all agreed though, it added grist to their investigative mill.

Tuppence, having a second cup of coffee and conscientiously leaving the biscuits alone, said that while what happened at the care home was pretty nasty she didn't think it proved any extortion was going on.

"Couldn't agree more," said Tony. He explained his bugging proposal.

"Hold on a minute, is that legal?" asked Henry.

"Bernadette, the care home manager, says there is a protocol for such a thing. She's got agreement from both Grace and her daughter. And our expert here," he indicated Wayne, "can set it all up."

"There is something we do need to consider," said Tuppence. "If we find proof that Enrici is trying to extort something from this Grace lady, then that is a separate crime for which he could be prosecuted. We have to ask ourselves, do we still want to go ahead with proving the blackmail considering the potential impact that could have on Harley?"

After a bit of thought, Wayne gave his opinion. "Harley has been swindled out of £150,000. In my view, if we only focus on Grace, there is no way he could get that money back."

"I agree," said Henry. "We started investigating the blackmail, I think we should finish it. We just need to work on minimising the impact on Harley."

There was a short silence, then Tony spoke up. "I think we should follow up on both. Saving Grace from Enrici's clutches is a good thing in itself and I think will add weight to the case against him for the blackmail." He added, "On that subject, I've got the bones of an idea that could bring these villains to justice and pay Harley his money back. It involves running a sting where we lure them into a new blackmail operation and then shop them to the police. I don't want to go into any detail about it now because it needs the cooperation of my company. I'm going down to London this evening and have arranged to meet some people tonight to talk over ideas. If you trust me to flesh this out I can come back very soon to discuss it."

There was both agreement and a collective sigh of relief. The meeting drew to a close and crockery was deposited in the kitchen. Willie, lying in his bed, glanced at people trooping in and out in a disinterested fashion. That was until he saw Harry. Willie's top lip quivered in the cat world equivalence of a sneer. One day, he thought to himself, one day. As they left, Harry apologised to Tuppence for his previous behaviour. He said it was totally in character but he would do better in the future. Tuppence laughed and said she'd forgotten about it already. As they left together, Harry thanked her for the invitation to the party. He and Sofia would love to come

* * *

That afternoon Tony motored down to London. He met Sandy the Creative Director and Finance Director Vijay at a favourite Chelsea restaurant. They were not long into their meal when he announced, "Prepare yourselves for something left field." He paused for effect. "I would like you to help me bring a bunch of criminals to justice."

"Yep! That's indubitably left field," said Sandy. "Excuse my ignorance, but isn't that what the police do?"

"It is indeed, but it's not quite that simple." He poured them another glass, "let me give you a complete rundown."

He did just that, warts and all, including his possibly illicit recording, Wayne's hacking and why they couldn't get the police involved at the moment. "I want to set a trap for the blackmailers which will provide hard and fast evidence for the police. And before you ask, I'll make sure there is nothing illegal involved that would cause Brodie Vellum a problem."

"Right," said Vijay, "so how are you going to set this trap and how on earth can we help?"

"Ha Ha," said Tony, "my plan!" He reached into the inside pocket of his jacket and held up his notes.

"Simply, I want to play these scoundrels at their own game. We'll get them to take part in a fabricated blackmail plot which will deliver enough cash to pay Harley back and, in the process, provide enough evidence for the police to convict them."

"Who's 'We'?" asked Sandy

"Myself and my little group of friends in Sheringham. We will persuade them that we are also a gang of blackmailers." He noticed Sandy's eyebrows raise. "Let me explain."

"We will approach Enrici with a business proposition. We'll say we are in the field of 'tax evasive blackmail' uncovering cases of real tax fraud within organisations and then demanding payment for our silence. We'll tell him we employ top-class financial hacking specialists but lack face-to-face expertise so we need to work with a professional like him to extract payment."

Looking a bit sceptical, Sandy said "You're going to have to provide him some sort of proof aren't you?"

"Absolutely. We will offer him the chance to join us on a real case we say we have in progress, which is extracting

£300,000 from a company currently defrauding the tax man. He will receive £150,000 for very little work."

"You sure they'll believe you?" asked Vijay.

"We will be able to show him fabricated, but totally believable books from a bogus company. We'll also create a website showing products and services, customers, management team, all that sort of stuff."

"So then what happens?" asked Sandy.

"We'll run the sting!" said Tony dramatically. "We'll tell them the company accounts team runs out of a serviced office. We will populate it with actors playing the crooked finance director and a couple of clerks. One of Enrici's hoodlums will make the visit, provide the evidence, and after a lot of argument, the finance director will agree to pay up. We will provide a bank account into which it is to be paid."

"This is going to cost a lot of money to stage. And you're implying that £300,000 has to be paid into a bank account. Where's that coming from!" asked Vijay.

"You're right, there are some costs. But the most important thing is, the £300,000 doesn't have to exist. I'll tell you why."

"I think we might need another bottle," said Sandy attracting the attention of their waiter.

"Part of the bargain with Enrici is that we would only involve him in the first scam if he agreed to sign up for much bigger future targets where he would earn upwards of half a million a go. I think he's sufficiently greedy to go for that. The cost to him of signing up would be £300,000. Half of that is his £150,000 share from the scam which we would keep. How he pays the other half is up to him, but he's just taken that amount from Harley. The reason we want that £150,000 is to return it to Harley. In other words, there is no need to come up with £300,000 cash in the first place." Tony sat back wearing a self-satisfied grin.

There were chuckles from both his colleagues. Then Vijay said "You've obviously put a lot of thought into this. I have a few questions. What evidence will you get to give to the police? Secondly, how is this going to help the old lady? And thirdly, where is the money coming from to build the website you'll need, populate the office, and create the false books?"

"Let me answer your third question first. That's where you come in."

"I had a feeling this was coming," said Sandy.

"I'm sure you know about the 'good causes fund'."

"Of course," said Sandy.

"Vaguely," said Vijay who hadn't been with the agency long.

"OK, I'll tell you about it. Several years ago I set up a fund to use for good causes. This started when a contract was delivered significantly under budget. I secured a lump of that to prime the fund. It was popular with the staff so from then on we usually added a small percentage to each contract. Unfortunately, I failed to put somebody in charge of making the 'good causes fund' fund many good causes. It's now got rather a lot of money sitting there doing nothing. It seems to me, we have here a genuine good cause.

"Sounds reasonable," said Vijay. Sandy just sat, glass in hand, grinning from ear to ear.

"In terms of how it helps Grace, if we put Enrici out of business it will take the heat off her. As for getting proof, I thought we could potentially film all the activity during the face-to-face blackmailing session and hand that to the police."

Vijay sat quietly for a few seconds, a slightly troubled look on his face. "I assume you expect comments rather than outright acceptance?"

"Of course."

"Well, I'm not so sure it would work. The trouble is, what you're proposing is not a real blackmail. It's just a staged one. So I don't think the police would take it up. Even if they did, a decent KC would get Enrici off."

"Um. Didn't think of that. But at least we'd get Harley his money back."

"And you'd have a group of hardened criminals on your back, having relieved them of £300,000."

Tony was deflated and sat silently contemplating his half-empty glass of wine.

Vijay broke the silence. "Your problem is, you've stopped before you've finished the job."

"How do you mean?"

"Well, the hook you dangled in front of these villains was for a large pay-out from a big blackmail. If you could make that a genuine blackmail from a real company and film that, then you really would have something to give to the police."

"How on earth would I do that?"

"I guess it would mean looking for a company that either is evading tax or would be prepared to play ball in some other way," suggested Sandy.

"We're not actually capable of investigating real company finances, so I don't think that would fly.

"What about the agency?" said Vijay.

"How do you mean the agency? We're not evading tax."

"I know that, but imagine if you told the villains that the 'good causes fund' had been accumulated illegally, then there would be good reason to blackmail us for the whole amount. You will then be doing what you promised them. That should interest the police."

Tony was rendered speechless. Sandy broke the silence, "I'd go with that and I'm sure the board would too. It wouldn't damage the agency and we might even get some good PR out of it."

"If you guys think that would fly, it would be fantastic. I'm still chairman so it would get my vote. I'd have to modify the emphasis on tax evasion but that would be easy enough. And do you think we could use the fund for the initial set-up costs?"

"I believe we could," said Sandy, "with one proviso. Remember when we spoke on the phone the other day I said I had an idea up my sleeve?"

"Yes, and I said I'm not coming back."

"You don't need to. We would like you to manage, on behalf of the agency, the 'good causes fund'. It would be a sort of voluntary, expenses-paid job. And this little scheme seems like a good place to start. Let's say it would contribute to your legacy!"

Tony laughed, "I've been shafted!"

"But in the nicest possible way," said Sandy.

"The first thing we have to do is to help you get your initial scam off the ground," said Vijay getting rather animated. "We could use one of our dormant companies and my guys can easily build a set of books for you."

"And we can populate a very creative website too," offered Sandy. "Where does the office need to be?"

"I was assuming London but somewhere in southern England would be OK."

"Great. I guess you remember PoliAds, the small outfit we acquired just over a year ago? Well, we've kept on their little industrial unit in Reading. We could use that as the front for your company."

Tony leaned back in his chair. "Am I pleased I talked to you guys! I thought I was being so clever. Just goes to show, nobody has a monopoly on good ideas. This is wonderful and I can't tell you how much I appreciate your help. I'm looking forward to getting back to Sheringham to discuss this with the team. We can put a detailed plan together. In the meantime my friends," he lifted his glass, "Cheers! I haven't been this excited about a project in years!"

CHAPTER 12

Bugging Grace

Tuppence spent a very pleasant weekend with Poppy and Trevor, met several old friends and stepped off the wagon for the occasion. On Sunday evening she took a cab to meet Bob at what had turned out to be an old watering hole of both of them on the Strand. It was local to Bob when he was at Scotland Yard and a haunt of Tuppence when she was on stage in the West End. They both arrived at the appointed hour. There were cheery greetings and Bob insisted on setting up a tab which he would settle at the end of the evening, "the least I can do for my old Auntie." Tuppence decided not to react but accepted the gesture gracefully. They had a long chinwag about the past, about their respective families and about what both of them were up to now. Beer and wine were consumed and each enjoyed a roast dinner.

Tuppence was about to bring up the subject of the investigation when Bob beat her to it. He asked how far her little team of snoops had got chasing down this band of iniquitous East End criminals. Tuppence was prepared, "I think you'll be surprised." She told Bob she could confirm the gang leader was Lawrence Enrici and that his sidekick was Michael Bradley. She showed him some photos Harry had sent her. "This younger man is somebody called Joe, who also seems to be part of Enrici's gang. And this older chap is implicated in some other evil doings that Enrici is involved in."

"Crikey! You sure?"

"Positive! We have another recording of them both and we're sure they are the same people doing the blackmail."

"And you believe you know the name of the victim?"

"Yes, I'll tell you if it won't go any further." Bob nodded. "His name's Harland Payne, known as Harley. He's an old school friend of two of the team and the father of one of them. And we know the ransom has been paid too."

Bob sat back, a thoughtful look on his face. "If you could get this Harley chap to come forward and testify, we might just have a case. However, there are problems. One is that the recordings were made secretly. A good KC may well get them excluded. Then, of course, it would come down to the victim's word against the other two. They can probably manufacture an alibi. So apart from the circumstantial sighting of a car numberplate, that may leave us rather short of evidence."

"So what you're saying is, without Harley's testimony there's basically no chance of the local police becoming interested. And even if he does testify, it comes down to his word against the villains."

"I'm afraid so. Sorry to be so negative."

Tuppence paused. "No problem! That's what we thought." Now was the time to tentatively introduce Tony's plan. "So what we have decided to do, is to run our own sting operation."

Bob was about to take a swig and his glass stopped just before he did so. "I beg your pardon?"

"Look, we have a situation here where a completely innocent man has been tricked out of £150,000. It's not only affecting his pocket, it's affecting his mental health and will have knock-on effects on his wife's health too. And, it's personal! We understand the police position but we are not prepared to just sit back and do nothing."

"And you want to take things into your own hands? Do you know who you're dealing with? These are very unpleasant people."

"We've thought about that. We will plan very carefully. Our objective is to get Harley's £150,000 back and in the process accumulate enough evidence for the police to become involved."

Bob looked rather worried. "I'm not so sure about this. I have to advise you against it. You could get yourselves into serious trouble."

"We'll take care, trust me."

Tuppence could see that Bob was thinking again and chose to stay silent. "I probably shouldn't do this but maybe you'd like to bounce your plans off me once you've got them thought through," he offered. "From what you've said, you do seem to have stumbled across some genuine criminals causing genuine harm in the community. That's something none of us want. However, I don't want you to put yourselves in danger or find yourselves on the wrong side of the law. That really would be counter-productive."

"That would be helpful, thanks."

"I also shouldn't tell you this, but I asked a few questions about Enrici. He's a career criminal. Mainly extortion. Always uses heavies to do his dirty work. Served a couple of terms in jug, most recently Brixton. He's now been out ten years and has been charged twice but he uses a good barrister and has so far escaped prosecution. Looks as if he's up to his old tricks again. According to my colleagues, he is absolutely driven by money and image. It would be good to get him but they won't push unless there is a cast-iron case."

"So if we can provide a portfolio of what they're up to, you think somebody from your side might get involved?"

"Probably. It would have to be sound stuff that's admissible in court."

"Fair enough. You're on!"

And with that, they agreed to stop talking about criminals, have another drink, and then call it a night. Tuppence took a taxi back to Poppy's, happy in the knowledge that she had something positive to talk about at the team's next meeting.

* * *

The next morning Wayne left Sheringham in his new sports car, a sleek red number with a BMW badge on the front. Previously, he'd not bothered to change from the third-hand Vauxhall Astra he'd had for years because he hardly ever drove beyond Norwich. But business was booming for Wayne and he'd always dreamed of having something classier. Now he had the money, he was jolly well going to make that dream come true.

However much he was looking forward to the drive though, he was concerned about going to the care home on his own. He imagined people shouting and behaving in embarrassing ways. He assumed it smelled unpleasant. This Bernadette woman also seemed pretty fearsome. So when he discovered Tuppence was visiting Poppy he suggested she join him and he would drive her back home in his new sporty number. Tuppence didn't exactly jump at the idea but felt this was a team thing, so she should help out. She made her way by Tube to Epping where Wayne had arranged to pick her up at 2 o'clock.

Having collected the camera equipment, Wayne got there almost dead on time and found Tuppence sitting on a bench outside the front of the station. From there it was a relatively short drive to the care home where they met Bernadette. She was surprised to see two of them so Tuppence jokingly explained that Wayne was the expert and she was his apprentice. With Dorota in tow, Bernadette took them straight to Grace's room. It was well appointed as it should be for such an expensive place. Grace was in the lounge watching an entertainer.

Between the four of them, they decided where Wayne would locate both cameras to get the best coverage and be camouflaged effectively. The first was tucked beneath a fluffy toy on top of the wardrobe at the intersection with the wall. The other was at the base of a large indoor plant on a shelf. Wayne had set the configuration up on one of his spare laptops, so now they tested it out in situ with Tuppence playing the part of Grace and the laptop securely hidden away in the nursing station. It all worked well.

On the way back to Bernadette's office they passed two elderly ladies who turned and one of them squealed, "Oh, look who it is!" and they both waved. "Are you moving in?"

"No, I'm just on a visit. Nice to see you."

Wayne hooted, "Could be just right for you one of these days."

"Don't start behaving like your grandfather!"

Bernadette looked confused.

Back in her office, pouring coffee Bernadette said "What was all that about in the corridor?" Wayne explained that Tuppence was a famous, now retired, actress. It was clear that Bernadette had never heard of her.

She was excused by Tuppence, "Don't worry, you're only famous to the people who know who you are. You're much too young."

Bernadette explained her surveillance plan. She said that when Enrici arrived he would be required to wait in reception because Grace was 'just having some personal care'. The receptionist would then call the nursing station and say loudly that Mr Enrici was here to see Grace. That would be the signal to start recording.

Tuppence sensed that this whole process was alien to Bernadette and her staff. "If it helps Bernadette, I had a conversation yesterday with a senior member of the Metropolitan police. He confirmed that Enrici is a criminal skilled in extortion. We don't underestimate how difficult this must be for you."

"You're right. Our job is to look after Grace, not spy on her. But then if we protect her, as we should, and in the process help put a criminal behind bars, then so much the better."

Very soon afterwards Wayne and Tuppence were on their way home. Tuppence couldn't remember having been in a car like this before. It surprised her how relatively easy it was to get in, and how smooth, comfortably and quietly it drove. The only downside was when they overtook large lorries. Her left ear seemed only inches away from enormous spinning wheels. This was much of the drive as the M11 had only two lanes a lot of the way and Wayne was mostly in the one on the outside.

Tuppence had spent a fair amount of time in Wayne's company over the last few weeks but hadn't really picked up much about him other than his capacity for computer hacking. "What got you into the cyber security world," she asked as another wheel zipped past. "I guess it wasn't just your experience with that company in Holt?"

"Oh no, I've been interested in computers since I was at school." He talked about his group of friends who played computer games competitively, and learnt how to program and build their own websites. "We all knew about hacking too. We thought it would be fun to break into one another's systems. Some of us were quite successful, me particularly."

"That led us down the route of finding out how to build in levels of protection. I got more and more interested and by the time I left school, I was a bit of an expert. I got a job in an IT network security company in Norwich. It turns out I knew more than half the people already there. I became one of their specialists in tracing and preventing security breaches. In the process of course I learnt how to get around security locks myself. Unfortunately, when I was hauled up in front of the beak, the company decided I was surplus to requirements. Fair enough I suppose."

"So what happened when you came out of clink?"

"One of the lecturers from the Prisoners' Educational Trust put me in touch with a contact he had in a big bank. It turned out they needed people to try and break their security systems. Two IT people sat me down in a room with a collection of equipment linked to the web, some bank statements, various letters, and a couple of cards. They gave me a cup of coffee and a sandwich and told me to see whether I could break in and transfer money between accounts. It didn't take too long to work things out."

"I transferred money backwards and forwards but any decent hacker could do that. So I fiddled with one of the dummy accounts they'd set up, transferred a hundred pounds from it into my personal account in another bank and then transferred it back again. Then I found out who the Chief Executive was and where he lived from their personnel files. I used one of the debit cards to send some flowers to his wife with a nice note from me telling her where I was and what I was doing."

"When the two guys came back I explained to them where their failings were and what I'd done minus the bit about the flowers. They checked and were gobsmacked. Apparently, the Chief Executive wasn't amused although his wife did like the flowers. He told them to offer me a job! I worked there for a couple of years but I got fed up travelling into London all the time and didn't want to live down there. So I set up on my own. I now work for banks, finance companies and the public sector."

"That's a real success story."

"I'm not sure success means ending up in gaol," said Wayne, his face creased with a smile.

"Maybe not. So what keeps you busy when you're not manipulating cyberspace?"

"I like sport. Watching rather than participating, although I'm pretty good at pool. Most watching is on TV, so in winter it's football and rugby. I like cricket in summer, although funnily enough, I prefer to listen to test matches on the radio. Anything else too if it catches my imagination, American Football sometimes, Athletics, Ice Hockey, Basketball."

"Do you ever go to matches?"

"Oh yes. A group of my friends have season tickets at Norwich City. I go to near enough every other home game. How much do you know about Norwich City?"

Tuppence pondered for a second, "They play in pretty colours?"

"They do indeed, yellow and green. The Canaries."

"I'm not a sporty person myself, although oddly enough I do like Rugby. I've been taken to Twickenham on a number of occasions. So tell me, watching sport can't take up all your time."

"No, not at all. Since I bought my house I've got into gardening. It's odd because in business I like immediate results. If there's something you never get with gardening it's immediate results. I think it's taught me the value of patience. It also gives you thinking time. I've solved lots of business problems while weeding my vegetable patch. I've also become a dab hand at DIY. I even managed to assemble an IKEA wardrobe all on my own! My brother was amazed. He said he didn't think people like me could do anything practical. Never trust a gay man with a hammer he used to say." Wayne smiled as he remembered the conversation.

Tuppence had known many gay men in her time. The entertainment business seemed to be a bit of a magnet. And in her earlier days, before the word gay had become ubiquitous, she had shared flats with several queers as they were then called. Generally, in her view, they were preferable to girls, keeping the place much tidier. So she felt completely comfortable and able to talk openly. "What do you do for friends in Norfolk?" she asked.

"Same as everybody else I suppose. Gay people do extend beyond the reaches of London you know. I've got a mixture of gay and straight friends, males and females. The only difference is, when I look for romance it's from the male side of the street, not the female."

"Do you come across much prejudice?"

"A bit, not a lot. I suppose that's because I'm not too obvious. I don't flounce. You will have noticed I don't wear particularly fashionable clothes. I don't carry a handbag, I don't speak with what some people identify as a 'gay voice'. But then in reality most gay men don't. It's just that we get stereotyped. I have absolutely nothing against anybody who does, but it's just not me."

"No, I would hardly have known you were gay if you hadn't said."

"And does it really matter?"

"No, not at all. I just assumed things could be a bit more orthodox, if I can put it that way, out of the big cities."

Wayne chuckled, "you're not the first! I don't think there's any difference. It's all about intolerance wherever you are. A lot of people can't cope with anyone different to what they consider normal. There's loads of it around, racism, xenophobia, religion, politics. There are cultures where being gay is punishable by death. Religion is the worst in my view. Why do Catholics hate Protestants despite believing in the same God? Why do Sunnis and Shias try to exterminate one another just because 1500 years ago the top job went to somebody who wasn't related to Muhammad? It's all about bigotry and people should be ashamed of themselves. Probably a bit a simplistic I know. Anyway, you're into rugby, why do Scottish and Welsh supporters hate the English?"

"That's different. You're talking about rugby. Everybody hates the English! We just have to get used to it!"

Wayne roared with laughter to the extent that Tuppence was concerned he wasn't fully in control of the car. "Anyway, what about you? I don't sense you are gay and there's no man around."

"I've had the odd fling in my time but sadly nothing that stuck.

"Oh dear. Tell me about it."

"It's not very exciting I'm afraid."

"I'll be the judge of that."

So Tuppence began her story.

She said that in the early days she had several on, but mostly off, relationships. Then, in her early 40's, she met someone who seemed ideal. He was a barrister based in London commuting back home to Cornwall at the weekends. He was very caring, accepted she needed to tour and had a very comfortable pad near Regents Park. She asked many times whether he would take her to Cornwall for a weekend but there were always good reasons why he couldn't, usually revolving around his mother, who he lived with. She was old, frail and didn't like visitors. That apart, Tuppence was truly contented and, she believed, in love.

"Then one day I was at his flat on my own and the phone rang. I heard a very posh voice record on the answerphone. It said, Sebastian it's your mother, call me at once it's urgent. I would have rung his office but he was in court that day. Half an hour later the same thing happened. The next time an exasperated voice insisted that Seb phone immediately, so I picked up the phone and interrupted. Who are you? she said. I said, I'm Tuppence. Tuppence, she said, is that the sort of name they give cleaners nowadays? Where's Sebastian I must speak to him."

Tuppence realised Seb's mother had no idea who she was. "I told her he was in court and offered to get a message to him. She said, tell him Jane's had a stroke. She's asking for him. God knows why, he's all but abandoned her. Jane? I said. Yes, are you deaf? she shouted. His wife! I was horrified, upset, angry, hurt, confused. Now tell him to call me straight away she blurted and hung up. Eventually I rang Seb's secretary, Peggy. It was difficult. I asked her to get an urgent message to him to ring his mother, his wife had had a stroke. There was silence at the end of the phone. What? Peggy eventually managed to say. I can't repeat it Peggy, just tell him, I said. And that was the end of a wonderful relationship. Seb tried contacting me but I refused to talk. I wouldn't answer my door or phone. If only he'd told me, I could probably have lived with it. But I couldn't handle the lies and deceit."

"That's really sad," said Wayne. "So that was that then?"

"Not quite,' said Tuppence. "He wrote to me. I knew his writing but wouldn't open the letter. I tucked it in a drawer and forgot about it. I came across it many years later when I was moving to my house in Chiswick. I plonked it on a table, looked at it several times, then poured a very large gin and tonic and ripped it open. He had explained how his marriage was one of convenience caused by his aristocratic family being made almost penniless by mismanagement of the estate and death duties. He had to rescue their fortunes by marrying the daughter of a neighbouring landowner. He said it was a loveless marriage from the start. No offspring."

"Divorce wasn't an option apparently. Then a year later his wife fell off her horse, was paralysed from the waist down and partially blinded. He was trapped and just couldn't abandon her. He said life was only made bearable by the times he spent with me during the week. He was sorry he hadn't told me before but was frightened I would leave him. He said if I didn't respond to his letter he couldn't blame me and wouldn't try to contact me again."

"And he didn't. I sat with the letter open on the table into the early hours. Did I make the right choice or was it a disastrous missed opportunity? Deep down, I know it was the latter." It was time for Tuppence to be silent for a moment and reflect. "I've never been one to say if only I'd done this or done that. I've learned in life you have to make decisions and you can't forever regret the road not taken." She smiled at Wayne. "I didn't throw the letter away though. It's in my keepsake box."

Wayne smiled wanly at Tuppence. "Sounds as if you both were the losers." The two continued their journey, in silence at times and at others chatting on all manner of subjects. It didn't seem long before they reached Sheringham. At Sillingham House, Wayne jumped out of the car to give Tuppence a helping hand. Getting out was not as easy as getting in. During the weekend Tony had fixed the team's next meeting to coincide with their return and Wayne said, "see you at Tony's," before driving away, feeling he'd grown distinctly closer to Tuppence as the day had passed.

CHAPTER 13

A Plan Of Action

There was an air of anticipation, even suppressed excitement, as the team assembled in Tony's apartment the next day. A month ago most of them were wondering what to do with their time. How things had changed. To help in the planning process, before he left London Tony had temporarily purloined flipchart boards and pads, marker pens, a projector and a screen. He wanted this to be a brainstorming session like he used to run in the old days.

This was a good day to stay indoors and plan a campaign. The North Norfolk coast was having another of its miserable grey days. It was distinctly chilly and steady rain was sweeping in from the sea soaking everything and everyone in its path. However, tucked up cosily in Tony's apartment, the assembled company had a panoramic view over the golf course to the west and through the murk to the east over the town and on towards West Runton.

Willie concurred with the indoor option. This was the second time his home had been filled with people. What on earth were they doing here. He decided he needed to take part in whatever was going on. He wandered around, imperceptibly sniffing feet, brushing against legs, accepting the occasional greeting and studiously avoiding Harry. His gaze settled on Tuppence and somewhere in his little cat brain there grew a warm, fuzzy feeling of recognition. So he climbed onto her lap, circled around, then settled down and began purring loudly.

Tony stood by one of the flipchart boards and called the meeting to order. "I believe our objectives are as follows,' he said. "We want to get Harley's money back and we want to get the criminals prosecuted. Everyone agree?" Everyone did. "I believe we also want to stop Enrici extorting money from the lady called Grace." More agreement. "Tuppence has checked with her contact in the Met and as suspected, the information we have is not enough for the police to get involved. So if we are going to achieve our objectives we have to do something ourselves." Tony paused and looked around the assembled group. "Is everybody up for that?" There were responses of enthusiastic agreement.

"OK," said Tony, "Harley first. I mentioned I had the bones of an idea. Unfortunately it requires logistical and financial capability we just don't have." He looked around the group, appearing downcast. Then a wide grin spread across his face. "However, the organisation I'm still chairman of, has. As you know I went down to London to talk to two of my directors and they've bought into it. Between us we have refined my original idea which has shaped what I want to talk to you about now."

Tuppence failed to supress a giggle. The group stared at her. "Sorry, sorry." She blurted. "I've been watching re-runs of Dad's Army and I'm hearing Captain Mainwaring."

Tony didn't look best pleased with the comparison, but continued, "put simply, the idea is that we set up a sting. We lure the villains into taking part in another blackmail operation. This will not be real, but a set up. We do this by persuading them that we are a team of financial blackmailers using sophisticated hacking techniques to identify and attack targets. We tell them we have had some success but lack the necessary muscle to handle the final extraction of cash from the victims effectively. We will offer Enrici the opportunity of partnering with us to provide that muscle."

"How on earth are we going to do that?" asked Tuppence.

"That's what I would like us to work on today. It's not going to be easy, but I think it can be done. I'll tell you where we're up to."

"The sting needs to be in two phases. For the first phase, we will set up a dummy company with dummy books, website, customers, premises and staff. I've called the company Scamco for the time being. Scamco appears to be cheating HMRC through failing to pay VAT. Also, cheating customers by charging them VAT on services that should be VAT-free. We will say Scamco has been making well over £250,000 per year in this way, which is creamed off by the owners. Enrici's job is to meet a director and demand payment of say £300,000. The threat will be to tell HMRC and the police. Enrici will keep 50%."

Tony surveyed the silent but now very alert group. "This phase is just to get them interested, demonstrating how our scheme works. His total investment in time would be no more than one day for which he will receive £150,000 with almost no risk. If I were him I would think it a good deal. Phase two will be the blackmail of a real company. We need to do this because as phase one is a complete setup, nothing actually criminal will have taken place. They need to break the law in order for us nab them."

"So for phase two, the company we will blackmail is my agency, to the tune of £2 million."

"What?" said Henry. "Two million quid. That's an awful lot of money to lose!"

"I suppose it is," said Tony, "however, we won't lose it because it will never be given to Enrici, it will just be dangled in front of him. We'll say we discovered the agency skims off a small margin from all their contracts to put in a charity fund. However, some directors pocket a large part of that each year."

"We will follow exactly the same process as Scamco, only this time it would be a real company being blackmailed, therefore criminal, so the police should be interested. Everything would be videoed and the only difference is that the money would not be transferred to them. I have to say we got no further than that because we need to get phase one thought through first. So that's where we are up to." Tony looked around enquiringly. "What do you think?"

"It looks good as long as these guys fall for it," said Harry. "There's a lot of effort involved. And money. Is your agency going to fund the £300,000?"

"Yep, they certainly are." Tony explained the agency's part in the venture and the 'good causes fund'. "It will cover our expenses and payment of the ransom. Brodie Vellum will fund the work they're involved in."

The whole group thought it was ingenious. They were concerned it could be dangerous though. Tony wrote 'Security' on a flip chart. "How will we persuade the villains to take part?" asked Tuppence. Tony wrote down 'Hooking the Villains'.

"Why don't we start by listing all of the things we've got to think about," suggested Wayne.

"Good idea," said Tony. "Just shout things out and I'll jot them down!" It took some time but everybody did and he ended up with a list as long as his arm ranging from 'who would do what' to 'legality' and 'building website' to 'rehearsals'.

"Let's talk about hooking the villains first," said Wayne. "If we don't get that right we're not going to get any further anyway."

"Sounds good to me," said Tony.

Harry put his hand up, "The first thing we have to do to is find a way of getting Enrici to even talk to us."

"You're right Harry. I would think the only place we could do that would be at his golf club," said Henry.

"Agreed," from Tony. "No doubt you can keep an eye on when he will be there Wayne?" A nod in response. "In my experience, you have about 30 seconds to get somebody's interest so we'll need to hit some hot buttons straight away."

Tuppence responded, "according to my friend Bob from the Met, two of them at least are greed and ego." Tony wrote that down.

The group bounced plenty of ideas around about what to say in those first 30 seconds. They listed everything they could think of which would attract Enrici. They also came up with lots of objections he might throw at them. It didn't take long before a flip chart was full. Tony said, "scripting the first couple of sentences very carefully helps. Why don't I take this away and come up with a structure?" They all agreed.

"Can we go on to security now?" asked Tuppence. "I got more background on him from my friend Bob." She told them about how Enrici worked, and his prison terms. "I've a feeling this meeting could be dodgy, especially if he has his henchmen with him."

"We will have to do this in a public place," said Tony looking thoughtful. "Golf club car park probably."

"If they don't buy into your idea, you're still in danger wherever you meet them." pointed out Harry. "Maybe there's something I can do to help. Have I mentioned

Anthony Christian to you?" There were a few shakes of the head. "He's my funeral director in Cromer, ex-marine, six foot something, tough as old boots. He spent time in Iraq and Afghanistan. Also places where we were not supposed to be apparently. If he's up for it I can have him on standby just in case they start throwing their weight around."

"Is he the big bugger who marches in front of your hearse?" Asked Henry.

"That's him."

"Christ, he's enormous. I wouldn't want to get on the wrong side of him."

"Sounds like a good idea then," said Tuppence.

"Right, let's get onto looking at Scamco now," said Tony. "The agency has a dormant company we can use and has offered to build comprehensive financials and a website. That's going to take quite some time I'm afraid."

"I think I can help there," said Wayne. "I've got tons of stuff from my little brush with the law."

"Brush with the law?" said a shocked Harry. There were chuckles from Tuppence and Tony and a weary sigh from Henry.

Tony explained, "Wayne tried to protect his cousin from some fraudsters but it backfired. As a result he served a small amount of time and they got away with it."

"They only got away with it temporarily. I think what they were up to could form the basis of Scamco and save a lot of effort. Why don't I tell you all about it?"

There was a groan from Henry, "I suppose it could be useful. This could take some time though!"

"In that case why don't we break now and you can tell us about it over lunch?" said Tony. "I've got some Pizzas and salad, fruit and juices." It was a suggestion welcomed by all except Willie who was unceremoniously dumped from

Tuppence's lap. Not being a pizza fan anyway, he pushed his way out through the cat-flap for a bit of damp fresh air.

They sat themselves round the dining table. "Go for it Wayne," said Tony.

"OK. When I came out after my little sojourn behind bars, the family just wanted to leave it and get on with their lives. I wanted some sort of retribution though. I'm not a vindictive person but those fraudsters were still in business and getting away with it. As some of you know, I broke into their payroll system and got Liz's salary paid but got caught. They hadn't a clue I'd looked anywhere else though. I popped back in and found they hadn't improved security and were still up to their old tricks."

"Liz pointed me towards the finance director, so I had a look at his email. There was nothing particular in there but he kept referring to things 'being in the other place'. After a bit of effort I discovered he had another email address on a different server. Now in there was all sorts of juicy stuff. It implicated him, the CEO and the operations director. I decided to report them to HMRC. I had a look at their website about tax evasion and it said 'Don't let anyone know you're making a report'. So I decided to become devious."

Wayne was getting into his stride now. "My past experiences could have made me reporting them a bit awkward. So I decided I would turn the finance director into a whistle-blower. I arranged that I would see all his emails from both servers and send mails on his behalf that he on the other hand would never see. I concocted one from him to the Inland Revenue. It said he was being blackmailed by the chief executive who had discovered some indiscretions he'd had with a girl in the office and had threatened to tell his wife. He said he made him run the fraudulent scheme. But he wanted to come clean and report everything. He said he hoped they would understand his position."

"In the meantime, I got Liz to build an up to date report on their misdemeanours which would make it look as if it had come from the finance director. I attached it to the mail, added a bit to say only contact him through his private email, and sent it off. Now!" said Wayne, "he, or rather me, was soon mailed back from HMRC asking a few more questions which Liz and I answered. It took a while but they got back and said they'd established the accuracy of his report and they would visit the premises unannounced in the near future. Of course he had no clue about the whole thing."

"So we waited and let things play out. Luckily Liz had a good friend still working in the company and one day she called to say the police and government inspectors had arrived at the office demanding to see the directors. They were about to confiscate files and computers. Liz called me and straight away I went into the FD's email system and unlocked everything so that all the mails I had sent and blocked miraculously appeared in his mailbox in date order. It would appear, he and the chief executive were taken away in police cars."

By now everybody was chuckling. "What sort of company have I got myself into? declared Harry. "What happened after that? I'm sure the FD didn't take it lying down."

"Well, in a way the FD did take it lying down. It turns out he was indeed having an affair with a PR consultant they were using and the two of them used to skive off regularly to a local hotel for a bit of lying down! I got questioned by the police but I'd managed to cover my tracks perfectly so nobody could see my involvement. It turned out their dirty deeds were much bigger than we had uncovered, money laundering and all sorts. They all got gaol terms." Wayne leaned back with a self-satisfied look on his face.

"You're a star, Wayne," cried Tuppence clapping her hands.

"The thing is," said Wayne, "I've kept all that documentation from the company digitally hidden away at home. With a bit of manipulation we could make Scamco look exactly like the outfit in Holt. It will save your people from inventing tons of stuff. I can also help build the website of course."

"Don't you have a job to do young man?" asked Henry.

"I can fit all of this in around my job, no problem grandad."

Tony suggested he spend time in the London office. Better for communication.

Wayne agreed. "All I need is a desk and the people to talk to."

"No problem, there's plenty of space. And we have a deal with a nice little hotel close to the office."

They went back to the comfortable seats and like a flash, Willie was back on Tuppence's lap. They then turned their thoughts to how to staff the scam operation. Tony said, "the agency can provide a few people but I don't think that can extend to the director. Maybe we can hire an actor to do the job."

"I beg your pardon," said Tuppence, "we already have an actor on the team."

"You can't do that. Too dangerous," said a horrified Henry.

"Precisely. That's why Equity would never stand for an actor doing it. Anyway, I can look after myself."

"Wouldn't they recognise you from the tele?" asked Wayne.

"Of course not. A bit of slap. A wig. A business suit. A posh accent. Plus of course, I'll know exactly what I'm talking about."

"I think you'd be great," said Harry.

"Brownie points awarded to that man!"

"We should hide Anthony away somewhere though, just in case." Universal agreement!

"Can I jump in here?" asked Wayne. "Who's going to do the confrontation with Enrici at the golf course?"

"I'm happy to," said Tony.

"You can't do it on your own. One of us needs to be with you."

"Well you can't, you'll be setting up Scamco."

"Tuppence can't either if she's going to act as Scamco director," said Henry.

"I'd happily do it," said Harry, "but I'm sure Anthony will agree to get involved and while I can get him covered on the front line, I'll need to step in on the business side while he's away."

All eyes turned towards Henry. "Count me in," he said, "as long as I don't have to run away from the buggers I'll be fine."

"Are you sure grandad? You might have to be diplomatic!"

"I'll give him some coaching," offered an amused Tuppence.

"There's something else," Wayne added. "Security-wise, we need to hide our real identities. You mentioned Enrici may have already clocked you at the golf club. If they're smart, they could get your name from the club's tee booking system. I'm afraid I've taken an executive decision. I got in and changed your name and telephone number." There were some wide-eyed looks from the others. "You are now Algernon Armstrong and if anybody dials the phone number on file, it will be unobtainable."

"Good thinking Wayne," said Harry.

"Algernon sodding Armstrong? Sounds like a second-rate thirties luvvie."

"I'll trouble you not to mock names from my profession!" said Tuppence.

"You'd better make one up for yourself grandad. It will probably be needed."

"I assume we'll go in your car. Say they see it. They might be able to trace you."

"Hadn't crossed my mind. Maybe the agency can get some false plates."

Wayne said, "they will need to contact us at some stage, so we need to get you a burner phone which you use for them and only them. I can give you Enrici's telephone number which I picked up from the membership file. By the way, I could give you his bank account details too if you like."

"That might just be useful," said Tony.

"So when are we going to do all this?" asked Henry.

"I've a feeling all the set-up's going to take quite a while. I would think we are probably talking a month or so before we can even approach Enrici. Then maybe a couple of weeks before we enact the sting."

"It's better we get it right than rush it though," said Harry.

Everybody agreed. Tony turned the flipchart back to the original list of items. "I'm not sure there's much more we can do today. I need to agree everything with the agency and get some idea of how their contribution will work and how we can link that with all the data you've got Wayne."

"Hold on a minute, we haven't talked about Grace at the care home." Wayne described bugging Grace's room but said he hadn't heard anything from Bernadette. It was agreed they couldn't do any more on that front until he had.

So they decided to call it a day. As they prepared to leave Tuppence gently removed Willie from her lap, made her way to the door and called out, "see you all on Sunday. Don't be late!" As they filed out of the apartment two of them particularly we're on something of a high. Tuppence was looking forward with glee to doing some real acting again. There wouldn't be an audience but she could already anticipate the surge of adrenaline. She would set about getting her props together, experimenting with her stage make-up, digging out her collection of wigs. All very exciting. Harry too was over the moon. He had somehow met a group of people who not only wanted to help his father but had truly welcomed him into their little group. Things were definitely looking up.

CHAPTER 14

The Party

In Tuppence's lexicon, party meant lots of chat, jollity, drink and food, liberally sprinkled with home-grown entertainment. She had held many parties over the years, mostly populated by people from 'the business'. They could be relied upon to be outgoing and happy to put on a turn when asked. She wondered how these Norfolk people would manage. She'd discovered Henry was in some sort of choir and played the concertina so asked him to be prepared to get involved. She guessed most others would be a bit reticent but, as she had found throughout life, people can surprise you.

She had stocked up on more wine than a whole busload of out-of-work-actors could sink. Her wine fridge was now full of Crémant. The fridge in her kitchen housed plenty of Sauvignon Blanc and lined up on the kitchen worktop was an equal amount of very swiggable Pinot Noir. Following a request from Trevor for some beer she had also stacked bottles of a Woodforde's Wherry in the fridge. There was a small supply of non-alcoholic booze, just in case.

Most of the food was coming from one of Poppy's local delis and would arrive with her and Trevor around midday. Tuppence felt she needed to reflect local tastes so in addition was making crab sandwiches, albeit very delicate and rather sophisticated crab sandwiches. Along with a collection of nibbles of various sorts to spread around the room, she felt the catering was just about right. Lots of preparation had been done the day before. The apartment had been cleaned and tidied. Tuppence's very best damask tablecloth was in place along with plates, cutlery and napkins. Serving plates were waiting on the kitchen worktop. She had bought several bunches of flowers, put them in water and lined up a collection of vases ready for Poppy to weave her design magic.

After breakfast Tuppence set off to walk over the cliffs towards Weybourne. The party was not going to disrupt the new exercise regime which she had discovered was not just good for her body but her mind too. She revelled in the view of the sea sparkling blue stretching all the way to the horizon and the gulls swooping and shrieking around her. It was sunny with a gentle breeze and due to get nicely warm, perfect for being out on the balcony later. All was well with the world. She hadn't been back to her apartment long when Poppy called telling her to get the kettle on, they'd be there in a couple of minutes.

After they'd had their tea accompanied by hot bacon rolls with copious brown sauce, Poppy quickly set to with her flower arranging, while Tuppence decanted all the canapés and other goodies onto serving plates. Meanwhile, Trevor set up his keyboard in one corner of the lounge. A half an hour before guests were due, Trevor poured three glasses of fizz and on the balcony, the three friends toasted the occasion of Tuppence's first party in her Sheringham home.

On the dot of start time, the entry phone rang. The planning and organising were now over and the party was about to get underway. The screen presented a smiling Henry at the front door. "Come on up," shouted Tuppence and a buzz let him in. Within a minute he and Elsie along with Wayne and his cousin Elizabeth were at the door of the apartment. Trevor took control of the drinks orders while Poppy started talking. It turned out that talking was an Elsie pastime too, so a competition for airtime began.

In no time at all Sangeetha and her husband Derek along with Deborah arrived. Like a well-oiled machine, they were passed from Tuppence to Poppy and Trevor who distributed chat and drinks in that order. From then on there was a constant procession of arrivals; Graham and Tilly from Sheringham Rep, Tuppence's friend Gilly along with daughter Lydia and Trevor's colleague John with his snooty wife Phoebe. They were quickly integrated into the growing bunch of partygoers.

Trevor took John and Phoebe under his wing. John was a recovered alcoholic and happily took a zero-strength beer. Trevor made sure Phoebe's glass was quickly filled with Pinot. He would keep his eye on that particular container over the next hour to make sure it was continually topped up. Experience had told him it was a sure way of taking the edge off her somewhat haughty behaviour.

Soon Margaret arrived arm in arm with Ken along with their son John. "Hello all, welcome, come in." On recent trips to the bench Tuppence had felt Ken looked ragged but today he had on a new pink and white striped open-necked shirt, fawn trousers and a pastel green summer jacket. His stubble had been shaved and his hair neatly cut. He gave Tuppence a big smile. Margaret was almost unrecognisable. Her hair had been expertly cut, her make-up was immaculate and she wore a smart grey floral patterned midi-dress. Tuppence led them through into the lounge.

Above the growing hubbub, Tuppence heard the doorbell again. It was Harry and Sofia. "Hope we're not too late," said Harry, "we had to deposit Adrian with the grandparents."

"Absolutely not, come in and we'll get you introduced to everyone. You must be Sofia."

"And you must be Tuppence. It is so nice to meet you. And so exciting to come to your party." Crikey thought Tuppence, where on earth did Harry find a stunner like you? She led them through to the lounge and was intercepted by Trevor, a bottle in each hand.

"This is Trevor, he's in charge of drinks. Harry and Sofia."

"Come with me and I'll get you a glass," he said, and they obediently trotted off behind him.

Poppy came over to join Tuppence, "where's your man?" She said quietly. "I hope he's going to turn up."

"I'm sure he will. I'd better circulate." Poppy paused her semi-hosting role, cast her eye round the gathering, and thought how good it was that her friend had settled comfortably in her new community. Then the doorbell rang again. Tuppence had disappeared, so she answered it. A tall, elegant man smiled at her.

"You must be Tony," she said.

"And I must assume you are Poppy", he replied.

"Got it in one! Lovely to meet you. Come in. Tuppence is nattering somewhere." And she proceeded to talk to him in her uninterruptable way as she guided him to Trevor's bar and then off into the throng to find Tuppence.

One of Tuppence's cardinal rules for running a party was that she didn't attach herself for too long to any particular group but drifted around, in and out of conversations, keeping everybody happy. Party conversations the world over varied from the inane and uninteresting, through gossip to absolute nuggets. Today was no different. As

146

she circulated she earwigged groups of guests, pausing occasionally to just listen or add the odd word. Sofia and Harry chatting to Margaret's son John were on her route.

" . . . Me? I was born in place called Nikel in northern Russia. My father worked in Nickel mine. Horrible place. Desolate. Badly polluted. The ground was black. No flowers. Trees all stunted. Everybody was poor. When I was 11 my father died in accident. We got no help. No compensation. My mother and I moved to live with her sister in St Petersburg. Two rooms. Shared kitchen in hallway. Sounds bad, but it became home. Are you from around . . ."

" . . . seems to have come down in the world. I believe she had a very nice Town House in Chiswick and now she lives in this tiny flat in the middle of nowhere. I suppose she doesn't have the income anymore. Are you two locals, or should I say yokels, ha ha?"

Elizabeth smiled. "Absolutely! But we're all used to living in squalor. Tuppence has become quite accustomed to it as well."

"And I'm an ex-convict. She's helping me rehabilitate," said Wayne.

"Oh, my goodness," said Phoebe. She moved away making a beeline for Trevor's refill bottle.

" . . . thought your face was familiar. What was it? I know, Body Shop. What else did you do?"

"Loads. A few travel ads. I liked those, needless to say. Although I would rather have actually gone to Thailand than film on a Hebridean beach in autumn! Luckily the camera didn't pick up the goose pimples." said Gilly.

At last Tuppence had caught up with her final guest. "Tony, glad you could come. Sorry I was tied up when you arrived. You've obviously met Gilly. And Lydia?"

"Lydia is chatting to the lady from your Pier Theatre," said Gilly.

"Ah yes. I see Trevor has sorted you out with a drink."

"He certainly has, cheers! I've just discovered Gilly did some work for the agency. Did you I can't remember?"

"Maybe. I was rather picky who I worked with though."

That put me in my place thought Tony.

" . . . costumes. Derek does the lighting. Have you never been to the show in Cromer? You know it's the last genuine 'End of the Pier' in the whole country? We'll be kicking off the season soon. It's really very good."

"When do you run to?" asked Lydia.

"September. It's a lovely old theatre. When the sea is rough the whole thing shakes. Adds a bit of spice. Are you doing anything at . . ."

" . . . Has Tuppence told you Ken's not well?"

"Yes she has. Nice to meet you Ken. I've refilled your glass for you." Trevor handed Ken the plastic beer mug Margaret had brought with her, half full of beer. Cheers!" Ken beamed. This was great. So many smiley people.

"How do you know Tuppence?" asked Margaret.

"She's Poppy's best friend. Poppy's my wife. It must be 50 years ago since we first met."

"Were you in the entertainment business too?"

"Still am. I started off as a jobbing pianist. I've no doubt I'll be called upon to play a few tunes later. Do you have any requests?"

"You don't do classical do you? Ken loves Erik Satie. Not exactly party stuff. He says he's a bit off the wall."

"Quirky definitely. I'm sure I can give it a go."

"Maybe Ken could play his violin."

"Ken's able to play the violin?"

"I know, amazing isn't it. You play a piece for me every evening don't you Ken?" He nodded, still grinning.

"That would be brilliant."

"I'll get John to fetch it."

" . . . she's Russian by the way."

"Ah, I wasn't sure," said Poppy.

"She'd married a worthless oik who sweet-talked her on a trip to Russia. She upped and left once she knew she could stay in the UK. It was tough but she wasn't penniless. When I first saw her in the office. I thought cor, I fancy you. Oh, I hope you don't mind me saying that!"

"Not at all, I can understand why!"

"Trouble was, I was no good at dealing with anyone let alone girls. Anyway, in the job we had to talk about business things a lot so we spent a fair bit of time together. It turned out we'd both had fairly difficult upbringings. Most importantly though, we were both really into art and bird watching. It took almost a year before I built up the courage to ask her out. I have no idea to this day how I managed it, but when her divorce came through I proposed. And she said 'Da'!"

"Oh, that's wonderful. I met . . ."

" . . . not at all like his reputation," said Elsie, nodding towards Harry.

"No, he's fine when you get to know him," said Tony. "He can be quite blunt and does have a brittle side though. When I was sitting in the garden last week he was playing with his son Adrian chucking a ball back and forth. An old misery guts called Freddy Barstead who thinks he runs the place went up to Adrian and told him that ball games weren't permitted in the garden. Harry picked up the ball, waved it in front of Freddy's face and explained in great technical detail exactly where and how far up he would shove it if he ever went anywhere near his son again."

"Good for him . . . . "

" . . . Don't have a nickname," said Phoebe, her voice beginning to slur slightly.

"Rubbish, everybody has a nickname. What did they call you at school" asked Henry.

"Not sure I want to tell you that."

"Come on, you're amongst friends," said Poppy.

"Alright. It was Snozzle. Because I had a big nose."

"You haven't got a big nose," said Henry, truthfully.

"I know. That's because I told John I wouldn't marry him unless he got me a new one!" She whooped with laughter.

"What about you? Henry" asked Poppy.

"My friends called me either Stumpy or Noxious," and in explanation, "I was short and stocky and a champion farter!"

"Oh, that's awful," cried, Phoebe, quickly, swallowing another mouthful. "What about you Poppy?"

"Various. Pea-soup was the most common although the sixth form boys had a less pleasant one."

"Go on," said Henry.

"Well, I was very thin, but with big boobs. They used to call me Tits-on-a-stick!"

Another whoop from Phoebe. The Pinot was doing its job.

Before another word could be said Tuppence, putting on her pub landlord voice, announced "food is served! If there are any vegans here the blue plates are for you. Vegetarians can have that and the food on the plates with the curly edges. Omnivores you can eat whatever you like." And it wasn't long before everybody was tucking in. Trevor took a glass of beer and plate of food over to his keyboard and began softly playing some old standards. He'd downloaded the sheet music for *Gymnopédie No 1* so after a while he propped his iPad up on the rest and slipped his rendition into the stream of music. He got both puzzled and approving glances from the partygoers but most importantly a thumbs up from Ken.

He soon morphed into a slightly jazzed-up version of *After You've Gone*. Elsie put down her plate and joined him.

"That's so clever," She said. "I wish I could play the piano."

"Years of practice! Any requests? Just don't make it anything too modern."

"I don't know anything modern. How about *I only have eyes for you*. Henry and I used to smooch to that in the early days." And almost imperceptibly he drifted from one piece to the other. Elsie shook her head in disbelief and Trevor smiled. He loved entertaining people, playing music that made them happy.

Wayne joined his Granny. "And your favourite, sir?" asked Trevor looking up and grinning.

"*Chasing Cars*. But I don't suppose that would work just on the piano."

"My dear chap, no problem at all. You know the words?"

"I only sing in the bath."

"That's about to change!" Trevor flicked a couple of switches on the keyboard. "I'll start, you join in at the first chorus, OK?" And with that he upped the volume, played the instrumental intro, then sang, "*We'll do it all, Everything, On our own*." Heads turned. Conversations paused. "*We don't need, Anything, Or anyone*. In you come Wayne." Together they sang, "*If I lay here, If I just lay here, Would you lie with me and just forget the world*."

By now everyone was listening. Those in the kitchen and on the balcony had joined the throng in the lounge. There was amazement and joy etched onto so many faces. Wayne was getting into it too, the decibels had risen and Trevor was giving the keyboard a run for its money. When they finished there was tumultuous applause. Trevor and Wayne took a bow and Elsie gave Wayne a big hug.

Tuppence went over and stood next to Trevor. "Thank you boys that was amazing! And then to the assembly, "Time for a bit more entertainment. Lydia will give us a song from her upcoming tour." Beckoning her over Tuppence announced, "The wonderful Lydia everyone." There was enthusiastic applause and Trevor played the opening bars of *One Day I'll Fly Away*. Her voice was pure, clear and resonant and she had her audience in raptures. Tony and Harry were standing by the door to the kitchen having refilled their glasses. "This is amazing," said Harry. "I thought we were just coming for drinks."

"Thank you, thank you," called Lydia over the applause. "The Theatre Royal is on the tour, so if you'd like to see the rest of *Moulin Rouge*, come along!" Tuppence collared Henry as Trevor plunged into a keyboard-rocking rendition of *Maple Leaf Rag*.

"I can't compete with these guys Tuppence," said a worried-looking Henry.

"Henry Bennett, you'll be absolutely fine. What are you going to sing?"

"I've got a couple that everyone can join in with," Henry said rather defensively.

"Well grab that squeezebox of yours and Trevor will introduce you when he's finished." With that, she gave him no chance to back out and sashayed off.

Ken's son John had overheard this exchange. "What are you singing Uncle Henry?"

"I thought I'd sing *Song of the Fishes*."

"I know that, you used to sing it to us when we were kids. Would you like a guitar accompaniment?"

"Too true young man!" John had brought his guitar when he fetched Ken's violin and collected it from the hall as Trevor acknowledged his applause.

"Now ladies and gentlemen, a real treat. We have a performance from Mr Henry Bennett, retired fisherman of this parish, who will accompany himself on his trusty concertina. Henry!" Clapping, whistling and cheers welcomed him.

"Thank you, thank you. I would like to sing you an old American folk song cum sea shanty called *Song of the Fishes*. The names of the fish change depending on where you are in the world. In the original they sing about bluefish, swordfish and whale. We don't have too many of them around here, so you will hear mention of herring, cod and crab amongst others. My friend John here will accompany me. They launched into the song, everyone joining in the chorus. After thirteen verses, the audience was word perfect and deafening. As was the reception afterwards.

During Henry's performance Trevor had spoken briefly to Margaret and with a bit of encouragement she stood up. "As several of you know, Ken is not all that well, but he would like to play something for you. Throughout his life his greatest love has been the violin. Each night, before bed, he plays for me. Sometimes he chooses, and sometimes I make a request. This afternoon I've requested that he play a little compilation he put together of some of our favourite show tunes. We hope you like it."

John helped Ken up and they walked over to the keyboard accompanied by polite, slightly anxious clapping from the assembled host. John stood close by, just in case Ken's balance faltered. He tucked his violin under his chin, moved the bow gently over the strings, and the sweetest sound drifted around the room. He expertly melded together snatches of tunes from *The King and I, West Side Story, Phantom of the Opera* and half a dozen other films and shows. When he finished the applause was spontaneous, accompanied by cheers from almost everybody in the room. The observant would have noticed Margaret, Tuppence and Henry discreetly wiping a tear from their cheeks.

After Tuppence had performed an appropriately dramatic version of *There are Worse Things I Could Do* from *Grease*, Henry took to the floor again. He was into this now and had recruited John once more to provide guitar backing to *The Mingulay Boat Song*. Trevor flicked another couple of switches and from the keyboard came a close approximation to the sound of bagpipes. "You can all join in again," shouted Henry over the hubbub and he launched into the first verse with gusto accompanied by guitar and pipes. Everyone duly joined in, finishing with two renditions of the chorus. Henry, John and Trevor bathed in the glory of the moment.

Tuppence was delighted that everybody was having a lovely time. After another hour or so people began drifting off. Soon the only ones left to help Tuppence finish the opened bottles of wine were Tony, Poppy and Trevor. Asked what everyone was doing for the rest of the week, Tony said, "I have to look after my twin granddaughters on Thursday. I suppose I'll cope."

"Well, I don't have any granddaughters myself, so if you like, I'd be delighted to lend a hand," offered Tuppence. "I assume there are no nappies to change."

"They're eight years old so I hope not!"

Tuppence didn't notice but a look of minor triumph shone from Poppy's face. Things looked as if they were moving in the right direction for her friend.

CHAPTER 15

The Operation Starts

There were a few sore heads on Monday. Henry particularly had come to the conclusion that excess alcohol was no friend of increasing age. He had to endure Elsie telling him it was all his own fault. Again and again. Tuppence was crambazzled, as her father would have said, having made absolutely sure there were no wine bottles left unemptied. Tony was surprisingly chipper though. He put that down to drinking nothing but fizz all day. In fact he was so chipper that he set up a Zoom meeting with Vijay and Sandy for the afternoon. He wanted to update them on progress and set a few balls rolling.

His two Directors were pleased that their ideas had been taken on board. "We think all the preparation is going to take around a month," said Tony. "There are a few things in the short term you could do if that's OK."

"Just give us the list," replied Sandy.

"Right, firstly we need to set up a real company for the first scam. I know we've several on the shelf so I'm hoping you can pick one that could masquerade as an import/export outfit. One of our number, Wayne, has complete financial details of a company who were committing a fraud of the nature we will be emulating."

"That will make life easier. How did he get hold of those?"

"It's a long story, and quite entertaining. You should ask him about it. He can help with a website too."

"Wayne can work closely with whoever you allocate so can we put him up for a few days and give him some office space?"

"No problem at all. I'll see who's available and we'll get him booked in round the corner."

"I think he's pretty flexible about time so I'll give you a call once I've spoken to him. Then we need to do the same thing for us as blackmailers. We are Business Consultants and Wayne has all the information needed. And then of course we will need bank accounts for both companies."

"Easy. I'll get my guys on to all of that," Said Vijay.

"In terms of premises, I really like the idea of the Reading unit. We need to make it look authentic though."

"We have somebody down there looking after the place and he should be able to do that," said Sandy. "What about populating it with staff for the operation?"

"I wouldn't want to put you under any pressure there, so I think we can do the whole thing ourselves. We have a professional actress to be the victim, and I guess we only need a couple of others to be closely involved. Maybe your man could be shifting stuff around in the background to give it a bit of authenticity?"

"I wouldn't have thought that was an issue."

"Great. That's about it I think for the moment. Thanks again."

"Okay Tony. Good to be working with you again," said Sandy. "By the way, I have all the formalities set up for you running the fund. I'll get it e-mailed to you. Just let us know when Wayne is arriving."

As soon as he closed down Zoom, Tony rang Wayne and talked him through what had been agreed. He was happy to go down to London tomorrow so Tony gave him the contact details for Vijay and Sandy and said he would let them know. He was sure one of the PAs would ring him to arrange accommodation and parking.

* * *

By the Tuesday Tuppence was back to normal. She needed to fix another meeting with Bob to get his opinion on their plans so rang and left a message asking him to call back. Within a minute her phone rang, "Hi Bob, thanks for ringing back so quickly."

"I've been called many names in my time but not Bob. It's Bernadette here from Burns Croft."

"I'm so sorry Bernadette. I should have checked. You've got some news?"

"I have indeed. Enrici has been in to see Grace. We managed to video the whole meeting."

"Well done. Anything interesting?"

"Maybe. He asked her to sign some forms. If Wayne could magnify what was on the screen it might be possible to see what they were."

"I'm sure he can do that. I'll call him. Did she sign?"

"No she didn't. However there did seem to be a veiled threat after she refused. He said he was getting some information that meant soon she would have no choice."

"I wonder what he meant by that. How is Grace by the way."

"She's well enough to go home. However Enrici is insistent she stays here until she's fully fit. Grace doesn't want to go anyway. I can't in all conscience keep her here for too long though, she's taking up a bed that somebody else could make better use of."

"Yes I can understand that. let's see what progress Wayne can make."

Tuppence immediately called Wayne and talked to him about the recording. "No problem, I've set up their laptop so I can access it from my system here. I'll give Bernadette a ring now. It was a great do on Sunday, thank you. How's your head?"

"It's fine now. I was a bit fragile yesterday."

"Same here. By the way, I'm heading off to London this afternoon to work on the website and so on for Tony's Scamco. Should be fun. They are putting me up so I'll probably be away for a few days."

"Great. See you when you get back."

* * *

A bit later on Tuesday the team received a WhatsApp from Harry. *Spoken to Anthony and he is keen to help! Would be good to organise a meet. Business is not too heavy at the moment and he could take a short time off Thursday afternoon around 2 pm if everybody is available?* Within an hour everybody except Wayne responded to say that would suit them. No doubt he was still driving. Tony suggested using his place again.

* * *

It wasn't until Wednesday morning that Bob got back to Tuppence. He was happy to talk over what was planned and said he had some information that could help. He said he happened to be visiting Cambridge next Tuesday to give a lecture at the Institute of Criminology. If that was convenient maybe they could meet in the evening. As it happened that suited Tuppence perfectly. She'd been promising herself a day out in Cambridge for ages. So they agreed a time and Tuppence booked a room in the hotel where Bob was staying.

* * *

Wayne called Tuppence back at lunchtime. "I've had a look at the video. Not a lot in it except I did manage to work out what the document was."

"Interesting?"

"I should say so. It's what's called a Stock Transfer Form. I spoke about it to Vijay. It turns out that you fill in one of these if you want to pass ownership of shares in a company from one person to another. The company concerned is Sub-Arctic Oil and Gas and it quoted 73,500 shares. Vijay had a look at the current value and each share is worth £5.23. That gives a total value of £384,405. We surmised that Grace probably owns the shares and Enrici is trying to get his hands on them."

"Bloody Hell! No wonder she doesn't want to sign. I'll call Bernadette."

She rang straight away and was put through quickly. "I've heard from Wayne," she told her and explained about the form and sums involved.

"Oh my goodness. I'll have a word with her about it. I'm also worried about Enrici's threat to come up with some sort of reason why she would have to sign. Somehow we need to nip that in the bud."

* * *

Tony's youngest daughter Jessica lived about 30 minutes away in Aylsham and worked on climate change research at the University of East Anglia. An offsite meeting coincided with her twin daughters' school being used as a polling station all day on Thursday so it was down to grandad to look after the girls. Before they were delivered he gave Willie his breakfast. "You're going to have a bit of company today, the girls are coming to play with you." Willie didn't react, partly because his breakfast was far too important but also while he could understand the meaning of some sounds, the English language itself completely defeated him.

It was a bit unfortunate that the team meeting coincided but it couldn't be helped. The girls arrived just after 10 o'clock. Once their mother had departed Tony said, "now, somebody else is joining us today." they looked quizzically at Tony. "It's a friend of mine called Tuppence."

"Tuppence? What a weird name" said Roxanne. That's the pot calling the kettle black, thought Tony, who had never been enamoured with either of the girls' names. "Is it a man or a woman?"

"It's a woman. She used to be a famous actress. Like me she's retired."

"You weren't a famous actress," said Harper.

"Is she your girlfriend?" asked Roxanne.

"No, she is just a friend who lives in this building."

"Why is she joining us then?"

"Because she'd like to meet you. She doesn't have any grandchildren of her own. Anyway, it will be useful having somebody help me look after you two pests. She'll be here soon. Also a few more people are coming in this afternoon for a while. You'll just have to sit quietly with your iPads."

It wasn't long before the doorbell rang. "Can you let Tuppence in please girls," Tony called from the kitchen. They ran to the door, opened it and stared at Tuppence who was wearing the bright yellow dress which had been cleaned after its behind-the-sofa experience.

"Hello. You must be, now let me get this right, Harper and Roxanne. You'll have to tell me who's who."

"I'm Roxanne."

"Most people call her Roxy. I'm Harper. I prefer to be called Harper but some people call me Harpie. What do you prefer to be called?"

"I'm happy just to be called Tuppence."

There was a pause until she added, "are we planning to continue this conversation on the doorstep or are you going to invite me in?"

"I'll tell Danda you're here," said Harper turning and running along the hall.

"Please come in and I will show you to the lounge," said Roxanne very formally.

Tony met them there, "you've met these two then? I hope you're not going to regret your offer of help."

"Not at all. I'm sure we'll get on famously."

"The first thing we'll do girls is take a walk along the prom into Sheringham, I've got a bit of shopping to do, and we can call at Henry's fish stall to get some crab for lunch."

"Who's Henry?" asked Roxy.

"Another friend, you'll meet him later. Then if the weather clears up we can have a picnic in the garden."

The stroll into town took some time. Tuppence bought the twins a cake each from the baker in the High Street and then they had fun trying to identify the fish on the stall. The sun was shining by the time they got back and the picnic was prepared.

"Thank you for doing a picnic Danda," said Roxanne "it's yummy!"

"Did you have picnics when you were our age?" asked Harper.

"Sometimes. My brother and I used to go into the field at the bottom of our garden. We would have a jam sandwich, a piece of cake and a bottle of cordial."

"We used to have lots of picnics," said Tuppence. In summer we often used to squeeze into the Shooting Brake and head off to the Dales."

Harper peered at her quizzically, "what's a Shooting Brake, Tuppence?"

"I suppose it's what you would call an SUV now."

"And what are Dales?" asked Roxanne.

"The Dales? It's an area of Yorkshire. Big green hills and deep valleys with fast flowing rivers. Fields separated by dry stone walls and lots of sheep. My sister and I loved it."

"What's your sister's name?" Roxanne asked Tuppence.

"It's Phyllis. She's a bit older than me."

"What's she like?"

"Very nice. She is much cleverer than me though. She took over my dad's market stall and expanded it from fruit and vegetables into exotic imported foods like fresh figs and marinated anchovies and German sausages. Eventually she had a chain of delicatessens all across the north of England."

"I like exotic foods," said Harper.

"I don't," said Roxanne. "I like beige food."

"Now Tuppence," said Roxanne, "you may not be very clever but Danda said you were famous in the old days."

Tuppence giggled. "That's very kind of him Roxanne. I suppose I was fairly well known as an actress in my heyday."

"What in movies?" asked Harper.

"Mainly television but I did a few films. What I really liked though was live theatre. I did The West End and touring productions. Pantomimes too. Do you like panto?"

"Yes!" shouted Roxanne. "We were elves in our school panto. What were you?"

"Usually the ugly, wicked queen."

"You're not ugly," said Harper.

"Or wicked," chimed in Roxanne.

"It's kind of you to say so, but that's the point. When you're acting you're not yourself, You're whoever you want to be."

"Were you ever an actor on stage Danda?" asked Roxanne.

"I've been on stage lots of times but I can't remember acting."

"You can't remember because you're getting old. Mummy says you're beginning to lose the plot."

"That's nice of her! I can tell you I still remember some things right back to when I was three or four years old!"

"That's about 100 years ago!" said Harper with a shocked look on her face.

"Would you like me to tell you all about bath nights when I was three?" The two children frowned and Tony smiled.

"Well, we had a bath once a week."

"Once a week?" said Harper,

"We didn't have a bathroom you see, we used the scullery." The girls looked nonplussed. "I suppose in your house that would be the utility room."

"There was a bath in the utility room?" said Roxanne.

"No, the bath was hanging on the wall outside."

"Danda you're telling fibs," she said.

"No I'm not. We had no mains water supply. Instead, at the bottom of our garden, we had a water pump. We filled a big jug by pushing the handle up and down until water came out of the spout."

"Now in the corner of the scullery was a big boiler we called the copper. There was a coal fire underneath it, and on bath night it would be filled up with jugs of water earlier in the day and the fire lit. It got very hot."

"When everything was ready the tin bath was unhooked and brought into the scullery. Then the hot water was taken from the copper using the big jug and poured into the bath. Just enough cold water was added until it was the right temperature. It was topped up with hot water from the copper every now and again to keep the water warm. My mum and dad and my brother and I then all had a bath, one after the other. All of us used the same water!"

"Urgh!" exclaimed Harper.

"My mum went first, then my brother, then my dad and last of all me. I remember very clearly that by the time I got in the bath, the water was grey."

The twins screwed up their faces. "That's horrible."

"Why did you go last Danda? Asked Harper

"Well according to my brother, it was because I weed in the bath!'"

The two girls jumped up and down, shrieking with laughter. "Harper used to wee in the bath!" shouted Roxanne.

"So did you," yelled Harper.

"Alright, alright. I'm sure all little boys and girls do at some stage."

The conversation continued until Tony, looking at his watch said, "we need to clear up now. There are people coming round for a meeting." It wasn't long before they were all back in the penthouse and the doorbell rang as the team started assembling. The last to arrive were Harry with Anthony Christian. Tony explained the presence of the twins who sat with their iPads on a sofa. Everyone said hello to them and they responded politely. Willie though was disconcerted; did he sit with them or on Tuppence's lap? In the end, the comfort of a lap prevailed.

Harry introduced Anthony. Only Henry had previously set eyes upon him. The rest were momentarily taken aback. Even Willie seemed transfixed. Anthony was enormous. Well over six feet tall, massive shoulders, close cropped hair, clearly looked after himself. In Tuppence's opinion he was 'dashingly good looking', enhanced in a strange sort of way by a scar extending down his left cheek. He was dressed smartly in a sober grey suit, white shirt and black tie.

"Good afternoon ladies and gentlemen. It's a pleasure to meet you." The group were once again taken aback. He spoke with a gentle Bajan accent in a voice unexpectedly soft for such a large man. "I'm sorry if I look like I'm dressed as if I've come from a funeral, but I just have. It goes with the job," and a broad grin spread across his face. "I'm afraid I have another to attend soon so I can't stay long I'm afraid."

"Of course. We appreciate you coming at all, and good to meet you," said Tony, "please sit down. Tea, coffee?"

"A tea would be perfect. Black if I may."

"White coffee for me please Tony," added Harry taking a seat next to Tuppence on a sofa. Tony poured from the pots on the table.

"We wondered whether you could give us some advice and maybe even help out if you can find the time."

"Harry has appraised me of the situation with his father. Anything I can do to help Harland out, I will. As Harry says, he can be a bit difficult at times, but deep down he is a fine man."

"Have you told Anthony about our little scheme?" Asked Tony.

"I have," replied Harry.

"I am very impressed with what you are planning to do," continued Anthony, "but I am concerned about your safety. These criminals could probably turn very unpleasant if they rumble you. I think there may be some times when you will need my assistance."

"That would be very helpful. Harry said you have people who can deputise when you are away."

"Indeed, given a small amount of notice, we should be able to add this project into my schedule."

Anthony continued, "in talking to Harry it seems to me there are in initially two phases where you could have difficulty; when you try to get them to agree to join you and when you run your first sting operation. You will need what I would call 'babysitting'."

"So you suggest being with us when we meet them for the first time?" asked Tony.

"I would be out of sight, keeping my eye on proceedings, ready to become involved if a problem arose." He paused. "This old body can move very quickly if needs be. I can assure you they would not enjoy the experience. I will need to recce the place of course and I understand a young man called Wayne can fix up some comms. If you keep me involved with your planning I can advise on how, and how not to, approach these people, where you do it and how you keep yourselves as safe as possible. I always think it's advisable to be prepared for the worst situation."

"Crikey, this is beginning to feel a bit real," said Tuppence.

Henry said, "Tony and I are planning how we will make the approach very soon now. Maybe we can bounce our ideas off you once we've done that?"

"Of course, contact me any time." Anthony pulled two business cards from his top pocket, wrote down his mobile number and personal email address and handed them to Tony and Henry. "I obviously don't have my mobile switched on while I'm with clients," he explained. "Now, I hope you don't think I'm rude but I must go." There was a chorus of thanks from the assembled team. Tony and Harry showed Anthony out.

"What a delightful chap," said Tuppence when they returned. "He can bury me any day."

"Not for a while I hope," said Harry. "By the way, he's a stickler for detail, so expect him to question everything you want to involve him in. I've given him some photos of the location I took. I'll also give him the golf club URL so he can look at the Gallery."

"I have something I need to bring you all up-to-date with," said Tuppence. "I've had a call from Bernadette regarding Grace at the care home." She gave the team a run-down of the surveillance and what Wayne had deciphered from the form. I'm meeting my friend Bob from the police on Tuesday to talk him through our plans. I could ask his advice on this too."

"Sounds good to me," said Henry.

A little voice from across the lounge spoke up, "are you private detectives?" The twins had been so quiet everyone had forgotten they were there. They were both staring, wide-eyed at the group.

Tony thought quickly on his feet, "We're running an undercover operation with the police. It's very secret. You mustn't say a word to anyone about it."

"You mean we have to keep schtum!" said Roxanne

"Until you nab the mobsters! added Harper.

"Absolutely. Can you do that?"

"Holy Mazzoly, we can!" concluded Roxanne, which seemed to satisfy everyone.

"I think we've gone as far as we can, don't you?" asked Tony. Just then his phone rang. "It's Sandy from the agency. He might have an update. Hi Sandy." Tony listened. A huge grin spread across his face and he looked around at the group. "Really? Well that's nice to hear." More talking from the other end of the phone. "He said he might do that. Ha, he's not in too much trouble I hope? OK, chat soon," and the call ended.

Tony chuckled. "Wayne has found all sorts of problems with our online security. Remember the trick he played on the bank CEO? He did the same to Vijay. His wife loved the flowers and instructed him to buy Wayne a good dinner! He's making a couple of simple changes but has told Vijay he needs to invest in some decent software."

Laughter and clapping from the assembled group. "Something else Sandy said. He has allocated a chap called Diego to work with Wayne on building the websites. They are apparently getting on very well together!" The clapping continued. "Vijay has instructed Diego to take Wayne for a slap-up meal!"

Willie, who had been purring contentedly on Tuppence's lap during the proceedings, glanced around at everyone cheering. Harry was about to ease himself up from the sofa when something must have clicked in the cat's little mind. A low-pitched rasping noise came from his throat and he leapt towards Harry's slowly moving hand, clamping his jaw around its little finger. He released it almost immediately and like a flash ran into the kitchen and dived out through the cat flap. Harry yelled "Ow, that hurt," as he pulled his hand up to survey the damage.

"Are you alright?" asked a slightly shaken Tuppence.

"Willie!" called a worried-looking Tony. "I'm sorry about that. Did it break the skin?"

"No, it didn't," said Harry shaking his hand. He looked up and laughed. "I reckon that's what you would call retribution!"

CHAPTER 16

The Met Onside

Tuppence was going to be a tourist for the day. She parked at the hotel, took an unhurried walk through Parkers Piece, strolled past Emmanuel and eventually arrived at Kings College. In awe, she wondered how on earth Tudor stonemasons could construct something so extraordinary. Inside, bathed in rainbow colours from the stained glass windows, Tuppence sat, closed her eyes, and let the music from the rehearsing choir waft over her. Eventually dragging herself away she walked along the river, found a pub with seating outside and had a salad helped down by a glass of wine. Punts were out in force and Tuppence made a failed effort not to laugh as a novice, slipping on the wet surface of the rear deck, clung on to his pole, and arced gracefully into the water. A slow walk back to the hotel and a short nap prepared her for the meeting with Bob. She had a feeling the future of the whole project might hinge on this being a successful evening.

Tuppence had met Wayne the previous afternoon to get an update on the work done at the agency. He showed her a very impressive website, built by plagiarising material from other import/export organisations. The agency had revived a dormant company called Maxadex to take the place of Scamco. Vijay's team had built P&L and cash flow statements using material from the Holt company. And they had opened a bank account in the Maxadex name. Wayne had copied everything onto a spare laptop for Tuppence to take with her. He had also run extracts from the recordings made at both the Maid's Head and golf club through a Voice Speech Analyser. "Looks like the voices tie up," he confirmed.

Tuppence arrived at the bar, laptop in hand, and commandeered a discrete corner table. Minutes later Bob appeared. He gave his auntie Dora a hug and said "I hope you don't mind, but I've asked one of my colleagues to join us. His team knows your villains. He'll be able to tell you whether your idea is a goer or not." Just as he'd finished speaking, in came a tall man, smart and forty something. "Dick, let me introduce Tuppence Halfpenny. Auntie Dora, this is Detective Superintendent Dick Sargent."

He smiled, "a pleasure to meet you and before you say anything, I've heard all the jokes. Commander Henderson has given me a bit of an insight into what you've been up to. I'm looking forward to hearing more." Bob ordered some drinks and Tuppence kicked off, "This might take some time so I suggest I talk you through from the beginning. I'm sure you will have all sorts of questions so interrupt whenever you want."

She told them about the events in the Maids Head bar and how they identified both victim and villain. She showed photographs and played a selection of recordings. She then brought up the care home adventure, playing extracts of the conversation with the barman and the episode in Bernadette's office. She finished with an extract from the video of Enrici talking to Grace about signing the stock transfer form. "So that's our evidence. Oh, and by the way, we've put the voices through a speech analyser and the people in the Maids Head were definitely Enrici and Bradley. So, any questions?"

Both policemen had been listening very carefully, Bob occasionally smiling and Dick making a few notes. He looked up at Tuppence, "If you'll excuse the expression, bloody hell! You've got material here my guys would give their right arm for. Tell me a bit more though about how you made the link between a random car number plate and observing Enrici at his golf course?" Tuppence hesitated. She knew complete honesty was needed about Wayne's flirtation with the law.

"This is just a little embarrassing," she said in a way that implied they'd been a bit silly but it wasn't that serious. "One of our number is a cyber security expert. He earns his living protecting businesses against fraud and malicious attack. He worked out potential names, then compared them with people who had booked tee times at all the golf courses within the right distance from Norwich. We whittled them down to just one, Enrici, and we decided to go and check him out."

"Are you telling me he hacked into golf course IT systems?" asked Dick pointedly.

"He may be guilty of a minor indiscretion in looking at booking times at a number of golf clubs but he has gone no further."

"So he's hacked their systems?"

"I suppose technically yes. But in a very good cause."

Dick turned his head towards Bob, raised his eyebrows then looked back at Tuppence. "I'm afraid that's no defence as you probably know. This puts a rather different perspective on the matter." A glum-looking Tuppence nodded. A silence that seemed to go on for an age was broken by Bob.

"Dick's right." He hadn't heard this part of the story before and looked serious. "Do you mind if the Detective Superintendent and I have a quiet word together?"

"No problem. I need to spend a penny anyway." Tuppence got up and headed for the Ladies. She had a horrible feeling Dick Sargent was about to blow the whole project out of the water. She decided to give them plenty of time to consider their response.

When she returned her heart was pounding. She glanced back and forth between the two stern-looking men. Bob spoke. "Breaking into someone's computer system without their agreement is a crime. However I look at this, your cyber security expert appears to have committed a crime. This puts us in a very difficult position." The bottom was rapidly dropping out of Tuppence's world. "I'm amazed you got mixed up in it." Tuppence stared helplessly at him and then held her head in her hands.

"That said," she heard Bob say, "there just may be a glimmer of hope." Tuppence looked up. "If I were able to vouch for your expert and persuade Superintendent Sargent here that he is scrupulously honest, we might have a way forward."

"He is," said Tuppence, "I totally trust him." Her whole being pleaded with the policemen.

"Dick will have to be the arbiter of that. Now this is going to seem a bit dramatic but I think it will be a good way to settle matters." He stared at Tuppence. "Tell us his name, this cyber security man of yours."

With some trepidation she answered, "It's Wayne Bennett." Dick Sargent took a folded piece of paper from his pocket and opened it up. He looked at it, burst out laughing and showed it to Tuppence. On the paper was written 'Wayne Bennett'.

Tuppence startled two ladies at a nearby table when she yelled, "How on earth did you know that?"

More quietly Bob said, "There are not many totally honest hackers around. We employ some and use a few sub-contractors. I checked while you were away and there's only one who lives anywhere near Sheringham. His name is Wayne Bennett. I don't know him personally, but he has an open contract with us and can be used whenever required. He is highly thought of. I'm sorry about the drama but I needed Dick to know that I was being totally honest too. If you'd said any other name, he would have been in serious trouble."

Dick added, "Am I pleased you got the name right! You've uncovered a lot of valuable evidence. It's not something I would wish to lose."

Bob spoke again. "First things first. If Wayne had done this under our auspices, there would be no problem. In some cases, verbal authorisation to look at someone's data can be granted with formalities dealt with later." A pause as Bob seemed to be weighing up options. "Right," he said, "after we spoke on the phone about this initially, I gave Wayne Bennett authorization within the terms of his contract to look at information on a selection of golf websites. This is the story we must all stick to. I'll make it formal tomorrow and he can put in his invoice. Anything else he does needs to be agreed with me in advance."

"No problem." Bob nodded although Tuppence suspected he'd gone out on a limb. "I'll speak to Wayne first thing in the morning."

Dick took over. "You said you had further plans."

"Yes we have." Tuppence explained the first part of the sting. She showed them the website Wayne and Diego had manufactured. "We will pick some random photos to masquerade as the directors although one of them will be a member of our team. She's a retired actress," she said grinning.

"What would you see as the outcome of this little exercise?" asked Dick.

"The idea is the villains become sufficiently impressed to pay a sort of joining fee to open the door to much bigger deals in the future. This joining fee will pay our victim back his £150,000."

"How are you going to persuade Enrici to take part?" asked Bob.

"Two of our team will intercept him at his golf course and put a proposal to him."

"Careful, they could get into a lot of trouble," said a worried-looking Dick.

"We've thought about that. We've got a minder. He's an ex-marine and you certainly wouldn't want to argue with him."

"I'm not sure you realise, but that at the end of this Enrici and his crew will not have committed a crime."

"Yes, we know. That's where the second stage comes in. Let me explain." Tuppence, now feeling a lot more confident, talked them through their proposals and the part the agency would play. "We were hoping at this stage, with all the evidence and information we had gathered, that maybe you could become involved."

"Well, we certainly need to talk about how we can progress this case without you guys committing suicide. Now, I don't know about you two but my stomach is rumbling. Why don't we do that over dinner?"

"Good thinking," said Bob.

Food and wine ordered, it wasn't long before they got back to business. "Before we go any further, I think you've told Bob the victim's name. Would you like to elaborate?" asked Dick.

"His name is Harland Payne, known to us as Harley. Local undertaker, churchwarden, pillar of the community. Went to school with two of our merry band and is the son of another. He is very worried about his father's psychological state. He believes he would rather pay up and nobody know about this than get involved."

"Pity. Never mind," said Dick. "From what you've told us so far I think your scheme is rather ingenious and might just work. Let's go into your plan to persuade them to take part."

"The fine detail hasn't been worked out yet but we understand Enrici is driven by ego and greed, so we will focus on what's in it for him. We'll say we picked him out as a potential partner because of his success and professionalism. We expect objections so we will be prepared to explain and show how our technical expertise opens up massive markets that he has no access to. We will rehearse the meeting with a couple of our team playing the baddies. Anthony, our friendly marine, will recce the area in advance and will be on hand if there's trouble."

"Where will this meeting take place?"

"In the Golf Club car park."

"Photographs?"

"I think so, hold on." Tuppence opened up the laptop and found car park shots.

"Looks like there are a couple of CCTV cameras installed. Make sure your meeting is in view of at least one of them. We can get a copy of the recording for evidence purposes. Don't get pressured into going anywhere else with them."

"The lads are also hoping to record the conversation with Enrici."

"We might be able to help if you're stuck for kit."

"Let's assume they agree to go ahead, when do you think your Maxadex meeting will take place?"

"As you can see we're pretty well down the line, so we think it would be one or two weeks later. The earliest we can organise the Golf Club meeting would be a week tomorrow as Enrici tends to play on a Wednesday morning. With your agreement Bob, Wayne can keep an eye on the tee bookings." Bob nodded.

"OK. I think we need to have a watching brief but not become actively involved," said Dick. "Your Part 2 is another kettle of fish altogether and I think we probably need to run it, obviously with your close involvement. You happy with that?"

Tuppence's heart skipped a beat. "That's exactly what we want, let's get these guys banged up," she said dramatically.

Tuppence attracted the waiter's attention, "another bottle of wine I think. On me, or I should say the ad agency," she explained the financial arrangement.

"Let me give you a little bit more information about these villains," said Dick.

"Lawrence Enrici isn't his real name, it's Lorenzo Enrico Ellis. Italian mother, English father. He's a career criminal. Been a member of various gangs in his time. He's had three terms in prison, most recently Brixton. Changed his name when he came out the first time to simply Lawrence Enrici. His focus is now on extortion, principally blackmail around doctored photographs. He's fairly successful and very careful. He spends a lot of time spotting and researching victims who have plenty of money and who he thinks will not come to us. Places like rugby internationals, horse racing, one-day cricket matches. Always where a lot of booze is consumed."

"He employs two fixers. Michael Bradley has been with him longest, quite tough but not seriously violent. He's quite perceptive and has a brain on him. Newer on the scene is Joe Pegg. Very nasty. Been convicted twice of violent crimes starting at the age of 16. Met Enrici in Brixton. He's not somebody you would want to mess with. Enrici also employs a photographer who takes photos and then doctors them. To our knowledge, Bradley is always involved in the set-up. Not sure about Pegg's wider role. Bradley seems to have a small network of girls, probably part of the night-time industry, who act as stooges. Enrici seems to do most of the planning but seldom gets involved on the front line. I guess he pays pretty well and Bradley is certainly loyal."

"I'm sure that's going to be extremely useful, thanks," said Tuppence. "You seem to know quite a bit about Enrici and his group. You've not had any success nabbing him?"

"No, he's careful as I said. It would be nice to close him down though."

"Who else is in the business then?" asked Tuppence. "Of course, I don't suppose you're going to tell me that are you? Although it might just help us if we knew the name of somebody in a similar gang to Enrici."

"No. I shouldn't." Dick paused, but then obviously thought what the hell. "There is a guy called Arthur Logan. Pretty successful in his field. He and Enrici used to work together but they fell out. Despite being a villain Arthur is actually quite a gentleman. Old school. Never resorts to violence."

"By the way what do you think we should do about Grace in the care home?" asked Tuppence. "We don't want her scammed."

"If we did anything proactive, that could affect what we've just talked about," said Dick.

"It's going to be quite a while before anything moves on the main project," said Bob. "Is there any way you can work with the care home manager to ensure she doesn't sign anything in the meantime?"

"I'll talk to her," replied Tuppence.

With that, discussions about Enrici concluded. Tuppence promised to keep in close touch with both about progress, and Bob concerning anything related to Wayne's covert activity. They finished their dinner, repaired to the bar for a nightcap and then called it a day. Tuppence, although by now rather mellow, was very excited. Before going to bed she sent a WhatsApp to the team *'Spoken to my contact. All systems go. Could we have short meeting tomorrow (Wednesday) 3 pm. Bench?'* By 9:00 the next morning everybody had responded and all but Harry and Anthony could attend. They would be at a Board Meeting. Things were looking up.

* * *

As soon as she woke the next morning, which wasn't early, Tuppence rang Wayne. She told him a bit about the meeting but importantly how he needed to clear with Bob any future cyber activity. Wayne called him straight away. He had a few ideas about picking up some additional information that might help and they agreed on a few actions. Bob also insisted he send his appropriately dated invoices in quickly. Wayne realised he needed the cover.

Back at the hotel, Tuppence didn't hurry. She'd picked up a newspaper and read it over a breakfast of some fruit and scrambled egg on toast helped down with several cups of tea. She was feeling very pleased with herself. Before she left Cambridge she called Bernadette. Tuppence told her of the Met's interest but that somehow they needed to head off any coercion from Enrici in the short term. "Whatever pressure Enrici exerts, Grace guarantees she won't sign anything," Bernadette said. "The pressure to release her room has decreased slightly too because other space has become available. An inevitable consequence of looking after old and frail people I'm afraid. Once it can be organised Grace will go to live with her daughter. They have instructed her lawyer to prepare to sell her property." Tuppence breathed a sigh of relief and said she'd keep Bernadette up to date with progress.

At 3.00 pm the group arrived at the bench with great anticipation. Tuppence summarised what had happened at her meeting and to keep it simple explained that the Met had given their blessing to Wayne using his skills to collect information. Everyone was over the moon with the police getting involved particularly about taking control of Part 2. They agreed they now needed to go ahead and fix a date to meet the villains. Wayne said he had looked at tee times and found Enrici would be at the golf course next Wednesday as expected and was booked in at 10.28.

"Better just make sure that Anthony is available," said Tony. "I'll text him and Harry." While he was doing that Henry said he and Tony had come up with a rough plan to hook the villains and they would continue working on it. Tuppence added that while the Met couldn't get involved in this part of the operation, Dick had given some good advice on how to proceed, which she'd pass on. She reminded them that they must rehearse. Tony confirmed the agency would produce false stick-on number plates for his car as a precaution. Then his phone pinged. "Anthony can be clear all day next Wednesday. We're ready to roll!"

Wayne took over. "Let me give you an update on my latest research. I spoke to Bob this morning and I'm now working with a guy I know well at the Met. I got Enrici's bank details from the Golf Club membership system and we had a quick shufty. There is often fifty or sixty thousand pounds a time going in. This is mostly from one other account. That made us think money being paid by people he is blackmailing probably goes to that account first and then it's divvied out between him and the people who work for him. So we had a look in that one and noticed two amounts paid in at around the time Harley was being blackmailed, the first for fifty grand and the other for a hundred. The total amount going in over the last 12 months was just over £500,000. He seems to pay himself 50% and the rest goes elsewhere. My colleague in the Met has started building a report. They seem to be taking this seriously."

He then told the team what he was doing while in London, including guiding them through the Maxadex website. He ended up on the 'our team' page. "This is the CEO. I looked for the slyest photo I could get from the agency's stock images. Then I found a suitably Scrooge-like photo for the finance director. The most difficult picture to find was for the real villain in their team though, the Operations Director. I wanted something evil and look what turned up!" With that, he scrolled down to reveal an image from a late 1980s Liverpool Empire production featuring Tuppence as Cinderella's Wicked Stepmother.

"Where on earth did you dig that up from?" cried Tuppence as Henry bellowed with laughter.

"Diego and I spent a very pleasant couple of hours in the hotel bar populating the website with pictures. There were plenty of you but we didn't want anything that Enrici and his lot might recognise. You never know they might be fans! So we need one with you done up near enough as you will appear on the day."

"Harry's got some decent gear," said Tony, "I'm sure he can take it."

"That will be fun. I haven't had a publicity shot taken for ages. Anyway, who's Diego?"

Looking slightly sheepish Wayne said, "He's a graphic designer allocated to the team by Tony's agency. He's from Argentina originally, then moved to Spain. He's been in London for the last seven years."

"And?" she encouraged.

"Well, we got on pretty well. Lots of things in common. We went to the Tate Modern. He's got a smart flat in the Barbican."

"When are we going to meet him then?" Tuppence didn't beat about the bush.

"We'll see. Which reminds me," he said wanting to change the subject, "I'm sure you remember that as blackmailers we said we would pose as a business consultancy and have a website Enrici and his crew could scrutinise. We started work on it and then realised we needed a name. Diego said to me he'd seen a film years ago about a bandit called Robin Hood, robbing from the bad and giving money to those who needed it. He said that's what we were about to do and suggested we call ourselves Robin Hood Consultants. I thought the principle was good but in the end, we settled on linking it to where we come from. So it ended up as Sillingham Robins Ltd. I'm afraid that's now embedded so if you don't like it, the changes will take some time."

"Forgot about that," said Tony. "The name sounds great to me. I've always wondered where the name Sillingham comes from. Anyone know?"

Henry provided the answer. "It was a previous name of Sheringham from around the eleventh century. I believe it was recorded in the Domesday Book."

"That's very appropriate," said Tony. "Most of us are pretty ancient."

"By the way, and one very last thing, the Met are going to get us hidden microphones that you two can wear linked to Anthony. They are also going to take a feed from the golf club CCTV system so they can keep an eye on what's going on."

With that, the meeting drew to a close. "Before you disappear, I just need to tell you something," said Henry, his face taking on a glum look. "Ken's had another of his bad turns."

"What's happened?" asked Tuppence.

"He's become a bit aggressive. Keeps throwing things around. He's pushed Margaret about too although his balance isn't great and she's managed to dodge any punches so far."

"That's awful. He was so good at the party."

"He's also trying to get out all the time. She's had to hide the door keys. He's becoming very stressed. And tearful. She thinks he's trying to go home, wherever he thinks home is. Anyway, chances are we won't be seeing him again for a while." He grimaced. "If at all."

Tuppence put her arm around Henry's shoulders. "It's horrible for you too, isn't it? Your best friend. I'll give Margaret a call." And on that rather downbeat note, the team went their separate ways.

CHAPTER 17

Hooking The Villains

The next few days saw a deal of activity in preparation for the meeting with Enrici. Wayne, Diego and the team at Brodie Vellum finessed the material needed to hoodwink the villains. They invited the Sillingham Robins to review everything and hammer both websites to see whether they could find faults. A few were discovered and corrected quickly. The clandestine recording gear from Dick Sargent's team was delivered to Anthony, who soon had it up and working. Tony and Henry worked on their script and, under duress, were subjected to a rehearsal by Tuppence with Harry tagging along for good measure.

This wasn't an overwhelming success. They had fine-tuned a couple of opening sentences and were both able to deliver them fluently. Unfortunately, aggressive responses from Tuppence left them both floundering. Tony, calling on his lengthy experience of tactful business negotiation coped marginally better than Henry, who called on his experience to deliver suitably basic nautical ripostes. Tuppence read the riot act telling them that if they couldn't do better they might as well back out now because they were unlikely to return in one piece. It was Harry's suggestion that they sit down calmly, look at all objections they could foresee, and then work out how to react to each. This took some time. Then he got them to re-run the rehearsal in as non-confrontational way as they could. It worked but Tuppence still had her doubts. Tony and Henry agreed to reconvene to keep running through the process themselves until they felt that they were less likely to put their lives on the line.

The week passed quickly and on the morning of the confrontation, the three cavaliers set off early. Anthony likened the expedition to a special forces sortie heading out into hostile territory. "When we are in theatre we have to keep our wits about us and our eyes open. Get in, do the job, get out. If things go wrong, know what our fallback positions are." Henry said that sounded very Buzz Lightyear, although he quickly added that it was a sensible precaution. "You will each have a small microphone hidden inside your jacket collar. I'll have the controller and earpiece. I should be able to hear everything you say and hopefully what the villains say too."

During the journey, they also discussed who would do what in the meeting. Henry felt that an amount of diplomacy was probably needed and sadly he wasn't graced with much of that. The other two politely agreed. So he suggested they should operate a sort of good-cop bad-cop approach. Tony could lead the conversation, being polite and even pleasant, with the aim of getting them onside. If they became aggressive, or dismissive of Tony's proposal, he could step in using more direct language that they might better understand.

They arrived at the golf course just after 12:30. On the drive up to the clubhouse Tony pulled over, unpeeled the backing paper from the false numberplates and stuck them on. He was pleased. Even from pretty close you'd never know. They discovered Enrici's Bentley conveniently parked directly in line with one of the CCTV cameras. At Anthony's suggestion, Tony was able to park eight cars away in the opposite rank. He would be able to sit in the back and watch proceedings from behind the tinted windows. They had time for some lunch before Enrici would finish his round.

Over lunch, they agreed on an emergency call sign. Henry's expletive-driven original suggestion was rejected in favour of 'Mayday', although Anthony thought he would see and hear if anything was going wrong so it shouldn't be needed. If he wanted to get a message to them he would either call or text on Wayne's burner phone. Henry was in charge of that and turned the sound off so it would only vibrate. At a quarter to two, they declared themselves as ready as they ever would be. The clubhouse overlooked the 18th green and it wasn't long before Enrici, Bradley and Pegg arrived. Both Anthony and Henry took a good look at them. "Time to go?" asked Tony.

"I reckon so," said Henry, "It's now or never." The adrenaline was pumping. They'd been working towards this moment for a long time. They only had one chance to get it right.

"Good luck boys, you'll do just fine," said Anthony as he clambered into the rear seat of Tony's car. Henry was clutching a document case containing some papers he hoped would be useful. He and Tony positioned themselves not far from the Bentley with a CCTV camera directly behind them. Then they waited. It shouldn't be long before Enrici came to load his clubs into the boot of his car. Nothing happened. The minutes seemed like hours, then at last someone came round the corner of the building pushing a golf trolley.

It was neither Enrici, Bradley or Pegg. As he came past Henry and Tony loitering in the car park he asked, "Are you OK, can I help?"

"Just waiting for somebody," said Tony. The golfer didn't look too sure, paused for a second or two, but then carried on towards his own car. "That didn't sound too convincing, did it? Where the hell is he?"

Just then another man appeared carrying a golf bag. It was Bradley. He crossed into a parallel lane of the car park. "Looks as if they've come in different cars," said Ian.

Bradley was piling his clubs into the back of his Audi as Enrici and Pegg appeared and walked towards Henry and Tony. "Right, here we go," said Henry, "Sock it to 'em." As the two villains approached the Bentley Tony took a deep breath, stepped forward and delivered his rehearsed first line. "Mr Enrici, I wonder if I could take a few minutes of your time. I have a business proposition to put to you which I think you might find interesting."

Enrici turned to face Tony and in his usual aggressive manner said, "Who the hell are you? How do you know my name?"

"I know your name because we are in the same business as you. We don't compete directly but we have an opportunity that I believe can significantly increase your income. My name's Armstrong, this is Mr Crabbe." Henry chose that pseudonym because he thought he might remember it.

By now, Bradley had noticed something was going on and had joined the other two.

Enrici snarled. "You have no idea what business I'm in."

"As it happens, we do."

Before he could get any further Bradley interrupted, "Boss, that one was here a few weeks ago. He was behind us and played through, remember?"

"You're right. He was in the clubhouse as well. I thought at the time they were listening to us." Turning back to Tony he said, "I don't know who you think you are, but you are getting yourself into serious trouble."

"Do you want me to get rid of them boss?" said Pegg. He pulled a golf club from his bag. Tony's heart was now thumping. Over Enrici's shoulder, he saw Anthony get out of his car. This wasn't going well.

Pegg moved towards the two men and raised his club. Anthony began moving faster.

Henry decided it was time to intervene. "I wouldn't do that if I were you, Mr Pegg." Using his name brought Pegg's evil intentions to a halt, a look of astonishment on his face. "Yes, we know your name and Mr Bradley's too. Now if you look at the corner of the building behind me you will see a CCTV camera. They come in very useful at times. That's why we chose to wait here to talk to you. Everything is being recorded."

"We can move somewhere else," blurted a slightly less cocky Enrici.

"The damage has been done I'm afraid Mr Enrici. You are already on record as being here with us. So I suggest you put that club back in your bag Mr Pegg."

Anthony was only a few yards from Pegg when Enrici nodded and the club was returned to the bag. He paused, then slowly backpedalled. Henry continued looking directly at Pegg. "We know all about you. First convicted for violent assault at the age of sixteen I believe." Pegg was glaring wide-eyed at Henry. "That's fine with us. We need arseholes like you. Now Mr Enrici, we also know the sort of money you make for each of your operations. We can help you increase that significantly."

"What are you talking about? You don't know anything about how much I make."

"I can assure you we know lots about you Mr Enrici." He paused. "Or maybe I should say Mr Ellis."

It was Enrici's turn to look stunned. "And we know you've been working with Mr Bradley for some time, and

187

if I'm not mistaken you first became acquainted with Mr Pegg when you both spent some time living cosily together in Brixton. Now the reason we know we can help you earn more is that we have had a quick look at your bank account."

"You've not seen my bank account," said Enrici mustering as much bravado as he could.

Henry opened his document case and pulled out a single sheet of paper. "I thought you'd say that, so I took the liberty of printing a copy of your bank statement." He handed it to Enrici. Stunned silence from the man in question. "We've made it our business to understand a lot about you and your operation. You are very observant Mr Bradley, Mr Armstrong played golf here recently as part of our investigation. We have done the same with other organisations like yours. Only we've chosen to talk to you because we think you are professional and vicious enough to provide exactly the sort of services we need. So I suggest you listen to my colleague."

There was no response from any of the three villains. Things seemed to be calming down so Tony took over where Henry had finished. "Now Mr Enrici, do you want to talk to us with your two employees present or would you like to do it more privately."

Enrici was obviously shaken. "They're staying. I'll give you two minutes to explain what this is all about. And don't think we can't find out about you. If I think you're a danger to my organisation then there are far more private places for us to have a conversation, if you understand what I mean!"

"It won't come to that I'm sure. We do basically the same as you. However, our business model is entirely digital. We employ some of the best, shall we call them cyber security experts, in the country. Instead of dealing with individuals we deal with companies. Or more specifically people within companies who are siphoning off money illegally. There's no danger of our targets informing the authorities or causing us any harm because we document details of all their crimes. They know we would provide that information to both the boards of the companies concerned and the police."

"Just to put the values into context, we have undertaken many projects recently all of which were two or three times the amount you seem to typically take. We are in the process of stepping this up and our next major project will have a value of around £2 million. And there are plenty more where that comes from. The reason we want to partner with an organisation like yours is that we are not experts at the final extraction process which has to be done face-to-face. You are. I think that's my two minutes up so if you have any questions please ask them now."

Tony stood quietly and held Enrici's stare. It was obvious he wasn't sure what to do. Eventually, he broke the silence. "I'm not saying we are involved in anything and I'm not saying I'm interested. I need a few minutes to talk to my colleagues."

Henry said, "take as long as you like. We're not going anywhere."

"In the car you two."

Once the doors had closed Henry turned away from them. "I hope you managed to pick most of that up Anthony!" The burner phone vibrated with a thumbs up emoji.

Tony said, "thanks for stepping in like that, I was hitting a brick wall. What do you think?"

"I've a feeling he must be interested, otherwise he'd have gone by now. I guess we'll find out in a few minutes."

It wasn't long before the three villains were back facing Henry and Tony.

"I don't believe a word of what you said. You're going to have to prove it," said Enrici, "and I don't know how you came across us but I'll bet you don't know anyone else in our business."

Henry answered, "finding out about you was not an accident. We have some influential contacts and one of them provided a list with you at the top."

"Really? Pull the other one, it's got bells on! Who's second on the list then?"

Henry gave Enrici the broadest of smiles. "A gentleman called Arthur Logan. I believe you are familiar with him." Enrici's face turned the colour of his hair.

"You're going to have to prove you're not bullshitting," blurted Enrici.

"Of course. We appreciate that," said Henry. He fished three single sheets of printed paper from his document case. "Here are some projects we have completed. The names of the companies are correct but we've changed the names of the individuals concerned. You'll see the numbers are small, the maximum is £450,000. That's why we need somebody like you to handle the front end." Enrici gave the papers a fleeting glance.

"These don't prove a thing. You could have made them up."

How right you are, thought Henry. Wayne and co had done a fantastic job. "I can assure you we haven't made them up. Go online and see the sort of companies we're targeting. However we do appreciate your concerns. So we have an even better way of proving that what we do works. We would like you to take part with us in a very manageable and low risk venture we have ready to go. That way, you'll see for yourselves."

"What? Risk our business, and us, without proof it works?"

"Well, how else are you going to know? What do you suggest?" The only response was a shrug of the shoulders.

"It's all about risk and reward Mr Enrici," said Tony taking over the conversation. "We are prepared to risk working with you. You need to decide whether you are prepared to work with us. This job is small, worth £300,000. You'd get 40%, so that's £120,000 for just a few hours work."

"No chance! You are expecting us to do the dangerous bit of the job. It would need to be 60/40 in the other direction."

"Not at all. I'm being very generous. We have invested large sums of money in IT, highly skilled staff and all the collateral necessary for us to support our case. Your job would be a maximum of two hours per engagement, plus briefing and wash up. You get the business handed to you on a tray. It's not negotiable."

Enrici sneered, "nothing's non-negotiable! You need us to do the dirty work for you. 55/45 in our favour!"

"Quite right boss. You tell 'em," added Bradley.

Tony decided to play for time. "Give me a couple of moments to speak to my colleague." He and Henry walked away from the group. "I decided Enrici was bound to negotiate so thought I'd give him the opportunity."

Henry said softly, "It makes no difference, they're getting nothing anyway. I've a feeling they are not going to go with the upfront payment though."

"I agree. We need to knock that on the head. I'm sure the Good Causes Fund can bear the cost. If I cave in on the split though we'll look weak. I'll offer 50/50."

They returned to the group. Tony stared at Enrici and took a deep breath. "Right. 50/50, and that's our last offer. If you won't accept that we'll take our chance with Mr Logan."

"I need to discuss this with my colleagues." The three villains walked away although it didn't take long before they came back. With a self-satisfied look on his face Enrici said, "OK, we'll go with that, as long as you can prove this thing is going to work."

"Done!" said Tony. And you really have been, he thought.

Henry took a two page paper from his document case. "Here is a summary project plan with details of what has to be done and by whom. You'll see references to other documents which include financial information, an analysis of the corporate accounts, details of the people we will be talking to in the company and so on. We use a business consultancy as a front for our organisation and you'll find website details and a telephone number you can contact us on included."

"When would this start?" asked Enrici.

"Hopefully in a couple of weeks or so," said Tony. "You will need to tell us your availability and we will match days and arrange a meeting with the appropriate Director. In the meantime we will send you the rest of the documents mentioned in the plan. Do you want them to your home address or somewhere else? I'm not sending them electronically."

"How do you know . . . . " Enrici had still not grasped the depth of knowledge the two had about him. "From now on you stop poking your nose into my affairs. I'll text you an address."

"Of course," said Tony, smiling. "We will then need to meet a day in advance to finalise arrangements and ensure that you've grasped enough of the details to be credible."

"Do you think we're stupid?" blurted Pegg.

"Not at all. We wouldn't be talking to you if we did. It's just that it's your first time and we have to be sure it's going to work."

"Well thank you for your time," said Tony. "I'm sure our partnership will be very lucrative. If you have no more questions we'll bid you farewell." There was nothing forthcoming from the three villains who collectively seemed unsure what had hit them. Henry and Tony started off towards the clubhouse. Henry spoke into his collar, "we'll go in for a coffee Anthony. Once they've gone come and join us." A moment later Anthony ducked down low on the back seat of Tony's car, a bit concerned as Pegg was heading directly towards him. Pegg stopped and stared at the big limo. Anthony didn't move a muscle. After several agonising seconds Pegg turned to the car next to Tony's, put his clubs in the boot and roared off towards the car park exit.

As Anthony approached their table, Henry was pouring three cups from a large pot. "Well gentlemen it seemed to me that was very successful," he said as he pulled up a chair and sat down.

"Certainly looks as if they've taken the bait," said Tony, a wide grin creasing his face. "A bit hairy at times though."

"That's true," said Anthony. "I don't think you saw but Pegg's car was parked next to yours!"

"You don't think he saw you do you?" Henry asked.

"No, not at all. I asked you to drive in forwards so the windscreen would be facing away from the action. All the other windows are tinted and it is very difficult to see anyone through those. Especially when you have a complexion like mine!" he said chuckling. The other two joined in.

"I knew I bought a car with tinted windows for a reason," said Tony.

"We should tell the others where we're up to," said Henry. "Shall we fix for tomorrow? "What are you like for time Anthony?" asked Tony.

"I'm busy during the day. Are you sure you want me there?"

"Of course. You're a fully-fledged member of the team now. How about trying to arrange something tomorrow evening?" That suggestion suited the others.

"I'll get a WhatsApp out," said Henry.

By the time they'd got back to the car, positive responses had come back from everyone. Harry suggested seven o'clock in the garden by his apartment, and he would provide the booze! The confirmations for that were immediate and enthusiastic.

* * *

Sheringham had experienced a warm spell over the last few days and the next evening was particularly balmy. Perfect for a few drinks in the garden. Harry and Sofia had set up a table and a collection of chairs outside their apartment. Harry had if anything overprovisioned on drinks and Sofia said she would bring some genuine Russian blinis out a bit later. The atmosphere was jolly and tinged with expectation. Tuppence's patience cracked first. "Come on then you three, tell us what happened yesterday."

Henry kicked off and Tony joined in, between them giving a comprehensive, blow by blow report, while Anthony threw in his tuppence worth every now and again. "So they didn't get nasty then?" asked Tuppence.

"One of them became a bit aggressive," said Henry.

Anthony jumped in, "Wayne's grandad was about to get clobbered with a golf club."

"What!" she bellowed.

"We were in good hands. Anthony was on his way."

"The day was saved by Henry using copious amounts of his inbuilt tact and diplomacy! I was able to go back and sit in the car."

"My Met Police friend and I were watching online at that point, and we both shouted 'watch out!'" said Wayne. "By the way, they're going to sync the video from the CCTV system with Anthony's sound recording. It can then hopefully be used as evidence."

"I've updated the agency," said Tony, "they're happy with progress on their side."

Wayne added, "Diego and I have tested out both websites and they stand up OK. Hopefully they are fooling Enrici and his crew."

"I've chosen my outfit for my role by the way and will use a particularly fetching wig and some stage spectacles. I almost didn't recognise myself in the mirror!" said Tuppence.

"We seem to be all systems go then," said Harry. "So when do we run the operation?"

Everybody's gaze fell upon Henry and Tony. "Well, unless anybody's got any great objection, once we clear it with the agency, how about two weeks from today?" Everyone was happy with that.

"We need to give Enrici a bit of notice so I'll call him next week."

And with that the business side of the evening was complete. Glasses were refreshed and Sofia brought out the blinis. She said, "there's a mix. Some caviar, some salmon cream cheese and some beetroot with quails egg." She turned to go back indoors.

"Aren't you going to join us?" asked Tuppence.

"You sure? You got things talk about."

"No, we've finished all that. It will be nice to have some sensible female company. Come and sit here." Harry poured her a glass of wine and she joined in with what became a very cordial evening for a group of people rapidly becoming best of friends.

At one stage Tony asked Henry how Margaret was doing. He said she had been advised to look at care homes. "Oh no. Are things so bad?" asked Tuppence.

"It would appear so. She's soldiering on but is struggling. The heart-breaking thing is he often doesn't recognise her now. The GP has prescribed some tablets which calm him down in the evening and help him sleep which is good. She's petrified. She wants to keep him at home, but . . . "

"Horrible as it sounds, there often comes a time when it's best for everyone involved," said Anthony. "The toll it takes on the person who does the caring can be immense. You can end up with two very ill people instead of one."

A sombre silence was interrupted by a buzz from Harry's doorbell. It was answered by Sofia who returned with a lady unknown to most of the group. "This is Alesha. She come to pick Anthony up."

Anthony rose, crossed over to her, gave her a kiss, took her by the hand and proudly announced "this is my lovely wife." Harry, definitely getting into the host mentality, introduced everyone to her.

"Come and join us," said Tuppence, pulling over a chair. "You don't have to drag him away immediately I'm sure."

As it began to get dark the garden was subtly lit by pedestal lanterns. Along with light from Harry's apartment, they provided just enough illumination. Tuppence set about interrogating Alesha. It transpired that she had met Anthony about 10 years ago after he was repatriated from an operation somewhere in Africa. She was a nurse at the Navy rehabilitation service in Portsmouth. He was tough and it didn't take too long for him to get over his physical injuries. But his mental anguish was another story. He'd lost a number of his men. She helped him through the recovery process and as she said, they just clicked. He was not there for long but that was the end of his operational role. So their relationship was able to develop and they'd been together ever since.

The gentle hum of conversation and the occasional clink of a glass was all that broke the silence of the early summer evening. First noticed by Wayne, this quiet was broken by the soft, velvety sound of a violin drifting down from above. Tuppence quickly explained Ken's evening ritual to Anthony and Alesha. The talking ceased. They all recognised the old romantic ballad, *The Way You Look Tonight*. As they listened, deep in their own thoughts, darkness hid the occasional tear trickling down the cheeks of some of Ken's unintended audience. The piece tailed off into silence. It was replaced by the sobs of a woman battling misery, heartache and ever swelling guilt.

Nobody seemed to want to break the spell. Eventually Tuppence spoke for them all, "Poor Margaret. Poor Ken. We have him to thank for us being here tonight, so we must do everything we can to bring these awful people to justice. Thanks for being such good hosts Sofia and Harry, it's time for me to head up the wooden hill."

"Me too," added Tony. "Harry has challenged me to a game of golf just round the corner in the morning. I shall need my wits about me." And with that, glasses and plates were stacked in the kitchen with Sofia insisting she would easily manage the rest. It had been a lovely evening. Just a thoughtful end bringing everyone down to earth with a bit of a jolt.

CHAPTER 18

Ken Escapes

On Friday at 9.14 Harry drove off from the first tee at Sheringham Golf Club. The sultry heat of the last few days had gone and a stern wind was blowing from the south over the course towards the sea. His mis-hit drive bounced along the middle of the fairway ending up neatly between two bunkers. Tony's on the other hand was caught by the wind and landed awkwardly beside the steps up to the second tee. On the second, Harry's ball flew low above fairway while Tony's was again caught by a strong gust, landing in a fairway bunker. Harry was amazed to be two up after two.

Then his luck changed. His sliced drive from the third tee was picked up by the wind and last seen heading over the cliffs towards the lifeboat station. Once on the green, Tony had already putted out as Harry managed to down his replacement ball. Tony was watching from the edge of the green and looked up as Harry's ball dropped. "That's not Ken is it?"

"Where?"

"On the cliff path." Harry turned to see a man in a floppy red jumper and jogging bottoms stumbling up the path. "It is isn't it? That's what he always wears. What the hell's he doing there, where's Margaret? Ken! Ken!" shouted Tony.

Oblivious, the man ploughed on. "He must have escaped. Christ, we'd better get him."

They left their trolleys by the fourth tee and struggled through the long grass up to the path. When they got there the man they assumed to be Ken had disappeared. They went as fast as they could up the hill, cleared the gorse and were almost blown off their feet by the force of the now howling gale. The path turned towards the cliff edge and they hurried on. It was then they saw a lady in uniform standing by the old Coast Guard Station shouting at the man they were chasing. He was balanced at the very edge of the precipice, swaying back and forth, staring out to sea.

"Ken! Get back from the edge!" called Tony.

The lady turned and called out, "He's not answering. I didn't want to get closer in case he jumps!"

Another strong gust blew and the man they now knew was Ken wobbled towards the edge, just managing to retain his balance before taking a small step backwards. He swayed gently, continuing to peer out over the cliff. Tony eased his way slowly towards him and shouted over the wind noise, "Ken. You come with us." At last he must have heard and turned his head towards Tony. A wide, excited smile filled his face. Tony held out his hand. "Here, let's go find Margaret." Ken looked again at the sea before turning back, holding out his hand towards Tony. "That's right. Let's get back home." As Tony stretched out to reach Ken, he was buffeted and knocked over by another vicious blast of wind. Just failing to grab Ken's hand he fell, sliding precariously towards the cliff edge. The same gust hit Ken full in the face. He lost his balance and arms flailing, he toppled backwards. A second later he disappeared.

There was a scream from the Coastguard Lookout as Tony felt hands grab his right ankle. It was Harry who had dived to catch him as he slithered towards the edge. With some effort he managed to stop Tony's progress. Then the Coastwatch volunteer grabbed Harry by the waist, heaving on him with all her strength. They all ended in a heap sprawled on the grass but Tony safely back from the sheer drop in front of him.

"It's 170 feet down to the bottom," she shouted, a look of absolute horror on her face. "I'll call the Coast Guard and lifeboat station," she got up and ran to the hut.

The pulses of both men were racing, "bloody hell, this is terrible. I'd nearly got him." Tony crawled back towards the cliff. "There may be a ledge."

"Careful!" yelled Harry as Tony peered over the edge.

"Can't see him," he called. Then, "oh no! There are people running up the beach towards the bottom of the cliff. That must be where Ken is." He shuffled backwards.

The Coastwatch volunteer returned, deathly white, "Someone from the lifeboat is going now and the Coastguard will call an ambulance."

"Thanks for your help, we need to get down there," yelled Tony over the wind, still furiously battering them. The two men started down the path as quickly as they could. Harry, a lot younger and a bit fitter ran ahead. "I'll ring Margaret," called Tony. "Harry hold on, wait. There's a WhatsApp from Henry. They're out searching. He asked us to help." He caught up to Harry, "My phone was on silent."

"So was mine. Better to ring him than Margaret."

Henry answered his phone immediately. "Where are you? Have you seen . . ."

Tony interrupted him, "Henry stop a minute. We didn't get your WhatsApp but we saw him on the cliff path and chased him. Look, this is awful. He's fallen off the cliff! Right by the Coastwatch station."

"No!" A desperate cry from Henry.

"We're going down there now. Can you tell Margaret?"

"Yes." There was a tremble in Henry's voice. "We're searching around town. I'll get her there as soon as I can." He ended the call.

The two men ran down the path as fast as Tony could manage. Harry shouted breathlessly, "There's a way down to the back of the lifeboat station. It's not a real path and it's steep, but we can manage it."

"You sure?" They reached a small fence and Harry hopped over. He began to descend what looked like an old gully. Tony followed. It was slow going at first. Then they both lost their footing and started slithering down. They grabbed at big tufts of grass, trying to prevent themselves hurtling out of control. Luckily the slope levelled out as they neared the roof of the lifeboat station. Harry stopped just feet from the edge. However he was clobbered by Tony following behind at speed. He was pushed towards the gap between the cliff and the building. Heading for disaster, he managed to grab a fortuitously placed iron stake. He swung round and hanging on for dear life, his legs dangling over the side, he came to a stop. Tony reacted quickly and pulled him back onto firm ground. They both slumped to the floor, breathing deeply. As they recovered, the sound of a siren approached along the promenade below. They set off again and cautiously made their way along the cliff towards the stony beach.

Two paramedics ran past them and unsteadily made their way over the shifting stones towards a small group of people gathered at the base of the high cliff. Tony and Harry made slower progress. They arrived to find the twisted body of Ken with the two paramedics kneeling over him. Full of dread Tony asked, "how is he? He's a friend of ours."

Without looking up, one of them said, "not good. Still alive though. Just trying to stabilise him."

Tony knelt down beside Ken. "Hold on Ken. These guys are looking after you. You'll be OK." Ken's closed eyes flickered. Then they opened and seemed to focus on Tony. He smiled. And then his eyes closed again.

Another siren could be heard and it wasn't long before two policemen arrived. "Hi Jeannie," said one of them, "Will he make it?"

She looked up, "Hello Kev. Not sure."

"What happened, do you know?"

"We do," said Tony.

"We'd better have a chat then."

Tony, Harry and the policeman named Kev moved a few yards away. Tony gave him a complete run down, including about Ken's state of health.

"So you don't think he jumped?"

"He absolutely did not jump! He was caught by a strong gust. It's blowing a hooley up there. He's quite frail."

Tony was telling Kev where Ken and Margaret lived when Jeannie the paramedic came over. She looked downcast. "I'm really sorry, but I'm afraid there's nothing more we can do for your friend. There's serious damage to the back of his head. Broken back too I think. That was one hell of a fall."

"Is he .. ?" She nodded. They looked over towards Ken as the other paramedic covered him with a blanket.

Kev asked, "would you be able to contact the family?"

"His wife with a friend are on their way now."

"Will you talk to her before she arrives? Better than just seeing him covered up," said the young policeman looking concerned.

"Of course," said Tony.

Kev said, "I'll contact the duty undertaker, we'll . . ."

"I'll do that," interrupted Harry. "I run Payne's. I think we're on duty today anyway."

"Please do. Let me know when your people are on their way."

"No problem. We'll go and intercept Margaret."

They started walking towards the lifeboat station and Harry put in the call.

It wasn't long before they saw the familiar figures of Henry and Margaret coming towards them. Henry struggling over the stones, Margaret holding on to his arm.

"I'm dreading this," muttered Tony.

"How is he?" called Margaret as she approached the two men, each with a bleak look on his face. Tony was about to speak when she said softly, "he's gone hasn't he?" Her shoulders heaved. She looked down, her falling tears forming dark spots on the grey stones. Henry took Margaret in his arms. Her body shook in silent grief.

Tony waited for a while then spoke softly, "I'm so sorry Margaret. He would have quickly lost consciousness. He wasn't in pain at the end." He took Margaret's hand, "Ken came-to for a moment. I think he recognised me. The paramedics did all they could."

Harry moved over to Henry, putting his arm around his shoulders. Henry's eyes had glazed over but he was doing his damnedest to retain some degree of control. "You OK?" he asked.

"Not really, but I'll manage."

Margaret lifted her head, "it's my fault he got out. I need to see him."

As they walked towards the bottom of the cliff, Jeannie approached them. "You're Margaret I believe. I'm really sorry. We did our best but his injuries were severe. We made him comfortable. He was not in pain. Would you like to see him?"

"Thank you. Yes I would please."

Jeannie turned the blanket down as far as Ken's shoulders and stepped back. His head had been moved so that the injury was not visible. They had also cleaned all the blood from his face. He looked peaceful. Margaret knelt down and then lay beside him. "I'm so sorry Ken. I should have looked after you better. I'm sorry. I'm sorry."

Henry said "we'd better call everybody."

"Have you spoken to Elsie?" Henry shook his head. "Well why don't you call her. We'll deal with the others," said Tony. Henry nodded, took his out phone and walked away to make his call. In the meantime Jeannie helped Margaret over to a blanket her partner had placed on the stones. She sat down and put her head between her hands. Once he had finished speaking to Elsie, Henry went over to sit with her.

Wayne had only just seen Henry's original WhatsApp when Harry got through to him. He told him what had happened. There was silence, and then Wayne burst into tears. Harry held on and slowly he calmed down. "How did he get out? I thought Margaret kept him locked in."

"Not sure. We'll find out soon enough."

"Shall I come over?"

"I wouldn't. Anthony is coming to collect Ken and your grandad's looking after Margaret. I'll get him to give you a call a bit later."

When Tony got through to Tuppence she was equally shocked, almost unable to speak. "What about Margaret?"

Tony explained what was happening, "will you be OK?" he asked.

"Yes. Yes I'm sure I will. Thanks for asking."

Anthony and a colleague arrived as they finished their calls. Anthony spoke first to Kev, then to Harry and Tony. "I take it that's Margaret speaking to Henry?" Tony nodded. "I don't know her surname. I'm hoping you do."

"It's Stevens with a V," said Tony.

"Thanks." Anthony went over to Margaret and crouched down in front of her. "Hello Mrs Stevens, I'm Anthony Christian from Payne's Funeral Services." A flicker of a smile crossed Margaret's face and she nodded. "May I give you my heartfelt condolences. I had not met Ken but I do know how much of a loss he will be to you and to all of his friends." Another wan smile from Margaret. "The time has come to take Ken from here to the Funeral Home. We will look after him and once the formalities are concluded we can take instructions from you as to how you want to proceed. Is that alright with you?"

"Yes, of course. You will look after him won't you?"

"You can be sure of that Mrs Stevens. Now you just wait here and we will do the rest."

Anthony's compatriot took a stretcher over to where Ken was lying. They gently lifted him, still covered by the blanket, onto the stretcher and then placed a thick green sheet over the top of that. "Would you like some help?" asked Harry.

"If you and Tony could each take a corner it will make it easier over these stones," said Anthony. And with that the four men picked up Ken and made their way back towards the lifeboat station, Harry doing something he vowed never to do. How his life had changed over the last few weeks. They were followed by Henry and Margaret, the policemen and the two paramedics. Ken was secured in the back of the black private ambulance, which was then slowly driven away along the promenade.

The police car and ambulance followed a discrete distance behind. Henry and Margaret walked to Sillingham House while Ian and Tony went to retrieve their golf trolleys. Their game was done for the day. Elsie was waiting on the bench. Margaret had become increasing agitated after the ambulance had gone. "I need to call everybody and tell them, fix the funeral, look at the insurance and pension. There's a lot to do, I must get on with it."

Elsie and Henry managed to calm her, saying nothing needed to be done immediately apart from telling important people. They went up to the apartment and within what seemed like minutes John, who had been alerted by Margaret early on, arrived. As soon as she saw him, his mum dissolved into tears again, saying over and over that it was her fault. Elsie stayed with her while Henry left the room to explain to John what had happened. They then said their goodbyes with Henry promising to call tomorrow.

Margaret told John what had happened that morning. Apparently, as usual she'd got Ken up at about 8:00, sorted his breakfast, got him showered and dressed and placed him in front of the television while she had her own shower. She got dressed and about 15 minutes later went into the lounge. Ken was not there. It took just a few seconds to find the front door ajar. She'd hidden the key behind a box in a draw, which was now open and the key gone. Ken must have found it by some fluke. She searched the apartment building and the garden. No Ken. She called Henry and the wider search began. Others were called in to help and they were out a good hour before Henry got the call from Tony.

As a paramedic John had become used to consoling people affected by tragedy. But this was different. This was his mum. It struck him that he'd hardly ever seen her cry. Today, distressed, she wept buckets. He spent the rest of the day comforting her, encouraging her to talk and guiding her away from making too many instant decisions. All the while dealing with his own pain and sadness. It was alleviated somewhat when Tuppence appeared at the door, gave both of them big hugs and spent a short time with them. They were grateful for the lasagne she brought which she told them just needed 30 minutes in the oven. It was accompanied by a bottle of Barolo she'd been keeping for a rainy day. If ever there was one, this was a rainy day.

CHAPTER 19

Preparation

The next day, a less than merry band of Sillingham Robins woke up to the stark reality of what had happened. None of them had slept well. Tony sat at his breakfast bar picking at his porridge, Willie gazing at him with his intuitive cat radar knowing something was not right with the world. Tuppence geared herself up to ring Poppy. Trevor and Ken seemed to have clicked somehow and she knew they'd both be upset. Wayne woke up angry. Life was just so unfair. Harry was determined Ken's send-off would reflect the debt his family owed him. And Henry prowled around his kitchen from first light with some serious concerns on his mind.

WhatsApp from Henry 8.45 – 'Been awake half night. Yesterday put everything in perspective. Don't have stomach to carry on.'

WhatsApp from Wayne 8.48 – 'Oh dear. How about delay?'

WhatsApp from Tuppence 9.03 – 'Don't want to upset Margaret and John by carrying on as if nothing has happened.'

WhatsApp from Tony 9.12 – 'Must be respectful. Will need to think of how we play it with villains if we delay.'

WhatsApp from Harry 9.17 – 'Very grateful for what you guys are doing. It's your call.'

WhatsApp from Anthony 9.21 – 'BTW, Funeral might clash with our timetable.'

WhatsApp from Tony 9.32 – 'Difficult. Why don't we let things settle and sleep on it. Better to talk face to face too. My apartment, 5.00pm Monday?'

* * *

At the appointed hour, everybody arrived. There was little of the usual banter. Willie, whose suspicions had gained traction in his little mind, positioned himself beside Tony. "I imagine we've all had a difficult weekend. I've had to deal with very few deaths in my time and to see a friend fall off a cliff is not something I want to repeat. If only we'd got there a bit earlier. We were so close. He missed grasping my hand by inches."

"You were lucky not to follow Ken over the edge," said Harry.

"Neither of you should feel guilty at all," declared Tuppence. "You did everything you could. I feel for Margaret. They've been together for nearly fifty years you know. Her life has been difficult over the last few but Ken going will leave a big gap."

Henry looked pensive. Tuppence spoke for all of them. "This must be particularly hard for you Henry. Ken was your best friend, wasn't he."

"He was that. Oldest and best. We had some good times together. We looked after one another." All eyes were on him. "It doesn't make it any easier that he wasn't the Ken who became my friend though. It's like his character had been shot to pieces. You know he was really smart. If he'd known that's how he was going to end up," Henry looked down at his hands again, "he wouldn't have wanted to be here." Nobody said a word. "It was a terrible way to go. I hope he lost consciousness straight away. Horrible thing to say, but in some ways maybe going quickly was for the best."

For a few moments they all sat quietly, deep in their own thoughts. Then Tony spoke. "We've got to decide where we go from here. Are we going to give up? Do we delay? If so for how long?"

"I can't even think about it," said Henry. "All I can think about is Ken toppling down that cliff. And poor old Margaret. I don't imagine I can just carry on," he waved his arm around, "with this stuff."

Wayne, sitting next to his grandad, rested his hand his shoulder, and speaking directly to him said, "we've done a lot of work to get these criminals banged to rights. Maybe we should put it on the back burner and once Ken's funeral is out of the way decide what to do then."

Tuppence added, "I really don't think we can do anything earlier."

"I hate to sound too practical," said Anthony, "but I do need to know. I have a funeral to plan."

Tony was about to speak when his doorbell rang. "That must be my daughter. She threatened to pop in today." He went to see, partially closing the sitting room door on the way. The silent gathering heard a faint welcome and woman's voice in response. Moments later Tony returned, "look who's come to join us." And in walked Margaret. She was dressed neatly although in sombre clothes, was devoid of makeup and her eyes seemed sunken and dark. She was in need of a hairdo but had done her best to tidy it up.

"I hope you don't mind but I wanted to talk to you all." She looked as if she was struggling to retain her composure.

Tuppence jumped up, "come and sit here Margaret." She indicated the chair next to her.

"No, I'll just stand for a few moments Tuppence if I may. I wanted to thank you all for your kind words and the cards.

They've all been much appreciated by John and I. I'd like to also thank Harry and Tony for trying to," she stalled for a second, "to save Ken from falling. It was very brave of you. And a special thank you to Anthony for your invaluable help and kindness over the weekend. Which brings me on to fixing the funeral. I don't want it to interfere with your plans."

"No, it's the other way round Margaret," said Tony. "The most important thing right now is to do what's right for you and Ken. What we are up to pales into insignificance."

What might have been a grimace crossed Margaret's face. "I need to tell you that John has been dealing with Ken's computer and phone. I didn't realise he was part of a WhatsApp group with all of you. I read what you said on Saturday. It's kind of you to be so thoughtful but if you don't mind me saying so I think it was all rather disrespectful towards Ken." This took everyone by surprise. They all thought the opposite. "I know he was not able to contribute fully but he did play a significant part, and without it I don't think you'd be where you are now. To me that is part of Ken's legacy. Something John and I can be proud of. Especially if you bring these people to justice. Abandoning it would be a kick in the teeth. That's why I've interrupted your meeting. I want you to carry on and we will organise the funeral around your plans."

Nobody knew what to say and Margaret's speech seemed to have exhausted her will power. Her bottom lip trembled. Henry jumped up, enveloped her in his arms, holding her as she wept onto his shoulder. Tuppence dived into her handbag for tissues and handed a bundle to Margaret. "Sorry," she spluttered, "I promised myself I wouldn't cry." She wiped her eyes, and recovering her composure let Henry sit her down next to Tuppence.

"It's all my fault," said Henry. "It was me that said we should call a halt. I thought that's what you would want. Maybe I should have had the sense to ask."

Margaret managed a smile. "I'm sure you're all trying to do what is right, but what's happened has happened."

As Tuppence held her hand she continued, "let me tell you something. John and I went for a walk yesterday. Do you know, we found the buses were still running. People were shopping. A postman was delivering mail. The sun was still shining. So we stopped for a coffee. The customer in front of us said to the lady behind the counter, did you hear, a man went over the cliff by the coastguard station on Friday? Oh dear, did he jump? she asked. Don't know. Dead though, the woman said. Ah well, never mind, said the serving lady cheerful as you like, what can I get you? You see, just because Ken's died, the world hasn't come to an end. Life goes on. And so must you."

A suitably chastened group fell over itself with apologies and thanks for her intervention. Henry suggested she take Ken's place on the team. She said she was a bit distracted at the moment but would like to help when she could. Wayne said he would add her to the WhatsApp group. Having said so though, it was like a punch in the stomach when he realised he would have to remove Ken. Tony said they would get on with some planning and asked Margaret if she would like to stay, but she declined saying she had a lot to do. With lots of best wishes and offers of help, she departed.

Tony stood beside the flip chart board flanked by a perplexed Willie. He looked round and decided the nice lady needed cheering up, so rubbed himself against her legs then jumped up and settled on her lap. "I must say, that well and truly put us in our place," announced Tony. "Why don't we use the time to decide our next moves?" There was unanimous agreement. Wayne asked Tony to set up his projector.

That done, Wayne kicked off. "Let me give you an update on what we now call Maxadex." He projected diagrams which explained in simple terms how the scam worked. He then talked through the deal that Enrici would be proposing to Florence Grant, the director to be played by Tuppence. "It is about arranging direct tea imports from Mali. Currently these go via South Africa but they have a way of cutting out the middle men. I'll give you a copy of Enrici's brief on this Tuppence. Vijay worked the whole thing through and I think it's watertight."

Tony stood up. "Unless I've missed something, it looks to me like we are ready to put some operational stakes in the ground," he said, crossing to the flip chart board. "I guess Enrici will want his game of golf Wednesday week as usual. Could you check Wayne? If so we could brief him in the afternoon and run the show on Thursday."

Wayne quickly interrogated the golf club website and confirmed Enrici's tee time of 9.28. "That's good. Let's look at the logistics of what needs to be done and who goes where, when."

He scrawled on a flip chart, *Briefing – Henry & Tony. Need Meeting room.* "There's a serviced office close to Brodie Vellum, we can book a room there."

"You'll need me as well," said Anthony.

"Yes of course." Tony added *Anthony.* "Now, people at the Maxadex meeting. He wrote *Maxadex Meeting, Tuppence & Anthony.*

"And me," added Wayne. "I need to set up cameras and make sure the bank transfer works. It's not straightforward." Tony added *Wayne* to the list.

"We'll need to set the Reading place up," said Wayne.

"OK." Tony wrote that on the chart.

"And me," said Anthony. "Security needs checking."

"Hold on a minute," interjected Harry, "this all looks rather complicated to me. Shouldn't we fix dates and times with Enrici before we go much further? I'd be surprised if he didn't want his say."

"You're right. I suppose there's no reason why I shouldn't call him now. I'll tell him 3.30pm Wednesday for our meeting and 11.30am Thursday at Maxadex. Everyone OK with that?" Agreement all round. "I'll call from my office."

While Tony was away Harry took to the board and they worked out who needed to be where on days and approximate times in relation to the briefing meeting. Wayne would go down to Reading two days in advance taking Anthony with him, "if you can squeeze into my car," he added

"I can get into a Bulldog, so I don't think your car will be a challenge."

"I beg your pardon? Bulldog?" Henry raised his eyebrows.

"Armoured Personnel Carrier."

"Thank goodness for that!"

Anthony would need to shuttle back and forth between Reading and London, so they looked at transport needs. Then Tuppence would need to get to Reading a day in advance for familiarisation and rehearsals. "I'll take advantage and go down to London a few days earlier and stay with Poppy," she said. "Gird my loins on her liquid hospitality."

Henry piped up, "I'll stay in London after the briefing and be ready for the pay-off when they get back from Reading. I guess Tony will do the same. We'll have to be able to transfer money to Enrici without you Wayne,"

"I'll set that up with Vijay and show you what to do," offered Wayne. "By the way, Diego will be in Reading at the same time as me," said Wayne with just the hint of a smile.

By then they were able to list all transport and accommodation required.

When Tony returned Henry said, "That took a while. Was he being awkward?"

"A bit, as you would expect. He wanted to know why it couldn't happen this week. I said Florence Grant was on holiday. You need to think about where you've been Tuppence just in case he asks. Then he said he had to scarper after golf on Wednesday so couldn't meet us 'till Thursday. I've fixed that for 2.30pm. I didn't want both things the same day, so I've fixed the Reading meeting for Friday. Hope that doesn't cause a problem with anyone." It didn't. He looked at the board, "I see you've been working. Looks as if we're getting somewhere. I'll get that into an email and get Sandy's PA to sort out all the bookings."

With that the meeting drew to a close. Tony said he would send off all the briefing material to Enrici. He had provided a PO Box in Brentwood for the purpose. "I wonder if that's because they've managed to evict him from Grace's house," said Wayne. "Hope so." Tuppence said she would organise a time for a rehearsal or two and asked for volunteers. There were plenty of offers. Anthony said he was seeing Margaret tomorrow to start making arrangements for the funeral. Willie jumped off Tuppence's lap and made his way to his door with the distinct impression that whatever had been wrong with the world had been ameliorated. Certainly the all-consuming gloom shrouding the start of proceedings had lifted as everyone said their farewells.

CHAPTER 20

Into Action

Tuppence spent the rest of the week working on Enrici's comeuppance and what she had begun to call her Lifestyle Plan. She was particularly pleased with progress on the latter, having lost a lot of weight, reduced her alcohol intake by half and become fit enough to walk ten thousand steps a day. On the Enrici side, she'd roped Henry and Harry into a rehearsal. It was more useful than their previous experience. The two men didn't have much choice, receiving a tongue lashing after their first effort and the threat of a clip round the ear if there was no improvement. On the following Monday, she packed props, costume and clothes and left for London. She was picked up at Liverpool Street Station by Poppy and for the next few enjoyable days, there was barely a quiet moment.

* * *

On Wednesday Wayne drove down to Reading with Anthony levered into the passenger seat. When they arrived at the agency unit close to Junction 11 of the M4 Anthony was pleased to get out of the car and persuade some blood to flow back into his legs. Diego arrived soon after, having taken a train from Paddington then a taxi from the station. He shook hands with Anthony and gave Wayne a hug.

They had a busy afternoon. Anthony assumed one of the gang, probably Pegg, would keep watch in case of emergencies so took a walk around the immediate area where he found plenty of roadside parking from which the building could be watched. There were vertical blinds at each window so he took the simple precaution of closing them all. A glass-walled office was in the corner of the floor above the storage area, the rest of which was open-plan. Desks, chairs, cupboards, filing cabinets, computer equipment and phones were stacked in a corner. They set about making it look more like a working office. Wayne managed to get most computers working with what looked like something relevant on the screens. Papers were placed on desks and in filing trays. They wrote what appeared to be a delivery schedule on a whiteboard. Diego half-filled waste bins with paper and other rubbish.

Anthony picked a desk for himself in full sight of the corner office so he could keep an eye on proceedings. He found a small kitchen and made up a shopping list of provisions. As he was finishing this, a man in overalls walked in. He turned out to be Joseph the caretaker and had been briefed by Sandy's team. Diego delivered him a smart new outfit including a jacket with Maxadex printed on the back. "That's yours to keep," he said to a delighted Joseph. He had been kept on part-time after the PoliAds takeover to keep the place secure and ticking over. "Let's decide how we want to set the store up," said Diego, and they all trooped downstairs.

The store was full of exhibition equipment and lots of cardboard boxes. They needed to make it look like an import export warehouse. Diego said, "The exhibition equipment is not a problem but we should make a feature of the boxes. We need labels."

"A printer is working upstairs so let's make a load and maybe you could stick them on Joseph," suggested Wayne.

"No problem, boss."

"How about making them in foreign languages," said Anthony.

"Good idea," said Wayne. "Chinese would be good."

The rest of the afternoon was spent by Anthony, Diego and Joseph rearranging the store to look as authentic as they could while Wayne produced a sheaf of labels chopped into various sizes with mainly Chinese script he had found online. He had no idea what it said, but then nor would the villains. Having done that, they called it a day.

In the morning Joseph would stick all the labels on. Diego would dress the main office with flowers, pictures and a photo of Florence with the local MP which had been beautifully fabricated by the agency. He would stick a name on the door 'Florence Grant – Director of Procurement'. The agency had already put up a Maxadex sign on the building. Wayne would set up all the filming and recording equipment and make sure the link to the bank worked. They were booked into a hotel by Caversham Bridge. At Anthony's suggestion Wayne drove Diego. He didn't want to be folded into that car again. Instead, Joseph gave Anthony a lift in his big old Peugeot. The number of times I've sped across the desert in one of these, he mused.

* * *

The next day Anthony caught a train to Paddington and met Henry and Tony at the agency's head office in Mayfair. Tony explained that the Enrici meeting would be in a serviced office a 10 minute walk away. Two adjacent rooms had been booked in the names of Sillingham Robins Ltd. and Ability-Icon, another of the agency's dormant companies. Anthony needed to arrive an hour before the meeting just in case it was being watched. Before he left he attached microphones to Henry and Tony as before.

Anthony, dressed in a smart grey suit, white shirt and regimental tie, carried a briefcase as he walked to the serviced office. Approaching, he could see no evidence of Enrici's gang. However, there was a coffee shop opposite. He stayed on that side of the road, crossing just as he reached it so that his back was to anybody watching. He walked swiftly to the door and through into reception. Only the receptionist was there. He signed in as Brad Bernstein from Ability-Icon and was directed to the booked room. The company names had been placed on doors.

From his briefcase he took out the recorder, then went next door to the room reserved for Sillingham Robins. He closed the vertical blind and placed a microphone behind it. Setting his phone to play BBC Radio 4, he went back next door to check the mic was working. It was. Collecting his phone, he left the light on so there would be no reason to open the blind. He then settled down to study the only other item in his briefcase, his newspaper. Tony and Henry arrived 15 minutes early for the meeting. They did a sound check then Tony went to reception to wait for the visitors. From near the reception desk he could see Pegg sitting at a window table in the coffee shop opposite. Enrici and Bradley emerged a few minutes later. Tony greeted them and they joined Henry in the meeting room.

"Everything's set up for tomorrow," said Tony to start proceedings. "You're meeting Florence Grant, the procurement director at 11.30, ostensibly to discuss setting up a tea import arrangement from Mali. I take it you've read the documents I sent. Any questions?" Bradley said he had read everything. "Quite clever. Looks to me like there may be a bit of money laundering going on too."

"Well spotted," said Henry, "There is. You can bring it up but only if they play hard to get. Have you checked their website?"

Enrici said it looked pretty professional. Bradley commented that all the directors look very old. "Feathering their nests before they retire I imagine."

"Maybe," said Henry, "but they're going to be three hundred thousand pounds less feathered once we've finished with them."

"Thought about how you will run the meeting?" asked Tony

Enrici said "That's his job. I'm observing."

Bradley said he'd engage in conversation about the business to start with. "Then I will explain we want to discuss the skimming off of money from HMRC. I'll give her a short explanation to prove we know all about it and hand her the single page document you provided as proof. There will be lots of objections but we can counter them with the background material you sent. I'll then tell her how much she owes us."

Tony explained they must get her to transfer the £300,000 there and then. He handed Bradley two sheets of paper. "Here are the bank account details for the transfer, and this is an invoice for Consultancy Services from Sillingham Robins Ltd. It will help them get it through their books. We need to meet back here between 2.00 and 2.30 so we can transfer your 50%."

"Play it as cool as you can," added Henry.

Enrici said, "We don't need you telling us what to do."

"I hope not. There's a lot of money for all of us hanging on you doing this right!"

Bradley added, "we will and I'll be very nice." He even managed a smile.

Tony said, "you've got the address and you should be able to park in front of the building. Text us when you're leaving so that we know you're on your way. There might be a few checks from banks but both organisations have clearance to transfer those sorts of sums. Any more questions?" There weren't and the meeting closed.

As they were leaving Bradley made a call and within a minute they were picked up by Pegg. Anthony emerged from the next room and collected the microphone from behind the blind. "That seemed to go well," he said.

"It did, didn't it," said Tony sporting a frown. "I don't trust them mind you. Anyway, I'll need to get going, I'm driving Tuppence to Reading so that she can do what she calls her technical rehearsal. I want a look at the place too." Henry and Anthony were staying in London and would join Tony in an evening meeting with Bob & Dick, who wanted an update and to start planning Part 2.

* * *

When the three of them got back to the office Tuppence was being entertained by Sandy and some staff who remembered her from her TV days. Tony whisked her off smartly though so they didn't get caught in traffic on the M4. On the journey Tuppence rehearsed answers to questions about Maxadex and how the scam worked from Tony. She passed with flying colours becoming Florence and speaking in a Yorkshire accent for the whole journey.

Wayne and Diego were waiting for them when they arrived. Tuppence wanted to check everything out – location, office geography, who would do what. They had a tour of the storage space and both thought it looked genuine. "The handyman, Joseph, will be here shifting things around," said Diego. Upstairs looked like an empty working office. Wayne pointed out where everyone would sit.

"Don't forget," Tony reminded them, "in an office people chat, get up, walk around. Make this as realistic as possible."

They went into Florence's office which was furnished with sofas and a coffee table. "Oh, very nice," she said still in character. Diego had placed photos of Florence's family on the desk. Pictures of foreign ports hung on the walls, along with the photo of Florence with the local MP and a framed certificate for 'Small Import Export Company of the Year 2016'.

"The internal wall blinds can be pulled to give you some privacy," said Diego.

Wayne stood by the window and twisted open the blinds while the other three sat down.

"You'll need to invent names for your relatives Tuppence," said Wayne.

"Florence from now on young man!" Wayne grinned. "Who's the chap I'm shaking hands with?"

"The local MP," answered Diego. "His name is Gerry Morgan, a Labour Party man."

"Enrici and Bradley will be here at 11.30," said Tony. "Pegg will probably be keeping watch outside somewhere." Tuppence nodded.

"The screen on your desk is where we'll do the transaction from. It's a bit tricky so maybe you should call me in to do it," suggested Wayne.

"Good idea."

Wayne asked Tony, "How do we recognise this man Pegg if he's hanging about?"

"He's about six foot something, solid, fairish hair, thug-like. I'm not good a describing people."

"What sort of car does he drive?"

"A black BMW I think. Why?"

"I've a feeling he's outside now."

Tony crept over to the window and took a sneaky look between the slats. "That's him." Pegg had parked outside the front of a building about thirty yards away. He was walking slowly towards them, glancing up at the window. "Christ, I hope he didn't see me coming in."

"He's only just pulled up. Just keep your head down." Tony did as he was told.

"Doesn't matter if he sees Wayne, Diego or I," said Tuppence. "Might even add a bit of authenticity. Pull the blind across can you."

Wayne did as he was told. Tuppence moved to the window looking up at the blind mechanism as if there was a problem. Diego joined her. "Pull it back and forth a bit." The blind swished. Out of the corner of her eye she could see Pegg looking up at them. "Close it now, I think he's had a good enough eye full."

Wayne left just enough of a gap to see Pegg cross the road and approach the unit. "Diego, you got the tracker?"

"On the desk."

"Grab it quick. If he goes round the back, you can get it on his car." Diego ran to his desk, grabbed a black object and sped down the stairs. Wayne watched as Pegg disappeared along a path at the side of the unit. He shouted, "go Diego, run!"

"What's going on?" asked Tony.

"Our friends in the Met gave us some vehicle trackers to stick under their cars if we ever got a chance." Wayne and Tuppence watched as Diego sprinted along the road towards the black BMW.

"He's fast," said Tuppence.

"Yep." Wayne chuckled. "Apparently he was Argentinian schools 100m champion!"

"Impressive!"

Reaching the car, Diego checked Pegg was out of sight then ducked down behind it.

"Everything locked at the back?" asked Tony.

"Yes. Blinds drawn too. Come on Diego, get a move on." Wayne began to look worried. "Oh shite, Pegg's back out the front again. He's walking towards his car." Moving faster than he had done in years, Wayne sped down the stairs and out into the road, "Hello, excuse me," he shouted at Pegg. Pegg slowed, looked around and then turned back to face Wayne. "I noticed you looking up at the office. Were you after something?"

"No," shouted Pegg back at him. Diego must have been watching. Bent over, he ran quickly in the opposite direction before straightening up and walking in through the entrance of the nearest building. Pegg put his phone to his ear and made his way back to the car.

"Well done Diego," said Tony in the office, "I don't think Pegg saw him. I guess he's reporting in. I wonder if he's staying in Reading. Maybe they all are."

Wayne returned, out of breath, "Let's have a look where he's going." He collected his laptop from one of the desks, clicked a few times and said "Don't know if this is working. Is he moving yet?"

Tuppence, looking from the window said, "he's just getting in the car. Hold on, yes he's moving now. Mad sod! It's a 30 limit!" she shouted at the speedily departing Pegg.

Wayne's screen showed a map with a red dot moving along the road that led out of the business park towards the A33. "Working!" he shouted. The dot moved right and when it reached the M4 went in an easterly direction towards

London. "Looks as if he's going home." Wayne took a deep breath. "That was close."

Diego reappeared. "Well done young man!" cried Tuppence. "We were worried about you for a moment."

"It was OK. I gave the receptionist of that company over there a bit of a fright though."

"Well," said Tony, "everything seems hunky dory here so I'd better head back to London." He got up to leave. "I'll drop you at the hotel Tup . . , whoops, Florence. I doubt you'll all squeeze into Wayne's little roadster." She thanked him and arranged to meet the others in the bar before dinner. "Good luck tomorrow!" called Tony as they left the building. He took Tuppence to her hotel, then made for the M4. Wayne and Diego closed up shop and headed back too. Tomorrow was going to be a big day.

CHAPTER 21

The Sting – Part 1

Tuppence arrived at Maxadex by taxi just after 9:30 am. Wayne and Diego were already there, having been to the supermarket on the way with Anthony's shopping list. While Diego was preparing coffee for everybody Tuppence became familiar with her office. The family photograph of an older couple and a girl in her 20's she would say were her parents and sister, and use their real names. She made up a few stories about the port pictures and characters in them. It wasn't long before Anthony arrived having been picked up by Joseph from the station.

The team set about checking everything was ready. The screens on the desks were all woken up and Wayne ensured they had what looked like real information on them. Anthony's was linked to the cameras in Florence's room which they tested to make sure everything worked properly. He gave Tuppence the same instructions used in the meeting at the golf club. They did a walkthrough of the villains' arrival and the beginnings of the meeting. Joseph had opened the warehouse door and was instructed that if the villains approached to tell them they can look but, for security reasons, not enter. He said he would stay in the warehouse and behave like a caretaker. The others agreed, not knowing quite how a caretaker behaved but trusting his judgement anyway.

Wayne took a quick look at the app on his laptop to find out where Pegg's car was. It looked to be approaching the eastern end of the M25. Still plenty of time. They agreed that when it came to the transfer of the £300,000 it would be perfectly reasonable for Wayne, who Tuppence would say worked in finance, to complete the transaction. He had set up a dummy one and they tried it out in situ to ensure a smooth run.

They thought they'd done everything when Tuppence piped up, "We've forgotten something! You are all using your real names. We said we wouldn't do that. I'm Florence Grant, so you'd better decide what you want to be known as." Diego was quick to settle on Carlos Sanchez, the name of his mother's father. Wayne decided on the first name that came into his head. He would be Jason Singer. Anthony became Charlie Griffith, an old cricketing hero of his from Barbados. "From this point on today we must only refer to one another using these names," said Tuppence sternly. "So I'm Florence, or even better, Ms Grant."

Jason kept an eye on Pegg's movements. He was part way round the M25 by 10.40 and at 11:15 Jason warned everyone he was turning off the M4. Carlos nipped down to tell Joseph. Charlie discretely peered between the blind slats in the main office and it wasn't long before he saw Pegg drive past, turn round and park in the same spot as yesterday. He stayed in the car. Charlie called to the others, "Pegg's on his own. The other two must be coming separately. Jason, have you got another tracker by any chance?"

"I certainly have. We could put it on the other car couldn't we. Job for Carlos." Five minutes later the Bentley pulled up and parked in front of the building. Out got Enrici and Bradley, the latter clutching a document case.

"Right, this is it boys, break a leg "said Florence. She was comforted by the adrenalin coursing round her body. She always gave a better performance if she was a bit on edge. Between the blind slats Charlie watched the two villains approach the store door and talk to Joseph. They peered around him into the warehouse. They then approached the main door of the unit, the bell rang and Carlos skipped down the stairs to let them in. He insisted they sign the visitor's book and noted they used their real names. He politely asked them to wait in the lobby while he found Ms Grant. Back in the office Florence said, "let them stew for a couple of minutes." Enrici was noticeably flustered when Carlos collected them but Florence was effusive in her welcome. She sat them on comfortable seats, got Carlos to organise refreshments and closed the internal blinds. Charlie moved over to his desk, put on his headphones and switched his screen to the video being recorded. The conversation in Florence's office was getting under way.

"This is a bit small for an import/export company isn't it?" commented Enrici.

"Not really, it's just our distribution centre serving the Thames Valley. A lot of our work is with Far East hi-tech companies although the material in this warehouse is relatively low value kit of various sorts. All the top end stuff is in a secure, bonded site at our HQ in Felixstowe. I work out of here mainly as I live locally. The Finance Director sometimes squats here too. He lives in Bristol." To shake off any concern about Tony's car being seen by Pegg she added, "in fact he was here yesterday".

Jason, keeping an eye on Pegg, saw he was leaning on the boot of his car facing the other direction talking on his phone. Speaking softly, he said to Carlos, "could you get that tracker onto Enrici's car now?" Carlos did as asked, managing to fix it beneath the Bentley. When he came back Jason was able to confirm it was working. "That's two of them we can keep tabs on now," he said triumphantly.

Tuppence continued her introduction to Maxadex. "There are eight people based here. Sales mainly plus two finance people. This is one of the most profitable units in the company so we are just left to get on with things." She smiled what she hoped was a devious smile. Bradley was glancing at the photos on the wall.

"Who is that you are shaking hands with?"

"Ah ha, that's Gerry, he's our local MP. He's Labour but still a good supporter of business. He's a good friend of ours. Well, mine actually," she winked at Bradley. "Best to keep your local politician in bed with you!"

"So tell me about your organisation. You're interested in tea imports I understand."

Bradley said, "we work for a Business Consultancy called Sillingham Robins. We help developing countries build trade links."

Enrici butted in, "I'm Manager for West Africa, Mr. Bradley here is our specialist in plant based exports. Tea, Coffee, Cocoa, Cotton and so on."

Florence thought to herself, they've done a bit of work on this. Not too much I hope. She said, "we are involved in a lot of that, mainly south east Asia though. Vietnam, Cambodia, Laos. Mostly rice." She had absolutely no idea whether these countries exported rice but in her mind it seemed reasonable.

Enrici interrupted, "Look, let's get on with the business in hand, we are busy people."

"Of course," said Florence, "I understand Mali currently distributes most of its tea through South Africa. What do you want to do? Why are you looking at us?"

Bradley said, "We are not just looking at you, we are choosing you. And it's got nothing to do with Mali, tea or any other fancy imports. We used that excuse to get through the door. We are here to discuss the little scheme you are operating to avoid paying tax to the revenue. We know that you have been taking well over £250,000 a year and sharing it with two other directors, a Mr Wallace the Chief Executive, and the Finance Director Mr Jablonski."

Florence, a shocked look on her face, declared "How dare you! That's a lie. Are you from the HMRC?" Her voice rose with the delivery of each statement. Charlie had seen and heard the whole conversation. Now the others were able to hear too. They glanced at one another with wry smiles on their faces.

"Here we go," said Jason.

"Now, I want you to leave immediately, before I call security." Florence stood up, pointing at the door. Enrici and Bradley stayed where they were. Bradley calmly pulled a single sheet of paper from his document case.

"Read this!"

"I'm not reading anything. I want you out of here!"

"If you don't read it I can assure you HMRC and Thames Valley Police will." He raised his voice slightly, "now sit down and read it, five minutes now is better than three years in gaol."

"What?" Florence snatched the document from Bradley's outstretched hand and reluctantly sat down to read it. "How did you get all this? Who have you been talking to?"

"Nobody," answered Bradley. "We have a very sophisticated system capable of uncovering schemes like this. We have a copy of your complete finances for the last seven years. We know how you move money and the bank accounts it's been paid into."

"No, this is all wrong. It's all been fabricated." Florence had become far less strident.

Enrici jumped in, "Stop pissing about. You know it's right and cheating the HMRC can mean a lot more than three years nowadays. It can go up to life! Mind you at your age, I don't suppose that would be too long. All that makeup doesn't hide anything."

Florence was taken back, genuinely. "Don't be so bloody rude." But she hesitated. "So what are you going to do? What do you want?"

Bradley continued, "luckily for you we are here to help. We won't tell anybody and you can have all the documentation back. As thanks for that, and our silence on the matter, you will need to transfer £300,000 of your stolen HMRC money to us. Today!"

"What! I can't come up with that much. Anyway it's all been spent." Florence appeared to be floundering. She paused and then burst into tears. Watching, Charlie saw a career's worth of experience come to the fore. "I only do this to pay for my dear father's nursing home fees. He needs specialist care. He'll be out on the streets."

Enrici barged in to stop her flow, "stop bullshitting you fat cow. Looking at how old you are I should think your old man's long dead. You've been up to these tricks for years now. You must have taken a million each. You can afford it."

"Oh this is terrible! How do I know you won't come back and demand more?"

Bradley took over again, "We guarantee silence. It's the way we do business. If we go back on our word, we get found out."

Florence had taken some tissues from her bag and dabbed her eyes. "I need a moment to think. I must talk to my fellow directors." Her assertiveness seemed to return. "Right, you stay here, I'll get Jason to sit in with you while I make phone calls. Do not say anything to him about this, understand?"

"Of course," said Bradley magnanimously, "discretion is my second name."

Florence got up, opened the door and called Jason. "Keep these gentlemen company will you for a few moments, I need to call Mr Wallace."

"Yes Ms Grant." Florence went out into the stairwell and closed the door.

"Would you like more coffee?" asked Jason. They declined. He perched on the edge of Florence's desk. Nobody spoke. Eventually Jason decided to break the silence. "Nice day," he said as pleasantly as he could manage.

"For some people," answered Enrici, who then laughed at his witty response.

Pointing at the photograph on the wall Bradley said, "Nice to see your MP is interested in the business," inviting a response.

Jason had to think quickly. "Yes. I believe he and Ms Grant are very close. I don't trust any of them myself. They're all in it for themselves. They don't know what it's like in business. They cheat and connive but we are completely honest. We don't cheat anybody." Enrici laughed heartily then everything fell silent again.

"How long is she going to be?" Enrici was getting impatient. "We're on a tight schedule."

"I'm sure she won't be long," said Jason, desperately hoping he was right.

Within seconds Florence returned, "thank you Jason, you can go now. Don't leave the building though, I will need you." She turned to the villains. "Alright, I have spoken to my colleagues. We are prepared to pay you something, but £300,000 is far too much."

"You can stop that stupidity straight away," said Enrici angrily. "It's 300K and if there is any more argument at all," he emphasised the at all, "the price goes up by £100,000. Immediately."

Bradley took over, "Ms Grant, we have looked at your cash flow and large amounts of money go in and out every day. You can sign off £300,000 pounds without blinking an eyelid. We will provide you an invoice for business consultancy from a legitimate organisation so you can make it disappear if you want to deal with it that way."

Florence decided it was time to stop playing the authenticity game and get the transaction completed as quickly as possible. "Business as usual might work," she said.

"Get on with it then, we haven't got all day," said Enrici, "We have bigger fish to fry."

"Give me the invoice please." Florence looked it over, "OK." She opened the office door and called, "Jason, come here a minute can you." He entered the office and closed the door. "We are going to do some business with these gentlemen. We need to pay a fee immediately however," a thoughtful look came over her face, "Mali legislation. Here's the invoice. Could you sort it for me please?"

"Who do you want the cheque made out to?" asked Jason wanting a bit of fun himself.

"No cheques. It needs to be a bank transfer," said Bradley.

"There are no bank details on the invoice."

"You get the screen up and I will enter all the details."

"That's very irregular."

"Don't worry Jason that's fine," said Florence. "We can do it in here"

"No problem." Jason sat at Florence's desk, tapped on her keyboard for a while, then said to Bradley, "you need to put your account name, number, sort code and reference in."

Bradley moved round next to Jason and entered the information requested. There was an immediate response from Maxidex's bank to say that the payee was legitimate. "Just check everything is right," said Jason. Bradley scanned the screen and confirmed all was correct. "Ms Grant would you like to just check?" asked Jason. She also scanned the screen and nodded. Jason hit the button and almost immediately a message shot onto the screen to say the transaction was complete. "All done," said Jason. He left the room and shut the door.

"Now that didn't hurt, did it?" said Enrici grinning from ear to ear.

Before Florence could react Bradley pulled a wad of papers from his document case and gave them to her. "These are the hard copies. Once I get back to the office I will ensure that all digital data is destroyed. You won't hear from us again."

Time to be a bit subservient thought Florence, "OK."

Enrici stood up, "if we get anyone nosing around, we will know who sent them. We will then be back to visit you and it will not be such a pleasant experience next time."

Florence opened the office door, "these gentlemen are leaving now Carlos, could you show them out please." Bradley shook Florence's hand as he left and said, "it's been a pleasure doing business with you." Enrici ignored her. On his way down the stairs Bradley made a phone call. Carlos heard him say, "all OK Joe, on our way now." When he got back up to the office, the other three were peeking through the blind. They saw Pegg's car move towards them and then Enrici's Bentley backing out of the parking space. Both cars then moved off together.

There were high fives all round. They watched Jason's screen until both trackers showed the cars to be on the M4 moving towards London. "Well done all, I think we pulled that off," said Florence who also said she now wanted to be known as Tuppence again.

"That was very impressive Tuppence," said Anthony, "You convinced me!"

"Years of experience young man. I'll give Tony a ring to say they're on their way."

"I'll make sure the money is in our account," said Wayne.

No more than 10 minutes later Joseph was giving Anthony and Tuppence a lift back to the station where they caught a train to Paddington, then made their way to the Brodie Vellum office. Wayne and Diego tidied up, leaving a bottle of Irish Whiskey and a thank-you card for Joseph on Florence's desk. Not long after, they left in Wayne's car for a restful weekend in London.

* * *

While everything was unfolding in Reading, Henry and Tony were telling Sandy and Vijay about their meeting with the Met last night. The proposal for Part 2 involved the Robins setting everything up with Enrici, and the Met providing the actors and security. Sandy and Vijay would support in the background and Wayne would be involved on the IT side. The plan was to arrest them immediately the money was transferred to the Sillingham Robins account. They wanted this to happen as soon as possible, hopefully within in a fortnight. Henry explained though that Ken's funeral date was sacrosanct. As they prepared to go for a bite of lunch, Tony received Tuppence's phone call. "Bingo!" he yelled. "It's all gone well apparently. We just need to transfer £150,000 to Enrici and then get him to agree to the next phase."

After a quick lunch Henry and Tony made their way to the serviced office for the pay-off meeting. Having been given instructions by Anthony, Henry set up the sound recording. They didn't have long to wait, the villains were on time. Maybe the thought of £150,000 going into his account had been an incentive to Enrici. Tony said to the villains, "how did it go? Give us a debrief."

Enrici described the operations director in unflattering terms and told them she was a witch and put up a fight. Henry looked forward to relating that to Tuppence. "It would appear she is bonking the local MP and said he would make sure the police and HMRC wouldn't become involved. I could see that was a bluff though and put her straight. Our professionalism means the job was successful. So it's worth more than 50%."

"We have our deal," said Henry dismissively. "You'll be pleased to know that the money is in our account. Give us your account details and we'll get £150,000 transferred now.

"You get it on the screen, and Mr Bradley will put in the details."

"As you wish." Henry had already got the appropriate page up on the laptop Wayne had provided for the purpose. He turned it round to face Bradley who typed in the necessary information. "That looks fine," said Henry. "I would bet that's the quickest 150 grand you've ever earned."

"Right," said Tony, "having seen how it works successfully, we need to arrange the next deal. That should be within the next two or three weeks. As you know, it's a much bigger earner."

"I'll think about it," said Enrici. He didn't notice Bradley looking askance at him.

"You've had plenty of time to think. And you can see the power of our process."

"Well maybe I don't like being rushed."

"I'm afraid if you don't commit now, it's likely to cause a significant delay."

"Why should I worry about a delay? We've got plenty of other business."

Henry took over the conversation, "Mr Enrici, we've invested a lot into this deal, and we want our return. Miss this window of opportunity, it could be gone completely."

Just at that moment Tony's phone rang. He looked at the screen, "sorry, you'll have to excuse me." He got up and left the room.

Henry continued, "If we lose this chance, that will be the end of our arrangement."

"Why? The job we did today, you couldn't do in a million years."

"That's as may be. But we want to work with an organisation we can trust, not somebody who plays silly buggers. You either agree to proceed now or we call it a day and find somebody else."

Tony put his head round the door and beckoned Henry, "can you join me for a second." They walked to the end of the corridor. Tony spoke softly, "that was Sandy. Dick Sargent has said Thursday or Friday in two weeks' time would be ideal. They can line the right people up then. We need to get Enrici to agree to that."

"I've just given him an ultimatum. He didn't look happy. Hope I haven't turned him off completely."

"Well, we said we had to keep control. Let's go back and see what happens."

Back in the room, Tony said, "that was a call from our undercover placement in the target organisation. Our operation has to take place in two weeks' time on Thursday or Friday." They kept silent, staring straight at Enrici.

"OK, have it your way. We're in."

"I'm glad you said that, I'll authorise your payment now." Henry opened up his laptop and pretended to click on the bank payment button he'd actually pressed a few moments ago.

"What?" said a horrified Enrici.

"We told you this was just a trial. You weren't getting paid if you didn't agree to do the full job. Now don't try pissing us about again. We'll call you in a couple of days with all the details. Now good day to you!"

It was obvious that was the end of the conversation. Enrici and Bradley got up from the table to leave. "You'll regret that!" sneered Enrici as he left the room. The two sat quietly for a few seconds before Tony checked they'd left the building and Henry collected all the recording equipment.

"Let's get back to the office," he said, "the others should be there by now."

He was right. Tuppence and Anthony were having coffee and biscuits with Sandy and Vijay. They were in a jovial mood. "I would have broken open a bottle of champagne," said Sandy, "but I know you've got to drive back home."

"I think we can have more than one bottle when we get that lot behind bars," said Tony.

"Enrici wasn't happy about the timing, but he agreed in the end. Anyway, I think we need to love you and leave you. We have a long way to go."

They decamped into Tony's limousine and Henry gave Anthony the recording equipment. It was slow going getting out of the city but eventually they were onto the M11 heading north. Anthony, through his headphones, was listening to the proceedings recorded earlier. "Would you like to hear what they talked about when you left the room?" he asked.

"That would be interesting," said Henry.

Anthony unplugged the headphones and pressed the play button.

At first there was silence, then Enrici was heard saying, "They've got a nasty surprise coming their way. What they don't realise is, I'm in charge. Those amateurs are not pushing me around."

"What are you going to do boss?"

"You'll see." Then before anything else could be said, there was the sound of a door opening.

"What do you think that's all about?" asked Anthony.

"No idea," answered Henry. "I knew he wasn't happy."

"We'll have to be ultra-careful next time," said Tuppence. "You'd better let our policemen friends hear that."

Their journey continued in comfort. They had a short break at Barton Mills and it was dark before Anthony was dropped off at his house in Cromer and Henry at his in Sheringham. "I don't know about you," said Tuppence as they approached Sillingham House, "but I'm knackered. I'm having an early night." It had been an eventful and mentally exhausting couple of days. They agreed to talk over the weekend.

CHAPTER 22

Ken's Farewell

While all the excitement was taking place in and around London, Margaret was coming to terms with Ken's death. John had taken leave of absence and between the two of them they tackled the multitude of legal and financial hurdles needing to be jumped when someone dies. It was made easier by what Ken had referred to as their morbidity planning. Ten years ago they'd consolidated investments, simplified bank accounts and filed everything logically. Moving to a flat on just one floor was also part of the plan. So was looking at how they would be dispatched, as Ken so delicately put it.

Margaret and John also planned the funeral. The morbidity plan stated it would be a burial not a cremation. Non-religious, although Ken had said the odd rousing hymn wouldn't go amiss. They would like it in one of those 'new-fangled natural burial sites', preferably near the sea. It would be limited to friends and close family and a celebration of a life well lived, delivered with the minimum of misery. There must be plenty of good music. Then a good booze-up afterwards. With Anthony's help they had found a Natural Cemetery near Norwich which, other than overlooking the sea, ticked all the boxes. He also introduced them to a Funeral Celebrant who would manage and conduct the ceremony. Between them they fixed the date. It would be on the Tuesday before the final showdown with Enrici.

Margaret made the invitation list. It consisted of the few friends who stayed in touch after Ken's illness became obvious, all the Sillingham Robins plus Poppy and Trevor, and what amounted to quite a small family contingent. John took on the task of organising the wake, enlisting Henry's help. The restaurant in Cromer couldn't cope because it was full of bookings. All the pubs would be full of holiday-making families so didn't seem appropriate. In the end they decided it should be at the apartment where it could spill out into the garden if needs be. Elsie arranged that the restaurant would supply a buffet with a couple of part time staff to serve and clear up.

* * *

On the Tuesday morning most of the group met on the bench for a catch up. Only Harry and Anthony were missing. Henry said, "Let me update you on the funeral. It's all sorted for a week today at a place near Norwich. I'll WhatsApp the details this afternoon. It starts at 1.00pm, so get there earlier. No flowers, just charitable donations. Trevor is helping with the music by the way Tuppence. Margaret doesn't want it too morbid, so wear some colour other than black. Afterwards it's back here at her apartment for a buffet and drinks. It's a burial not a cremation so some of it will be outside. Bear that in mind if the weather is iffy."

"So what do we think about these scoundrels then," asked Tuppence. "I think Bradley is in possession of a brain. Within the context of being a criminal he was polite and relatively easy to deal with. Enrici was just an unprincipled, thoroughly unpleasant, bully. And he was extremely rude about me! I'd like to think one day he'll pay for that." Nobody disagreed and Tony added "Enrici is totally untrustworthy. We'll have to be extra vigilant."

Wayne then said that he'd had a call from Sandy to say that the Met's preferred day was Thursday next week. Tony said he'd call Enrici now and tell him. He moved away from the group and used his burner phone to make the call. It only took a few minutes.

"That's sorted," he said. "Both Enrici and Bradley will be there. No doubt Pegg will be hanging around outside. The only people on duty will be Wayne on site and Henry and I doing the pre-brief in the same way as before. There will be no pay-off meeting because once the transfer of cash has taken place, the police will nab them."

"They will also shadow Pegg," added Wayne. "They'll know where he is because of the tracker on his car."

"What about the plan for this part?" asked Henry. "We don't seem to have done much."

"This one is much easier grandad," said Wayne in explanation. "They'll be ripping off a real company so no need for fabricated accounts, websites, setting up premises and so on. The meeting will be at Brodie Vellum's city office in Canary Wharf. Sandy and Vijay have worked out how money could be siphoned off and are already talking with people from the Met on making it look authentic. The Met have officers who will act as the agency bad guys. We've produced drafts of the documents to go to the villains. They will be ready later this week."

"There is one little problem however," said Wayne. "We've got rid of your mug shot from the whole of the Brodie Vellum website Tony, but you do appear throughout the Internet associated with the company. Once we tell them who the target is I wouldn't be surprised if they search and discover your face."

"Do we have to tell them the name of the company?" asked Henry.

Tony considered for a moment. "Maybe not until the final briefing. We could say because the company is so high profile it's very sensitive."

"I suppose if the worst came to the worst, we could say you had been sacked as chairman and had gone rogue in retaliation."

"True. Anyway we can't change anything now so keep fingers crossed."

Tuppence then said she'd heard from Bernadette. "Apparently Enrici went to visit Grace last Friday late afternoon. That would have been after we'd paid him. He gave her an envelope which contained some papers he said she needed to read. He also told her he had some good news about his fortunes and said he would see her again soon to talk about plans. Bernadette is not allowed to look at private correspondence and Grace has not been willing to talk about it either. She's been a bit down since though."

"Do you think Bernadette could be persuaded to take a sneaky look?" said Wayne

"Doubt it. However there is some good news. Grace is definitely going to live with her daughter. She's just gone away for another fortnight but will be moving Grace in when she gets back."

"There is something else actually. It would appear I have a bit of a fan club at Burns Croft and Grace is one of them."

Henry laughed, "Well it is a home for the elderly and disillusioned after all."

"Cheek! Admittedly my fans are dropping off their perches in increasing numbers, but there are still some out there. Anyway, I have been asked to visit and provide a bit of entertainment. We've agreed Thursday week, because

Grace will be moving out a few days afterwards. Of course that's the same day as Part 2."

"Oh dear, I'll be tied up, otherwise I would be there to watch," quipped Henry to a withering stare from Tuppence

* * *

The days preceding Ken's funeral heralded a hive of activity in Sheringham. Mild panic set in for Tuppence when she tried to work out how to get to the care home. She could drive there in her little Smart Car. No chance! Luckily she was rescued by Anthony who said Alesha had been badgering him to take her to visit an old aunt in Theydon Bois and he could drop her off before taking Tuppence to Burns Croft. Perfect. Then Poppy and Trevor arrived on Saturday to stay with her. On several occasions Trevor absented himself from the continuous chatter to rehearse funeral music with John.

While they were in Reading Wayne, Diego and Anthony had talked about Ken's funeral. Anthony had told them that the practice of using a pallbearer to operate the sound system could easily go wrong. He recalled a time when the curtain closed round the coffin at a crematorium and the deceased was sent on his way by AC/DC with *Stairway to Hell*.

"Diego could do that," said Wayne. "My mum's been pestering me to invite him up for a weekend."

"I'm sure Margaret would appreciate that," said Anthony.

So another weekend visitor was Diego. On the Sunday Wayne hosted a BBQ for his mum and dad, granny and granddad. It turned out well. The ladies were charmed, Henry couldn't believe how an Argentinian could understand his humour and his father shrugged his shoulders and just got on with it.

* * *

The day of the funeral was sunny and warm with not a breath of wind. The hearse carrying Ken in a wicker coffin adorned with a casket display of white lilies and roses arrived at Sillingham House at 11:30 a.m. Five minutes later the cortege departed. Residents of Sillingham House, both those attending the funeral and others on their balconies, watched in silence as they left. Anthony, dressed in black morning suit with grey pinstripe trousers, white shirt and his regimental tie, shiny top-hat and silver walking cane, slowly led the way on foot until the road turned away from the sea. Their journey took the coast road to Cromer pausing at one of Ken's favourite vistas, the view from cliffs at the west of the town towards the pier. It then turned inland for a sedate drive to the cemetery.

A few minutes after the cortège departed Tony left by a more direct route with Harry and Sofia as passengers, followed by Trevor driving Poppy and Tuppence. Wayne and Diego got to the cemetery early. Diego prepared the sound system for music to be played as people arrived. Wayne linked his laptop into the projection system to be used for a slide show of photographs from Ken's past. They got text warnings from Anthony so music and slide timings could be orchestrated. The family arrived to *The Way You Look Tonight*, the tune Ken played to Margaret the night before he died, while a photograph of them on their wedding day was projected onto the screen.

As the song faded away, Trevor at his keyboard took a deep breath, nodded to John, then gently began the repetitive arpeggios of *Spiegel im Spiegel*, one of Ken's favourites. After a few bars John joined in with the meditative rise and fall of long steady notes on the violin. A couple of minutes later the Celebrant, who had been sitting opposite the musicians facing the congregation, got to her feet. Everyone followed suit and turned towards the rear of the hall. A few moments later Anthony, hat now held in his crook'd arm, entered walking very slowly followed by Ken's coffin on the shoulders of four pallbearers.

The coffin was carefully lowered onto the waiting catafalque. Anthony at its head and two pallbearers on each side bowed slightly, then maintaining their slow pace, they walked to the back of the hall. The Celebrant moved to the lectern as the music came to its gentle conclusion. She welcomed everybody and gave a short introduction to Ken mentioning his love of music and of the sea, his success in technology including the proud day at the Palace, and his passage into dementia which eventually cost him his life.

She then introduced John who spoke about being brought up in a loving household, about holidays in Norfolk with the Bennett family, and how his father encouraged him to engage in sport and art and music. He concluded by saying his dad had given him a mantra for life, which was to not compromise his happiness through an excessive desire for money. That's why he said, to a laugh from the congregation, he was simply a poor paramedic who played the violin.

The Celebrant then announced that while Ken was not particularly religious, he adored stirring church music. So could everyone join in a hymn led by what she referred to as Ken's Impromptu Choir. It was a surprise to everyone present when Tuppence, Poppy, Alesha, Sofia, Henry and Wayne left their seats to stand by Trevor at his keyboard. He immediately, and loudly, played the introductory bars to *How Great Thou Art*. The choir pitched in and the whole congregation, hesitantly at first, joined them. They finished with a rousing chorus, Tuppence and Poppy contributing an impressive descant.

Once the choir had returned to their seats and everyone else had sat down, Margaret walked to the lectern. "I just want to say a few words. I've written them down so I get them right. Ken didn't want a depressing, miserable funeral. That's why we're not dressed in black and why we've just had that lovely, uplifting hymn." She looked up, "I didn't know we were going to have a choir. Isn't it lovely what friends do for you." She looked back at her notes. "I just want to tell you a tiny bit about our life together. Our life before dementia took over. We met at a school cricket match and while I can't say it was exactly love at first sight, it was certainly love within the first half hour. I had another year at school and Ken went off to work in London, which made it difficult, and then impossible. We separated. But we remained friends and met occasionally when he came back to Norfolk. Every time we parted I knew we'd made a mistake."

"Then one Saturday I was walking along Bridge Street in Thetford and I heard someone shouting my name. It came from a car in the usual holiday traffic jam we had in those days. It was Ken. He shouted wait there! The traffic moved off, he turned left at The Bell and within a few minutes was running back along the road. He said as he came through Thetford he was thinking about our times together and how he missed them. Then miraculously, there I was. It was meant to be. We walked and talked and decided we really wanted to be together. Permanently. It was like starting all over again. Love at second sight. For years afterwards I had recuring nightmares that I didn't go to Bridge Street, or there wasn't a traffic jam, or he didn't see me. I'd wake up in a sweat. When the panic subsided, there were always butterflies flapping around in my chest. Everything was all right."

"We had a lovely life together. Then when John came along I had a mini-Ken to look after. He's not quite so mini now, but he's the spitting image of Ken at that age. Life was always fun. Like everyone else we had trouble paying the bills at times, but we got through it. Holidays were up here or as we got more adventurous, camping in France. As you know he became very successful in the IT world. I've decided to have his OBE framed and it will hang in a prominent place on the wall."

"I can remember much of the time the house was full of music. Ken played the guitar and was a brilliant violinist. I believe he could have made a professional career out of it. As you have heard today John is a chip off the old block. Ken did play semi-professionally in a string quartet. Also he and some friends formed a jazz combo and even made a few records. A few years ago he was diagnosed with that awful disease. Just about the only capability he didn't lose was playing the violin. I think it was a celebration of him having a small victory over that curse, that every night before bed he played it for me. I miss that."

"Ken was kind and caring. Always. He never forgot a birthday or anniversary. In fact it was our forty eighth wedding anniversary last month. I bought a card for him to give me and he managed to write a squiggly X on it. It's now in a box with the other forty seven. A month or so ago I was asked by a fellow dementia carer what the best part of my day was. I said it was exactly as it had been for the last forty eight years. It was when I woke up in the morning and turned my head to see the most wonderful man in the world laying there beside me." There was a pause. "I've now lost the best part of my day."

Margaret stood motionless, gripping the sides of the lectern. She had managed well but now a tear and then another spread over her notes. John walked over to her, took her arm and gently led her to her seat. The Celebrant quickly took over. "Margaret spoke about Ken's jazz combo. Let's listen to a piece he recorded in 1998." Diego pressed the button and the sound of the old standard *All of Me* filled the hall. As it finished, the Celebrant asked Henry to say a few words about his friend.

Margaret had asked him to keep it light, not soppy or sentimental. So he told stories about growing up in Cromer. He told about the times they hid in the bushes at Cromer Golf Course and crept out to steal balls, or replace them with different ones, or drop them all in the hole. They didn't get caught because they could run faster than the golfers. Then he spoke about how they gave up smoking when they were nine. They'd stolen a packet of ten Woodbines from a shop then perched up on the cliffs and smoked one after the other. They'd felt so ill they never touched another cigarette. He also told them about Ken's first ever car. He paid £60 for a big old black Wolseley 6/90. It had a three-speed column gear-change and a leather bench seat in the front, which he kept polished. Henry said Ken used to take left turns very quickly which meant the girl of the moment used to slide over to join him on his side. No seat belts in those days.

Henry had done his job. Talk about Ken but keep people amused. "Anyway, I hope that gives you a feel of how Ken was. Those of you who only knew him during his illness didn't see the funny, eccentric individual who could be serious when he needed to be but most of the time took life with a pinch of salt. He was my friend and life is poorer without him." Henry looked over to the coffin. "Goodbye old mate." And with that he walked back to his seat next to Elsie.

The Celebrant took over explaining that Ken would be carried into the garden to be buried and that everyone should follow behind. They would be handed sprigs of rosemary as they left the hall. She said that in ancient times this was cast into the grave to help the deceased on their way. It is also for remembrance, so if people wished they could keep it to remind them of Ken. With that, Anthony moved towards the catafalque followed by the pallbearers. As they lifted Ken onto their shoulders, the sound of another of Ken's favourite pieces began to echo around the hall. Trevor played Satie's *Gnossienne No 1* as Anthony slowly began the walk to Ken's final resting place.

Once everyone had assembled around the grave, the Celebrant said a few words. Then Tuppence, standing beside Anthony, spoke as the pallbearers lowered Ken's coffin into the grave.

Sunset and evening star,
And one clear call for me!
And may there be no moaning of the bar,
When I put out to sea,
But such a tide as moving seems asleep,
Too full for sound and foam,
When that which drew from out the boundless deep
Turns again home.
Twilight and evening bell,
And after that the dark!
And may there be no sadness of farewell,
When I embark;
For tho' from out our bourne of Time and Place
The flood may bear me far,
I hope to see my Pilot face to face
When I have cross'd the bar

CHAPTER 23

The Sting – Part 2

Super Thursday, as Wayne had begun to call it, arrived with everyone apprehensive but excited. This was it, all being well by tonight the blackmailers would be in custody. The active protagonists, Tony, Harry and Wayne, had all journeyed to London the previous day. Tony had arranged for the set-up meeting to be at another serviced office, this time close to Brodie Vellum's City Office at Canary Wharf. He and Henry arrived early, installed the recording system, and waited.

They were surprised when Enrici and Bradley arrived on time, and even more so when they saw what they were wearing. Enrici had on a yellow golf shirt under a light blue summer jacket with khaki slacks and tan loafers. His grey hair seemed much shorter than before and plastered back. Bradley sported jeans and trainers with a black T-shirt and prominent gold necklace. His previously receding hairline had receded completely. He was now as bald as a coot.

"I trust you received all the information we sent you?" said Tony in welcome.

"We did," said Enrici gruffly. "The company you gave us all the information about doesn't exist. What are you playing at?"

"If you'd read the whole document you would have seen. It was clearly explained," interjected Henry. "This is a FTSE 100 corporation. We couldn't risk the information we gathered accidentally falling into the wrong hands. We'll tell you who they are now."

Before Enrici could bellyache further Tony continued, "the company concerned, Brodie Vellum, is one of the largest advertising agencies in the country. Their city office is the other side of the shopping mall from here."

Henry handed Bradley a Brodie Vellum brochure with a business card of one of the supposed directors attached. "The address is on the card. You check in on the ground floor and the security guy will send you up to reception on the 7th. That director, one of the fraudsters, is expecting you."

"So are you comfortable with what you have to do?" asked Tony.

Bradley responded, "It looks pretty straightforward. We are talking about a lot more money though. Do you think this lot will kick up more of a fuss than the last one?"

"Quite the reverse," said Tony. "These are senior people, very respected in their field. They have a hell of a lot to lose. They will recognise very quickly you've got them by the short and curlies and will want everything tidied up and you out of there as quickly as possible."

"OK, Michael?"

"Yes boss, I think everything's good."

"Then let's get going. I'm looking forward to making a lot of money today."

"Excellent!" said Tony, "we'll see you back here after your meeting and transfer your share of the cash as before. The appointment isn't for nearly an hour. What are your plans in the meantime?"

"None of your business," said Enrici. "Just make sure you're here when we get back."

"You don't seem to be dressed for a business meeting," pointed out Henry.

"That's because we're professional and you're useless," smirked Enrici. "We're lefty do-gooders working for a charity so playing the part." He got up, "Michael, let's go. We've got work to do." And he swept out of the office with Bradley close on his heels.

"So that's what lefty do-gooders look like," observed Henry, "I've often wondered."

* * *

While that meeting was going on, Tuppence was being driven to the care home by Anthony. Bernadette had invited them for lunch and then Tuppence could spend an hour or so with the residents. During the journey Tuppence engaged in one of her favourite hobbies, interrogating people. Alesha was in the spotlight today. "So tell me Alesha, where were you born? There's a bit of a West London twang there I think."

"Well spotted, Notting Hill. Bevington Road actually. We lived in the bottom flat of one of those old Victorian blocks. I was very young when it was demolished and we were rehoused in Trellick Tower. It was pretty dire at first but by the time I was in my teens, things had really improved. My old mum still lives there. It's a grade two listed building now."

"Do you still have a dad?" Tuppence wasn't at her most diplomatic.

Alesha chuckled, "no idea. Shall I tell you all about it?" That was exactly what Tuppence was after. So she explained that her grandparents came to England from Trinidad after the Second World War. They were part of the Windrush Generation although didn't come on the ship itself. She told Tuppence how tough it was with lots of discrimination. They were often shouted at in the street and told to go back where they came from. They scraped a living. Her grandfather was an accountant but the only jobs he could get were manual and low paid. Alesha went on to tell stories about the difficulty of getting accommodation. Signs in windows usually said 'Room To Let, No Blacks or Irish'. Initially, they lived in one room, with a bathroom shared by four families, two from the West Indies and one Scottish. Their saviours were the Scottish family. The man worked at the docks in Tilbury and got her grandad a steadier job there.

Her mother, Marjorie, was born five years after they arrived in England. After a while they were able to move from their one room to the flat in Bevington Road, which made bringing up a baby much easier. Marjorie trained as a nurse and according to Alesha had a wild social life. It was the Swinging Sixties after all, her mum used to say. She went through a whole collection of boyfriends apparently. Some of them were white, which caused a bit of a stir at the time. She was very careful and ensured the right precautions were taken. Until, that is, she went to a party thrown by some junior doctors.

It was quite a party it would appear. Many of the men there were ex-private school. A lot of alcohol and some strange substances were consumed. Marjorie spent most of the evening with a very nice doctor. She was still with him in the morning along with a total memory lapse. The now not-so-nice doctor disappeared like a flash. The only things she remembered were his first name, Hugo, and his auburn hair. It wasn't long before Marjorie discovered she was pregnant. It could only have been this Hugo chap. She made enquiries as to who he was. Nobody seemed to know apart from a fellow nurse who thought he was a gate-crasher believed to be the son of a Lord somebody or another.

"So you've never tried to trace your father?"

"No, maybe one day. All I know is he's posh, with maybe some blue blood in him and he had auburn hair. That's no doubt where mine came from."

"Well that is a story," said Tuppence.

"So I was brought up in Notting Hill. I loved it. I used to get little jobs working on the stalls in Golborne Road market. Lots of interesting characters. Real wide boys some of them but hearts of gold. Then I also became a nurse. The first in the family to go to university! I liked nursing but I wanted a bit more adventure than I got at St Mary's Hospital. So I joined the Army and after a while specialised in mental health. A lot of it about in the forces, PTSD and all that. And then, I met this chap," she said pointing at Anthony. "That was it. We left the Army together and haven't looked back since."

They chatted away merrily until Anthony dropped Alesha at her aunt's house. Then in next to no time they arrived at the care home. They were greeted by Bernadette and were joined in her office by Dorota and the home's senior nurse, Makena. The chef brought in a very impressive looking spread for lunch. "No different to what the residents have," explained Bernadette. After an early breakfast and long drive, the travellers were in need of sustenance and tucked in.

Over lunch Bernadette updated them on the situation with Grace. Two days ago she had told Dorota about the mysterious envelope left by Enrici. Dorota persuaded her to let Bernadette look at it. It included a document looking like the report of an official investigation which mentioned bank accounts held and share dealings undertaken by Grace's late husband. It concluded he had been involved in insider trading and transferred profits illegally to offshore bank accounts. "There was a separate note from Enrici," said Bernadette. "In it, he told her that if the police found out, it would result in all Grace's savings and investments being sequestrated leaving her with nothing and her husband's name would be dragged through the mud. He said that if she made over the portfolio of shares in Sub-Arctic Oil and Gas to him, he would destroy the report and not give it to the police."

"Up to his usual tricks then," said Anthony.

"I showed it to our lawyer. He said the document contained no actual evidence of wrongdoing. The note from Enrici on the other hand was clear evidence of criminal activity. His conclusion was that Enrici was just trying to frighten Grace and was stupid to have written the threat down."

Dorota chipped in, "I've told Grace and she's cheered up a lot. She's really looking forward to moving in with her daughter next week and hopes Enrici won't turn up beforehand."

"Well let's just hope he doesn't," said Tuppence.

* * *

The stage was set at Brodie Vellum's Canary Wharf Office. Tyrell Gilpin, a detective sergeant, and detective constable Liam Andrews were playing the roles of the errant junior directors. Each of them was experienced working undercover. Detective constable Rhys Evans was inconspicuously lurking outside the 8th floor conference room where the meeting would take place. Other plain-clothed officers were stationed at strategic points around the building. In cars, but hopefully away from the expected prying eyes of Pegg, were plenty of uniformed officers. A call had been made to look out for all three villains, describing the clothes Enrici and Bradley were wearing.

The conference room was normally used for executive meetings so was luxuriously furnished and equipped with the latest audio and video technology making it very easy to bug. Listening in and watching from a meeting room on the 10th floor were five others. Dick Sargent had taken charge of the whole operation. He wanted to be in at the kill. Detective sergeant Ruth Gibson was in charge of communications and Wayne would be monitoring IT activity. Sandy and Vijay were there in case agency involvement was needed.

Dead on time Enrici and Bradley arrived at Brodie Vellum's office, each now carrying a large briefcase. They were directed to reception and asked to wait. After a few minutes, Liam collected them and they sat in comfortable chairs around the meeting table. Once everyone had introduced themselves, Tyrell kicked things off. "Gentlemen, I understand you are involved in advising companies how to effectively run charitable programmes and you want to know how we run ours. Is that the case?"

"It is," said Bradley. "We are partially grant aided from government to help companies decide the right way to set up this sort of scheme. Staff involvement, the sort of numbers involved, governance, I'm sure you can understand what I'm talking about."

"Of course," said Tyrell. "We've been doing this for many years. My colleague Liam here and I manage it on behalf of the agency. I'll give you a quick rundown shall I?"

"Please do."

"Quite simply, we add a very small percentage on to the price of each contract and that income, when it arrives, is channelled into a separate ring-fenced account. Customers have the option of declining the charge, but most don't."

Liam took up the story, "staff get involved by recommending good causes. We do our best to make sure that these are the ones that get the go ahead. Typically in a year we accumulate about three million pounds to distribute."

"That's very interesting," said Bradley, "you will appreciate we did some investigation before we came to see you."

"I'm sure you did," said Tyrell. Looks like they want to get down to business, he thought.

Bradley opened the pocket on the side of his briefcase and took out a small sheaf of papers. "We've looked at the recipients of your funding over the last three years. Quite a lot of it has gone to organisations that either don't exist anymore or are shell companies that receive multiple grants. These ones seem to have directors who are closely related to you. Maybe you'd like to have a look." He handed Liam a single sheet.

The script said at this stage Liam and Tyrell had to object, but not too much. "This is ridiculous. Where did you get this information from?"

"We have some very advanced technology and very clever cyber investigators."

"Hackers you mean," said Tyrell.

"If that's what you want to call them," sniggered Enrici.

"I can assure you there is a lot more where that came from." Bradley handed Liam some more papers. "Particularly how much of this charitable money has then been paid into accounts belonging to you two gentlemen."

At that moment Enrici's phone rang. He looked at the screen, "I need to take this." He got up and left the room. There were slightly nervous glances between Liam and

Tyrell but they knew Rhys was observing outside. The two police officers scanned the documents with increasingly concerned looks on their faces. They had of course seen it all before.

"Christ!" Said Liam.

"Bad bad." Added Tyrell. "So what are you after?"

Enrici returned and looked at Bradley, "Joe's finished." He turned towards the other two, "one of my men has just completed another job." Then back to Bradley, "have you told them what they need to do?"

"I was about to do so." He turned his attention back to Liam and Tyrell. "Now, we are aware that each of you takes about £500,000 a year for yourselves. So what you need to do is to pay us two years' worth of your fraudulent income."

"What?"

"Don't even think of arguing. I have a complete portfolio in my briefcase here of all your dirty deeds. If we leave here without the money it will go both to your Board and the Metropolitan Police. I don't need to tell you what the impact of that would be." Liam and Tyrell did their dramatic best to look a combination of angry and frightened.

"We know you take all the grant decisions so we'll make it easy for you. You are going to invest £2m into Sillingham Robins. This is for seed-corning a whole series of charities which is a good cause in itself so won't come under scrutiny." He handed Tyrell another small document. "Here is the proposal and agreement. You just have to sign and transfer the cash. And before you tell us you can't do it now, we know you can."

After a pause, Tyrell said, "I don't suppose we have a choice do we?"

"You don't," spouted Enrici in a return to his normal character, "now just get on with it." He turned to Bradley,

"I'm feeling really ill now. Those bloody mussels I had. I'm going to have to go and get rid of it. You carry on. I won't be long." He picked up his briefcase and made for the door. "The Gents is in the lift lobby I noticed," he said to Tyrell.

"Yes that's right. There's one on every floor."

Where all had been quiet and calm on the 10th floor, this turn of events caused a bit of a kerfuffle. Ruth quickly relayed a message to Rhys to follow him and for everyone else to be aware. Rhys had already seen Enrici leave and was on his way when the call came through. He was able to clock him entering the toilet in the lift lobby, where he waited a second or two before following him in. There was only one cubicle in use. Rhys went back out and reported to Ruth, "he's in the little boys room and groaning unpleasantly". There was a sigh of relief upstairs. After a quick discussion Rhys was told to return to his position and a call was made for one of the officers on the ground floor to get up to the 8th and escort Enrici back to the conference room when he emerged.

While all this was happening Liam got into the Funding Application on his laptop and started completing a payment schedule. It took a minute or so and Bradley sat impatiently tapping his fingers on the table. After a while Liam said to Bradley, "I need your bank details."

"I'll fill them in," he said getting a card out with the details on. Liam turned the screen towards him and he entered the information. "Done," he said and pressed the Pay button.

Dick, two floors up bellowed, "Gotcha! He's pinched the money. Let's go nab him." He and Ruth made to leave the meeting room telling the others to wait there and he'd call them down once it was safe. Meanwhile a confirmation request came through on screen in front of Bradley, he clicked it and saw that £2m had been transferred successfully.

He grabbed his briefcase saying, "I need to check on my boss, he's not well," and rushed out of the office.

"Stop!" shouted Tyrell, but he'd gone. He ran towards the lift lobby. Rhys, taken by surprise, followed as fast as he could. When he got to the lobby, he pushed between several people waiting for the lift. None of them was who he was looking for. Then a voice called from next to the Gents, "he went into the stairwell. I'm waiting for Enrici to come out." It was the officer from downstairs.

In the stairwell Rhys faced a conundrum. Did he go up or down? Down would be more logical, so down he went. Meanwhile the officer guarding the 8th floor gents decided to get Enrici out. Only one cubicle was occupied. He banged on the door, "come out of there Enrici, police!" Nothing happened so he hammered the door and shouted again. The door gingerly opened to reveal an elderly gentleman doing up his flies.

"What's happening?"

"Sorry sir. Police enquiry." He quickly glanced in the other cubicles. No Enrici. This was not good. He knew things were happening in the conference room on this floor, so he made his way there.

It was then that the fire alarm sounded.

As it did so, Dick and Ruth were about to enter the 10th floor lift lobby. They faltered for a moment, then carried on anyway, they needed to arrest Enrici and Bradley. Quickly down to the 8th floor, they were met by Liam and Tyrell. "We've got a problem sir," said a worried looking Tyrell, who then fell silent.

Dick stared at him. "Go on then, what?"

"We've lost them."

"You've done what?" shouted Dick. "Who was guarding the men's toilet?"

The officer in question had just arrived. "Me sir. PC Goffin. I was waiting for Enrici to come out but he didn't. I went in and checked but he wasn't there."

"What? He can't disappear into bloody thin air, go back and look again." PC Goffin duly trotted off, tail well and truly between his legs. He had a feeling this was going to end in a bollocking.

"What about Bradley?" yelled Dick.

"He ran out. PC Evans chased after him but I haven't seen him since."

Ruth put a call out, "PC Evans, check in. Where are you?"

"Right, you two. Go check the gents two floors up and two floors down. Pronto!"

This turned out to be easier said than done. The stairs were now crowded with staff evacuating the building.

Things didn't improve when Dick and Ruth were pestered by a man wearing a yellow safety jacket. "Leave please. Immediately," he insisted.

Dick said, "hold on, I know you're doing your job but we're police officers." He held out his warrant card.

A call came in from Rhys, "In building lobby. No sight of Bradley. Me and two officers are now checking faces going out. Hundreds of them. Yellow Jackets are not letting us stop them so we're missing most."

A call then came in from Liam, "checked gents on 7th and 6th floors. No sign of either of them. Being stopped from coming back up. I'll try to check all others on way down."

This was followed by a call from Tyrell. "Nothing on 9th sir. Just got to 10th and I can see the fire alarm box on the 10th floor has been smashed open."

"Of course, yes. Bugger! Bradley will have set that off to cause a diversion. Well it worked. Ruth call down and get someone to tell whoever is in charge it's a false alarm."

The man in the yellow jacket was now shouting at them to move. "It's a false alarm," Dick shouted back.

"It may be a false alarm to you, but it's my job to get you out. So effing well move!"

"All right, we're on our way." They headed to the stairwell.

Tyrell was still on the call, "I'm afraid there's another problem, sir," he said. "When I checked the data entry after Bradley had scarpered, I noticed the sort code and account number were different to the ones we had on our brief."

"What? You were supposed to …. Christ. If we don't catch them we are going to be very unpopular."

* * *

Having watched Dick and Ruth leave the 10th floor conference room, Sandy had said to Vijay, "Looks as if they've got them," and turning to Wayne, "well done Wayne."

There was no response from Wayne who had his head down tapping away at his laptop and appeared not to hear him. And that was when they heard the fire alarm.

Vijay said, "right guys, it's probably another false alarm but we need to get out of here. Wayne, you'd better leave everything and you can pick it up later."

"Sod that, this is coming with me." He picked up his laptop and joined them walking towards the stairs. Somehow, on the way down the ten flights they got split up and it was only Vijay and Sandy who managed to meet up with Dick and his team outside the building. With a bit of trepidation, Dick gave them the bad news. "They seem to be a bit smarter than we thought but don't worry, we'll catch them." There was a horrified look on Vijay's face, "What about my two million pounds?"

CHAPTER 24

Escape

Tony and Henry had irritated Enrici since the first day they'd met. Then it was an insult to his self-importance when he found he became answerable to them. Things came to a head during the payoff meeting following the Maxadex scam when Henry had told him he wouldn't have been paid if he hadn't agreed to the next deal. That was it, he would find a way of reasserting his position as top dog. He started scheming immediately he left the meeting. Not being the sharpest knife in the drawer it took him a few days to come up with a ploy. His first decision was to continue with this second phase of the operation. However, there would be a twist in his favour. Mind you, it was highly likely this twist would also require him to leave the country. That wasn't so bad, he thought. Retiring comfortably in the sun, joining other old colleagues who'd escaped UK justice, was quite a pleasing prospect.

He would have to bring Bradley and Pegg into the plot of course, but they needn't know all the details, just enough to secure him a large income and the opportunity to scarper if necessary. He was not intending to tell them about this last bit. He would pay them well, but if and when the time came for an escape, they would have to make their own plans. By then he should be well away.

Not only did he plan to double-cross the Robins, he also had a lingering suspicion this whole thing was a setup. He believed the police would want to get an important figure like him behind bars but didn't think they'd go to these lengths. However, stranger things had happened. So he'd have to prepare for that possibility. He called Bradley and Pegg into a meeting. He explained to them what he wanted to do and his concerns about a police stitch-up. They needed to work together to create a perfect master-plan.

So between them, the three villains schemed. Their plan assumed police involvement with a simpler option if they weren't. The key principles were worked out and the finer details would be added at the last minute, once they had been briefed. Enrici then brought a new element into the equation. This involved the final stage in the process of extracting shares from Grace which, he explained, he had been working on independently for some time. He told them this was now in the bag and in exchange for a small bit of assistance, he would very generously share a portion of the proceeds with them both, as a nice little bonus to their venture.

Their carefully laid plan was put into operation the moment Enrici and Bradley arrived at the preparation meeting with Tony and Henry. Pegg had dropped them a block away from the serviced office, then parked in Canada Square. They'd hired a vehicle for the purpose just in case the police were involved and knew his car. A good decision, as unbeknown to them the trackers were still working. Enrici delighted in having an opportunity to put them down over the subject of the clothes they were wearing. He made sure the meeting was as short as possible to give them maximum time to finesse their plan based on the new information provided.

They met Pegg at Pret in Cabot Square Mall for coffee and a sandwich. Pegg had brought with him two briefcases and gave one each to Enrici and Bradley. He planned to scout around the area keeping watch for anything untoward until he heard from them that they were leaving the Brodie Vellum office. They agreed to reconvene outside Waitrose in Canada square before getting away from the area as quickly as possible.

So the operation began. The meeting with the two agency so-called directors was going as expected when Enrici's phone rang and he saw on the screen it was Pegg. He answered it outside the conference room and Pegg immediately started speaking. "Boss, it's a setup. I've been looking into this Brodie Vellum outfit. Not much to worry about on the website but when I look around the web I come across pictures of the chairman. His name is Anthony Goodman. He is the same guy as one of them we've been dealing with, the one who calls himself Armstrong. Not only that, the place is crawling with police, two in the foyer and several circulating. You need to finish and get out of there. I'll be at Waitrose as we agreed."

When Enrici returned to the meeting and said "Joe's finished", it was pre-arranged code telling Bradley the police were involved. Immediately the full plan was put into action. As soon as he knew the financial transaction was taking place Enrici feigned illness and left the room taking his briefcase with him. He hurried to the lift lobby. Out of the corner of his eye saw a man following him. He rightly presumed it would be a plain clothes copper. The larger disabled cubicle was free, so he took that. He heard the outer door open and decided to groan for authenticity's sake. The door then closed again. He just hoped his tail wasn't waiting for him to emerge. The next three minutes were hectic but had been practised many times at home.

He removed his shoes, jacket, shirt and trousers. From his briefcase he took out a business shirt mostly buttoned up already with a tie tied loosely round the neck. This he slipped over his head and tightened the tie. He took out and put on a pair of suit trousers, followed by some black slip-on shoes. A suit jacket followed. He then reached in and took out a dark haired wig which fitted neatly over his slicked back grey hair. Lastly he added a pair of spectacles to his ensemble. He checked his look in a hand held mirror. He almost didn't recognise himself. For security purposes he pulled a cosh from the briefcase and slipped it into the inside pocket of his jacket. His other clothes and mirror were put in the briefcase, which he placed beneath the hand basin.

Now he had to get out. He heard no more sounds from outside the cubicle but to be safe he pressed the flush, then unlocked the door and purposefully strode out of the cubicle with his head down and hand ready to draw the cosh if needs be. Nobody was there. Hopefully his tail had returned to keep watch on the conference room. On the other hand he could be waiting outside in the lift lobby. So once again he swiftly opened the door and keeping his head bowed walked directly to the lift call buttons. He was in luck, nobody there either. He pressed the down button, stepped away, kept his back to the door that led out of the lobby to the offices, and waited.

A moment later he heard that door open. He stood stock still, waiting for the feel of a hand on his shoulder. After a couple of seconds a woman walked past and pressed the up button. He heaved a sigh of relief and over the next minute they were joined by four or five other office workers. A lift going up stopped. The woman got in and it deposited a man who looked at everyone waiting but then parked himself outside the door to the gents. Enrici's suspicion radar clicked in, so he kept his head down. As the lift doors closed he heard someone crash through the main door and rush straight into the stairwell. The down-going lift arrived just as another person banged through the door and hurriedly scanned the lobby. Enrici stepped into the lift and as the doors were closing heard the man by the gents shout, "he went into the stairwell. I'm waiting for Enrici . . ." He couldn't resist a smile as with a hum, the lift began its descent. At the ground floor, the doors opened and Enrici stepped out to the sound of a blaring fire alarm. There were a few people in the lobby looking around wondering what to do. There were also two uniformed policemen, but their attention seemed to be concentrated on the apparent emergency. He casually walked past everybody and out through the main doors.

* * *

While Enrici was doing his quick change act, Bradley was managing the ransom payment. The card he pulled out when Liam turned the screen towards him contained details of an account operated by Enrici. It was in fact a joint account originally set up by Grace's late husband. He had used it as a repository of profits from equity transactions and the like and it included a facility to transfer funds simply, and perfectly legally, to an offshore account. Early in their relationship Enrici had persuaded Grace to let him become a signatory on both of those accounts. There were few funds in them at the time and he explained that he would find it very useful for his business purposes to retain them. At that stage she believed he was a successful businessman and gladly agreed. The offshore account was in Mauritius. It had already allowed him to accumulate a nice little nest-egg out of the way of the UK tax authorities.

Having completed the data entry on screen Bradley had expected Liam to turn it back and complete payment himself. But he paused, so Bradley happily clicked on 'Pay'. Once confirmation came through he rushed out of the conference room and ran to the lift lobby. He knew he would be followed, so instead of going into the Gents he quickly pushed through the exit door to the stairs. He hoped the tail would either go into the Gents on the 8th floor looking for him or down the stairs assuming he was trying to escape. So instead, he ran up two flights to use the toilet on the 10th to undertake a similar transition to Enrici. Before going into the toilet, he noticed the red fire alarm point on the wall, punched it to break the glass, which released the button. That should keep them occupied for a while, he thought.

Bradley followed the same procedure as Enrici but with a different coloured suit, shirt and wig. In addition, he stuck on a small false moustache. He checked everything looked acceptable in his little mirror. It did. The mirror along with everything else was stuffed into his briefcase and shoved behind the bowl. By now fire marshals were banging on doors telling people to get out. "On my way, one second," he shouted back. As he exited the Gents he thanked the marshal directing people to the stairs. He joined an army of other office workers making their slow journey down the stairs to the ground floor. Once there he made for the exit. He heard a Yellow Jacket call "assemble where you see your floor number displayed." Keeping his tall frame stooped, he headed for a big sign with the figure 5 on it. In the confusion nobody took the slightest notice of him walking straight past the assembling office workers and away from the building in the direction of Canada Square. He pulled out his phone and rang Pegg.

* * *

Bradley hadn't noticed that floor 10 were congregating next to floor 5 and without knowing passed within feet of Sandy and Vijay. Having received the news from Dick, Sandy was nothing if not phlegmatic. "Oh dear. I'd better call Tony. He won't be too happy." He made the call and it was answered quickly.

"Is it all sorted?" said Tony excitedly. Sandy gave him the whole story and said Dick seemed to have started organising a search for Enrici's gang.

"Get Wayne to have look where their cars are, they've got trackers on."

"We seem to have lost Wayne for the moment. He said earlier that Pegg's car was still in East London. They must have used one without a tracker."

"I would guess he may be heading for it though. He may know where Enrici's car is too."

"Good idea. I'll find him."

Sandy called Wayne's mobile. He answered quickly, "where are you Wayne?"

"I'm right next to the man holding up a sign with a big ten on it."

"I'll be over." It took Sandy only seconds to get to him. "Enrici and Bradley escaped. Dick is initiating a search now. Can you look at the location of the trackers."

"No problem, I'll link my laptop to the web through my phone." He found a nearby low wall on which to rest his laptop and rapidly woke up the app. "Pegg is still parked in Upminster. Let's see where Enrici is." There were the usual few taps on the keyboard. "Very interesting. He's parked at his golf club." He looked up at Sandy, "heading there do you reckon?"

"Wouldn't be surprised, let's tell Dick"

"Sandy, there's something I need to talk to you about."

But it was to Sandy's fast disappearing back. Wayne followed him, pushing through the crowd.

By the time he'd caught up, Dick was standing with two sorry looking policemen. After finding the alarm that had been set off on the 10th floor, Tyrell had checked the gents and found Bradley's briefcase. The other one was in PC Goffin's hands who, on rechecking the disabled cubicle, had discovered Enrici's. "They changed clothes, look." The briefcases were opened to reveal their original outfits. "They could be in this melee somewhere or already well away."

"Wayne knows where Enrici's car is," said Sandy hopefully.

"And Pegg's," said Wayne. He showed the locations on his laptop. "The trackers are still working so they must have used different transport."

"That's all we've got to go on at the moment. Ruth get this area searched just in case, and we'll get after them." She issued instructions then organised a car to take them to Enrici's golf club. While they waited for their car, she got the local Met boys to go and find Pegg's. "I'll deal with Essex liaison on the way. Wayne can you keep a look out for any movement with those cars and call me if there is." With that their police car arrived and Dick and Ruth were gone, a siren fading into the distance.

Sandy and Vijay looked around rather helplessly. Then Vijay's phone rang. "We've been summoned," he said to Sandy. He turned to Wayne, "It's all been a bit of a shock to the company. We have an urgent senior management meeting about how to handle any fallout. Can we leave you to sort yourself out? This is likely to go on so let's talk tomorrow. Sorry."

"I just wanted a quick word," said Wayne, but as before it was to the backs of the two departing directors. Ah well, tomorrow it is then thought Wayne. Nothing else to do here then, I might as well go home. And that's just what he did.

* * *

While all the action was going on Tony and Henry had filled in time. Tony had given Henry a mini guided tour of the area and then they stopped for a bit of lunch in Cabot Square. They'd almost finished when Sandy's call came in. Henry got more alarmed as Tony's end of the conversation progressed. "Looks as if they've escaped with the money," said Tony as he finished the call.

"That's terrible. After everything we've done," said Henry feeling and looking distraught. They sat in silence for a while. Then cheering up a bit he added, "we do know a lot about him though. He's going to find it hard to disappear. Just have to leave it to the boys in blue I suppose." And with that, like Wayne, they decided to make their way home.

CHAPTER 25

Retribution

Blissfully unaware of fire alarms, millions of pounds being stolen from under the Met's noses and ingenious escapes, Tuppence and Anthony had enjoyed their lunch at Burns Croft. Between the five of them they decided that Tuppence would talk a bit about her life and sing a song or two. "I brought some backing tracks," she said.

"There will be quite a few who won't recognise or remember you I'm afraid," said Bernadette, "although Grace is a big fan!"

Makena added, "I should also warn you that a number of them are rather uninhibited so don't get upset at what they might say or do. If they get fed up they'll probably just leave. Oh, and they don't know you're coming, so it will be a surprise to them."

"Hopefully a good one," said Tuppence laughing.

"I'm sure it will be. We should get going," said Bernadette.

So as everybody at Brodie Vellum was walking downstairs, the little delegation at the care home walked upstairs to the second floor lounge. "You wait here," Bernadette said as they reached the door, "I'll introduce you. I can't stay but I'll see you afterwards." She entered the lounge and stood at the front. "Good afternoon everybody. We have a very special guest here this afternoon who some of you will remember from her acting days. Please give a very warm welcome to the wonderful Tuppence Halfpenny!"

There were a few squeals of delight as Tuppence made her entrance along with the odd 'who' and 'never heard of her', but there was a generous round of applause. A male voice piped up with "nice pair of bozoomers."

"That's enough Eddie," called out Dorota. She looked at Tuppence, smiled and raised her eyebrows.

Tuppence focussed on the source of the comment and said, "Thank you." Her audience was scattered around the packed lounge on easy chairs, sofas and an occasional wheelchair. In the background were three other carers.

"This is a real pleasure," she said, "Bernadette has asked me to tell you a bit about my career and she wondered whether maybe I could sing a song or two. Would you like that?" She heard 'yes please' and 'that would be lovely' along with an 'if you have to', from Eddie. "Why don't I start with a song from Oklahoma?" There was a big chorus of 'yes's'. "I'll sing you the opening number, *Oh What a Beautiful Morning*. Anthony, music please." The backing track started, Tuppence launched into the first verse and an increasing number of voices joined in the choruses. There was long applause at the end of the song. She went on to recount her journey from working class Leeds, through local productions to theatre school and beyond. She told stories about people she'd acted with and the idiosyncrasies that made them seem more accessible. With a couple more songs, an hour seemed to pass in a flash. Only a few residents fell asleep. Two needed the toilet and were helped out by carers and one walked out saying she thought it was supposed to be a magician today. Dorota interrupted eventually and said, "maybe five more minutes Tuppence?"

"OK Dorota. A long while ago I toured in *Sweet Charity* and my favourite song was *Big Spender* so why don't I finish on that." Anthony started the music and Tuppence launched into a rousing rendition. She bobbed around in front of the audience and the second time she got to not popping her cork for every guy she saw, she leant over and ruffled the few locks that still clung to Eddies head. He dropped his walking stick much to the amusement of all. At the end there was lots of clapping and cheering. Everyone seemed to have enjoyed themselves. Tuppence had had a lovely afternoon too.

* * *

While all the fun was going on upstairs Bernadette was head down in her office running Burns Croft. There was a tap on the door and Amy, one of the carers, popped her head round and said that Tuppence was about to finish. "Thanks Amy, are the flowers sorted?"

"They're in the linen cupboard by the lounge."

Then as Bernadette got up to leave her desk there was a crash as the external door flew open and hit the wall. A voice the two of them recognised immediately shouted, "I need to see Grace, and now!" It was Enrici.

Initially startled, the receptionist regained her composure quickly, "I'll see whether she is available," and picked up the phone.

Enrici reached over the counter, grabbed the phone from her hand and threw it into the umbrella stand. "I've had enough of you lot telling me when I can see her and when I can't, she's mine and I'll see her when I want. Now open the door!"

"Mr Enrici. Stop threatening my staff and leave Burns Croft immediately or I'll call the police." It was Bernadette standing beside the now-quivering Amy.

"No you won't," sneered Enrici as Pegg and Bradley entered the building, "open this door." He banged on the door through from reception.

"No. There are vulnerable people here and I'm not having you put them in danger," yelled Bernadette

Enrici responded by grabbing Amy and pushing her against the reception counter. He gripped her throat with his hand, "code, or she's going to get hurt."

Bernadette took a step forward but was stopped by Pegg who had pulled what looked very much like a police baton from his pocket. He lifted it up to his shoulder, "Move, and you get this in your face."

The receptionist called out the code, Bradley entered it and opened the door. "Michael look after these three. Joe, come with me. If she won't sign, we'll take her with us." And with that Enrici, Pegg in tow, went to find Grace.

"Right, in there, all of you, then nobody will get hurt." Bradley indicated the door to Bernadette's office. Daphne, the receptionist, and Amy moved hesitantly. "Hurry, or you'll regret it" shouted Bradley. Bernadette, now standing square on to Bradley, didn't move. She looked him in the eye and said, "You stay out of the way ladies and let me discuss with this animal who he thinks may get hurt."

"What?" He was taken aback by this woman's arrogance.

"You heard. Why don't you leave now and make a run for it, you might be able to get away before the police arrive." As she was speaking she edged slowly towards Bradley, keeping her eye on him all the time. He stared at her incredulously. "Go on, out of that door. Then you won't get hurt," she said.

"Hurt? Who's going to hurt me? You?" Bradley threw his head back and laughed. That was not a good move. Like lightning, she skipped on her left foot and brought her right up into the very tenderest part of his groin with a force neither he, nor the ladies peering through the open office door, could believe. No sooner had he bent double in agony than she landed her left foot on his jaw which lifted his head and he began to topple backwards. Before he could get far, her right foot again caught him square on the nose with the heel leaving a wedge shaped gap where seconds earlier teeth had been.

Accompanied by groans, the spitting of pieces of teeth from his mouth and spurts of blood from his nose, Bradley collapsed in a heap. "Quick Amy, bandages. We need to tie him up. Daphne, call the police." She retrieved the phone from the bottom of the umbrella stand and called 999. They quickly tied Bradley's wrists together, not easy as he was desperately clutching his groin. Then they did the same with his legs. "Add an ambulance to that Daphne," called Bernadette. She dashed into her office, coming back with a large black torch she kept in case of power cuts and emergencies. She gave it to Amy. "If he moves, hit him with it. Hard!" And with that, she chased after Enrici and Pegg.

* * *

Once Enrici and Pegg got through the security door, they had quickly reached Grace's room on the first floor. They found it empty of course as Grace was in the lounge. At the nursing station the duty nurse, seeing Enrici arrive without prior warning was worrying enough, but to be accompanied by another thug was frightening. She sneaked out, ran up the stairs and into the lounge to warn Grace and Dorota, arriving just as Tuppence's applause was dying down. Dorota and Makena were mystified but decided they needed to hide Grace somewhere.

Overhearing the conversation, Anthony instantly clicked into security mode. Enrici was supposed to be in police custody, what was going on? Not only did Grace need to be hidden, so did Tuppence. She was not keen but recognised Anthony was deadly serious and they decided on a communal bathroom next to the lounge. The nurse's description fitted Pegg and the two of them needed to be stopped. Dorota told him where Grace's room was and to take the emergency stairs, it would be quicker.

Down went Anthony. Grace's corridor was deserted. He moved quickly and silently to Grace's room. The door was open. His best hope against the two of them was surprise. In his time he had faced this situation in war zones where usually he had a weapon. Today it would have to be bare hands. He stood back to the wall beside the door. Deep breath. He twisted and rushed in shouting their names loudly. Nobody there, damn! He turned quickly and dashed out to see Pegg emerging from the nursing station stuffing drug packets into his jacket pocket. "Who the hell are you," he shouted,

"Someone who's going to see you locked up," said Anthony in a much calmer voice.

"Really? You think so?" Pegg drew the truncheon from his pocket, flicking it to make it extend. "Not if this has anything to do with it."

Pegg started moving forward, pushing out his left arm and raising the truncheon in his right ready to strike. Face on, well balanced, Anthony waited. He knew the most dangerous part of a weapon like a truncheon was the end furthest from the hand. It moved quickest. So you either stayed out of reach, or got in too close for it to hit you. That was Anthony's plan. Pegg was getting closer and his right arm moved back ready to strike. Just as he began to bring the truncheon down, Anthony leapt forward, his left arm up and turned outwards so any contact would be with the fleshy rather than bony part. He was so quick, it was Pegg's arm that made harmless contact, the truncheon dipping uselessly behind Anthony's left shoulder. At the same time, the base of his right palm came up and struck Pegg squarely under the chin. He was knocked back. In one smooth movement Anthony turned, grasped Pegg's right wrist and twisted it backwards causing him to drop the stick. Anthony seized it, swung round and slammed it into the side of Pegg's head.

That was Pegg's last vertical activity for some time. As he lay flat on the floor, Bernadette arrived having run up the stairs. "Well done, thank you for helping," she said still under the impression that Anthony was just there to put some music on. "Two down, one to go. Where's Enrici, and more importantly, Grace." Anthony explained. "We've called the police," she said.

"We need to secure this guy. Any rope? Maybe bandages?"

"Tons, hold on." She ran to the nursing station.

"I need to find Enrici," said Anthony as she returned. "If he arrives here, you just scarper and find me. I'll sort him out." Bernadette smiled a that-won't-be-necessary type of smile. Anthony ran to the back stairs.

* * *

Enrici, who had come up the main staircase, strode into the lounge just as Anthony reached Grace's room. The worried staff where trying to keep the confused residents calm. In his usual impolite manner he shouted at the nearest carer, who happened to be Dorota, "Where's Grace? I need her here now."

Rapidly thinking on her feet she answered, "her daughter has taken her out for a drive."

"Don't lie to me you foreign bimbo, where is she?" He pushed Dorota over and strode around the room looking at all the residents. Of those who had an inkling of what was happening, a few were whimpering, and a couple were yelling at him to go away. One of those was Eddie. Enrici grabbed him by the scruff of his neck, pulled his face close and screeched, "tell me where she is or I'll rip your eyes out you old fossil."

"I'm already half blind so that won't do any good. Now just bugger off and leave us alone you arsehole." Enrici threw him onto his chair which tipped backwards but narrowly failed to topple over.

"Enrici! Leave these people alone!" He recognised that voice from somewhere.

He looked around to find the source of the call. It was coming from the open doorway.

"You!" he said. "I knew there was something fishy about you."

Tuppence had heard what was going on, told Grace to stay where she was, and went back to the lounge. She repeated in her Yorkshire accent, "leave these people alone. They've done you no harm." She walked towards Enrici, stopping a few yards away.

"Get Grace here or someone's going to pay. My boys will leave this place, and a few of these half dead morons, smashed to pieces. You too, you ugly fat cow."

"Don't let him talk to you like that Tuppence," It was Eddie, brandishing his walking stick.

"Don't worry Eddie. Come here and say that Enrici, you conniving little shit."

Enrici strutted towards her. She could smell his breath and feel drops of saliva hit her face as he spat out, "Where's Grace you ugly fat cow!"

Tuppence's left foot shifted forward, her right arm went back, then with all her strength she delivered a right hook to his nose and left eye. There was a cracking sound and Enrici rocked back on his heels. A cut had opened up on the bridge of his nose. He was dazed and shook his head. Tuppence held her right hand gingerly a bit worried that he hadn't gone down.

Enrici pulled the cosh from his inside pocket, stepped towards her and lifted his arm. Tuppence recoiled. There was then an almighty thump as Enrici disappeared from her eyeline. Eddie had wrapped the handle of his walking stick round Enrici's right leg, heaved with all his might and down went the nasty little man. As he hit the floor, Anthony arrived and with all his weight landed his knee into the middle of Enrici's back knocking the air out of his lungs. He pushed his arm up to his shoulder blades. Enrici squealed. "Move and I'll put your shoulder out of joint." The cosh meanwhile had rolled away and been picked up by one of Grace's friends. She dropped it in her handbag.

Bernadette arrived, "Malcom the porter is looking after Pegg," she said to Anthony. "I guess we should wrap him up like the others. Dorota can you get bandages." It wasn't long before Enrici became the last of the trio of trussed up criminals. "I'll leave you to it, the police should be on their way." She left the lounge.

"What happened?" Anthony asked Tuppence.

"I tried to flatten the little sod but I'm out of practice. Eddie upended him."

"You're hurt Tuppence," said Makena, "let me have a look." She gently took Tuppences hand.

"Ow," winced Tuppence.

"You've probably broken a finger or two. We'll need to get it X-rayed."

* * *

The 999 call made by Daphne had been connected quickly. "Police," she had said, "oh, and an Ambulance." She explained that three men were attacking the care home, had assaulted staff and were threatening residents. Could they hurry please. Needless to say this went straight to the top of the controller's list. Asked a few more questions, Daphne mentioned Enrici's name. This rang alarm bells, they had only recently issued instructions to watch his car. Three police units were immediately dispatched to the scene along with two ambulances.

Dick & Ruth had almost reached the golf club when the call came through. Their police driver had made up lots of time with the judicious use of sirens, blue lights and a flexible attitude to speed limits. He made a quick adjustment to their destination. "Six minutes sir," he said confidently accelerating past a line of traffic.

A couple of minutes later a local police car, siren blaring, careered into Burns Croft car park followed almost immediately by a second. Their occupants jumped out and ran to the front door to be greeted by a very calm Bernadette. "That was quick," she said smiling as they stopped in front of her looking perplexed. "Really glad you're here. We've got things under control. Three of them are trussed up and waiting for you to deal with. Two need hospital treatment. The residents have had a traumatic experience so please don't upset them any further. Follow me."

She turned and led them into reception as the first ambulance arrived. "This is Michael Bradley." They were greeted by the sight of a man bound up like an Egyptian Mummy. Amy had obeyed her instructions diligently. Bradley was still groaning from the damage inflicted to his body.

"What did he do to deserve this?" asked the first policeman.

"We'll give you a complete rundown" said Bernadette, "myself, Daphne and Amy are witnesses to this one. During our scuffle he appears to have lost several teeth. Daphne standing behind the reception counter, rattled them in a plastic cup and handed it to one of the policemen.

Two paramedics walked into the reception area and stared in disbelief at the scene. "I'm afraid he's not very well." Said Bernadette. "Amy, could you explain what happened here and I'll take the policemen upstairs." To the paramedics she said, "there are others needing medical treatment on the 1st and 2nd floors. Daphne, could you get someone to escort them please."

Before she could go any further though, the car carrying Dick and Ruth skidded to a halt at the door. They surveyed the scene and Dick spoke to Bernadette, "Can I assume you are Ms Dixon?"

"I certainly am."

He smiled, "a young man called Wayne has told me all about you. I assume you were responsible for this?" He pointed at Bradley.

She smiled, "yes officer. Self-defence and protecting vulnerable patients."

"And capturing a wanted man in the process. Is Enrici still here?"

"He's upstairs, as is a chap called Pegg, I don't know his first name."

"Maybe you could lead the way. Ruth, could you handle the technicalities please."

"A pleasure boss."

"Pegg is on the first floor," she said as they climbed the stairs. They were confronted with another tightly bound body, this one with a long cut and a large purple bruise on the side of his head. Malcom was standing guard with the truncheon in his hand. Pegg was conscious but at a loss to know what was going on. "He's had a bang to his head from that," she pointed to Pegg's truncheon. "It's his, and one of our visitors relieved him of it." As she spoke Amy arrived with two more paramedics and three police officers. Dick told one of them to secure Pegg in a more conventional manner and stay with him. He, Bernadette and two of the officers then made their way to the 2nd floor.

They heard Enrici shouting before they got anywhere near the lounge. "I recognise that voice," said Dick, "he doesn't sound very happy." They walked into to the room to see yet another reprobate trussed up with bandages around his legs, and wrists tightly bound behind his back. Grace had been given Enrici's cosh by her friend and was standing over him pleading with Anthony to let her use it. So far he had persuaded her not to.

"Let me go you bastard. She owes me money. I'll see you pay for this. Wait til' my boys get their hands on you." Completely unmoved, Anthony had his foot placed securely between Enrici's shoulders.

"Well if it isn't Lawrence Enrici," said Dick bending down in front of the prone captive. "You and your little gang seem to have met your match."

"You've got nothing on me!"

"Well, in addition to a size 10 boot, we've got a list as long as your arm." Ruth had just joined him, "Book him would you Detective Sergeant." He turned to Anthony, "is your name by any chance Anthony?"

"Indeed it is. I'm here with Tuppence who walloped Enrici and is just having her hand bandaged up. She's been entertaining the residents. We thought these guys would have been locked up by now. By the way, have a look in Pegg's pocket. I think he stole some drugs from the nursing station." Ruth made a note.

Dick chuckled to himself, things were falling into place. "The local force can deal with Enrici and the others. I'd better update you on what's been going on."

Bernadette said, "use my office. I'll need to spend a bit of time here sorting things out."

Ruth merrily booked Enrici and took control of supervising his departure to the local police custody suite and the other two to hospital. Dorota took Anthony and Dick downstairs where Tuppence was already sitting in Bernadette's office.

Daphne brought them tea and biscuits and Dick relayed the story of the day's action. "To be honest, we should have caught Enrici and Bradley before they left the building but we delayed just a bit too much. I'm afraid we were too late to stop them diverting the money into Enrici's own bank account too. Hopefully we'll be able trace that and recover it at some stage. The local boys will need to take statements from you before you leave."

"I'd better call my wife, we are picking her up on the way home," he explained to Dick. He looked at his phone which like Tuppence's was on silent, "some missed calls from Henry," he told her.

Before Anthony could make the call to Alesha, Bernadette appeared. "Well, what a day," she said. "We have a few distressed residents but some very excited ones too. They've never seen anything like it and as Eddie put it, the bad guys lost! Lots of them were delighted to meet you as well Tuppence. We really appreciate you making the time, and if it hadn't been for you and Anthony, those guys may have got away and taken Grace with them." Bernadette paused then called, "Dorota, can you come in." And in she came with a huge bunch of flowers to present to Tuppence.

Dick explained that he and Ruth had to tie up loose ends with the Essex police, thanked everyone for their help and said he would be in touch. It didn't take too long for Tuppence and Anthony to make their statements and they were soon saying their goodbyes to Bernadette and the staff. Anthony behind the wheel, they left to pick up Alesha. On the way Tuppence read a WhatsApp from Henry saying things had gone wrong and the gang had escaped. He said it was too depressing to talk on the phone and would update everyone tomorrow. Tuppence decided not to reply that they had some better news, it could wait. It wasn't long before one came in from Wayne requesting an urgent meeting tomorrow afternoon. Henry responded fixing 2.00pm at Tony's. As they began their journey up the M11 Tuppence and Anthony regaled Alesha with the story of the day's events. However, it wasn't long before the strong painkillers she had been given by Makena saw Tuppence fall fast asleep. It had been a tumultuous day.

CHAPTER 26

Reflection

Not everyone slept well that night. Anthony woke up in a hot sweat from a bad dream, hand to hand fighting in a jungle somewhere. Tony laid awake worrying that it was all his fault that 2 million pounds disappeared into Enrici's evil little hands. And Tuppence found it difficult to keep her right hand comfortable, although that was alleviated somewhat by the satisfaction she gained from walloping Enrici. In the morning she was picked up by Alesha who took her to the Minor Injuries Unit at Cromer Hospital. The x-ray revealed only one broken finger. It was strapped to the adjoining one and she was told it would probably be like that for six weeks.

Tuppence hadn't been back long and was just pouring her and Alesha a cup of tea when Bob Henderson rang. "How's your hand auntie Dora? I hear you floored Enrici."

"I did, with a bit of help from one of the elderly residents. I broke a finger but that was my fault, I'm out of practice."

"Well I thought you'd like to know, everybody's elated around here. About the arrests that is. There's a bit of sheepishness about the misplaced two million mind you."

"Not sure what our friends in Brodie Vellum are going to say. Do you reckon you'll be able to trace it?"

"I'm sure we'll get it back, although I don't know when. Anyway, thank you for doing our job for us. All we had to do was pop in and arrest them."

"You're very welcome. I need to thank you too Bob. Goodness knows what sort of trouble we would have got ourselves into if you hadn't become involved. So what's happening with those scoundrels?"

"Enrici is going mad, threatening us with everything under the sun. The other two are in hospital, although Bradley should be out this morning. He's tried to speak apparently but most of what he says comes out as whistles. Pegg's had a scan but it doesn't look as if there's any permanent damage more's the pity. None of them will get bail, so they've each started a long stretch. Anyway must go but I'll get back when I have more news."

A bit later Bernadette rang to ask how her hand was and to thank her for entertaining the residents. She said Eddie's kudos had gone through the roof and that Grace was a changed woman looking forward to moving out on Monday. They took their leave of one another, promising to keep in touch.

* * *

The team assembled in Tony's apartment at 2.00pm. There was a mix of exhilaration, concern and consternation, depending upon who you were. Everyone welcomed Margaret for the first time who was there not knowing quite what to expect. Tuppence held a small scarf in her hand hiding her strapped-up fingers. She would pick the right moment to reveal it. Wayne appeared with a large document case which he placed beside his chair. Willie, now used to these gatherings, settled comfortably on Tuppence's lap.

Tony, not his normal ebullient self, stood up and said, "ladies and gentlemen, before we go any further I need to apologise. It was me that came up with this hair-brained scheme and I should have known it was fraught with risks and very little chance of success. I have to report that yesterday we failed to capture Enrici and his gang. Not only that, they got away with two million pounds of my company's cash." The only two Robins who were totally in the dark were Harry and Margaret. They were both crestfallen. None of the others said a word. "I can only tell you third hand what happened because Henry and I were not there. I'm sure Wayne can throw more light onto it. But putting it simply, Enrici and Bradley, having ensured the ransom had been paid into their account, not ours, got out of the room, changed clothes so they could blend in with other office workers, set the fire alarm off as a diversion, then got away in the confusion. I've not plucked up enough courage to talk to my agency colleagues yet, but I don't think they will be too pleased.

Margaret particularly tried to console a clearly upset Tony, and Harry said there was always a chance this would happen and that everyone had tried their best. Tuppence and Anthony trying not to smile, glanced at one another surreptitiously. Tuppence spoke first. "Actually Tony, things are not quite as bad as you think." In the blink of an eye, she had the floor. "When Enrici and Bradley escaped from Brodie Vellum's office they met up with Pegg and went to the care home to get Grace to sign over the shares."

"Hold on, you were there then weren't you?" said Henry looking concerned.

"We were indeed, I'd just finished my performance. The applause was ringing in the rafters when they burst in. I'll tell you now, they did not enjoy their visit to Burns Court as much as I did." She didn't need the encouragement she received to continue.

"I'll give you a chronological analysis of what happened. Enrici and Pegg violently broke through the security door while Bradley tried to imprison Bernadette and two staff in her office. His downfall was he didn't realise she was a kick boxing champion. She broke his nose, rearranged most of his front teeth and seriously limited his potential for future procreation. Then they trussed him up from head to toe in bandages. Upstairs a nurse rushed in to tell us Enrici and Pegg were on the loose and after Grace. So she and I were bundled unceremoniously into a bathroom by this man here," she pointed at Anthony. "He then went to confront them. Anthony tell everyone what happened next."

"I went down to Grace's room to find them but they were not there. I went back into the corridor and there was Pegg. He'd been stealing drugs from the nursing station. He pulled a police truncheon out and tried to hit me with it. Unfortunately for him he committed the cardinal sin of failing to think about defence as well as attack. So he lost. Somehow he received a heavy blow to the side of his head with his own truncheon and went to sleep. Bernadette arrived and tied him up with more bandages." By now Henry and Tony were cheering up somewhat and joined the others with applause and congratulations.

Tuppence took over. "While Anthony was doing his demolition job on Pegg, Enrici arrived in the lounge. He threatened the old people and carers and demanded to know where Grace was. I could hear all this from the bathroom and wasn't having that, so came out and told him to stop. He recognised me from Maxadex and called me an ugly fat cow." Henry couldn't resist a chuckle. "Ugly I can cope with. Even cow. But fat, no chance. I've lost 2 stone. So I punched him. Trouble is I didn't get the swing quite right. He was about to hit me back when an old gentleman called Eddie took his feet from under him with the handle of his walking stick and he ended up flat on the floor. Anthony arrived just in time and sat on him. That was the end of Enrici. Unfortunately it left me with a broken finger. Hence," she revealed her hand and held it high as a trophy.

Amid much whooping and clapping along with some sympathy for Tuppence, Willie decided it had now become too raucous, jumped from her lap and made his way out through the cat flap. Tony took over. "So, against all the odds, we achieved two of our objectives by landing Enrici's gang in custody and preventing him taking money from Grace. The only problem is, they now have my company's two million pounds hidden away somewhere."

"That's terrible," said Harry. "After everything they have done to help us."

"Could I say something?" It was Wayne interrupting the proceedings. "I'm sure you remember that during the Maxadex pay-off meeting Enrici seemed to issue some sort of threat." There were a few nods. "That worried me, so last week I inserted a bit of technical jiggery pokery between the laptop the Met would use and mine so I could keep an eye on what was going on. So I was able to see that Bradley entered different account details. Before the message went to the bank I quickly changed it back to what it should be. The £2 million isn't lost, it's sitting in the Sillingham Robins account."

There were gasps of disbelief, then cheers and Henry did a jig round the room. Tuppence jumped up and gave Wayne a squeeze. "You really did that?" said an incredulous Tony. "Have you told Vijay and the police?'

"I rang Vijay just before I came here. He seemed to be quite pleased."

"I bet he is!" Tony said to Tuppence, "why don't you call your friend Bob. I'm sure he'd like to know."

"Great idea." Tuppence put her phone on speaker and dialled Bob. It was answered very quickly.

"Hello auntie Dora, how's your hand?"

"It was painful but now it's getting better by the minute. Bob, you know our little group of mainly decrepit old aged pensioners captured that gang of extortionists for you."

"Ok, don't rub it in."

"And the Met's main contribution was misplacing two million pounds."

"Where are you going to with this auntie?"

"Well, we thought you'd like to know, Wayne diverted it to the Sillingham Robins account."

There was a lengthy silence and then the sound of someone desperately trying to stifle laughter, finally giving up. "How the hell did he do that?"

"I've no doubt he could run some seminars for you on the subject."

"Has anyone told Superintendent Sargent?"

"No, we thought we'd give you that pleasure. Now I must go, I think we might just be about to have a celebration."

"Thanks, Auntie Dora. I'll be in touch."

"There is something else," said Wayne. The room quietened. "Remember our original objective? It was to get Harley's cash back." There were nods of agreement round the room. Well, while I have been working with my friends in the Met over the last few weeks, we've talked about how that could happen. Firstly, Harley would have to come clean about losing it in the first place. Then they'd have to find out where Enrici's money was. After that there would be a long drawn out court process to get it. So I came to the conclusion that there was only a small chance that Harley would ever be repaid and none at all if we couldn't find where Enrici had stashed his loot." There was a bit of discussion on the subject but essentially everyone agreed.

"So a few weeks ago I asked Bob's people whether they'd like me to start the search for Enrici's cash and they gave me their blessing. We already knew about a couple of bank accounts of course and it didn't take me too long to find another one. I discovered that funds paid in to that account were transferred almost immediately to a bank in Mauritius. I followed the trail of Harley's two payments and that's where they ended up. The Mauritius account was stacked full of cash. Now what's really interesting is that those two accounts are held jointly with Grace although there is no evidence she's accessed them, certainly not for at least three years."

"So I contacted Bernadette who put me in touch with Grace's daughter. I explained the situation and she is so grateful for what we've done she offered to help. She holds Grace's power of attorney and presumably unbeknown to Enrici has access to these accounts. So I asked her to transfer some money back to the UK. I created an account in a fictional name in a different bank and she transferred £150,000 into it. This was then drawn out in cash and the account closed. It's unlikely anyone will notice it ever existed." Wayne flipped opened the document case, "and here it is. Over to you Harry."

Initially, there was a stunned silence. Then there was a loud shriek from Tuppence. Anthony and Tony doubled up laughing. Henry clapped and cheered. Margaret, not knowing quite what to do, sat with her mouth wide open. Harry, initially wide-eyed and giggling said, "What happens if you're found out? It's illegal Wayne!"

"Technically that's true, but ethically in my view, it's not. Anyway, I covered all my tracks so won't be found out as long as it stays between these four walls. Grace's daughter won't say a word. I just wanted to honour our Robin Hood credentials and leave a legacy for Ken." That swung it. They all bought in. Margaret spoke up, "This is quite a baptism of fire. You're on the moral high ground Wayne and I appreciate your thought. My mouth is firmly shut."

"Right," said Tony. "It looks as if that's our job done and as Tuppence has just said, it's time for a celebration. Tuppence, as you're standing up could you get the glasses, I'll get the champagne." She could only manage one glass at a time and that was left-handed, so Harry helped. Within a couple of minutes a cold bottle was opened and everybody toasted the success of the venture. Willie's cat radar had obviously clicked in as he returned to sit contentedly in the middle of the gathering.

"We should have a photo," pronounced Henry.

Harry said," I'll pop down and get my camera, we'll need time lapse if we're all going to be in it" It didn't take long for him to fetch the camera, set it up on a tripod and take several time lapse pictures. Willie took centre stage in Tuppence's arms. "I'll download them and send copies to everyone."

The celebration extended to another bottle and then another. Not a lot was going to get done by anyone this afternoon. Henry, for quite some time, sat quietly with a broad grin on his face. After a while, he stood up, "Ladies and gentlemen, there were many others involved in the venture beyond us in this room. Without them, we would never have succeeded. I propose that we have a celebration party sometime in the not-too-distant future and invite them all." It was a suggestion endorsed by all present.

* * *

Over the next few weeks a grand event was arranged for a month's time on the Sunday. The two senior policemen were invited along with the two Brodie Vellum directors, Diego, Bernadette and Poppy and Trevor. Partners were included of course, along with Margaret's son John. Michelle had agreed to close the restaurant for the day and Brodie Vellum insisted on funding the whole occasion.

In the intervening period, the Sillingham Robins began to return to their normal lives. However, for all of them, normality would never be quite the same. Wayne was seriously benefiting from the adventure. Vijay had contracted him to put in place a top-end security system and more work appeared from the Metropolitan Police. An added benefit was that he could spend time in London with his now very good friend Diego.

Harry was a changed man. He still liked being a bit prickly in his business dealings but he had a bunch of friends who he was able to join on the bench occasionally and they had instituted a regular Friday night visit to the pub. He and Tony replayed their foreshortened game of golf and the handicap system being what it is, he won. And as part of a private resolution to relax a bit more, he and Sofia spent more time on painting expeditions along the north Norfolk coast.

Tuppence energetically pursued her sensible eating and exercise regime, often walking along the path to Weybourne and always pausing for a few moments by the spot where Ken fell from the cliff. An unintentional impact of her regime was that she now needed a new wardrobe of smaller clothes. So there were plenty of visits to Norwich often alongside Alesha, Sofia or Margaret. These four, and occasionally Elsie, also instituted regular coffee and bubbly outings.

Tony was busy handing over to the new Chairman. He also formally took control of the Good Causes Fund and began to think about the best way to run it. Then his daughter had a weekend away and wondered whether he could look after the twins. He asked Tuppence whether she could help out again and she jumped at the opportunity. She rather liked the pseudo-Granny role. They had a lovely time travelling along the coast, bathing at Holkham, and taking a boat trip to see the seals at Blakeney Point. The highlight was a trip to the End-of-the-Pier show in Cromer.

Henry had taken on the job of organising the celebration and very successfully dished out all the jobs to everyone else. He would however chair the whole event. Following his sartorial success at Tuppence's party, he wanted something special for this role. With difficulty Elsie persuaded him against a bright red suit because, she said, it made him look like cabin crew from a budget airline. Instead, he got away with a green velvet dinner suit with a frilly shirt. Having gone through this trauma, she did at least get something special for herself too.

Margaret was still coming to terms with life without Ken. She found the freedom unsettling. For years she had never been able to do anything spontaneous, always had to put the care and safety of Ken first and had almost no time to call her own. She felt guilty about shopping for a new party outfit. This was where Alesha came into her own. She'd spent years dealing with serious cases of mental anguish. She was able to gently guide her through the minefield of putting herself first. She also turned out to be a top-notch fashion advisor and made sure Margaret found something that was perfect for the occasion.

On the surface, the least affected was Anthony. He still had a full-time job. But he did manage the occasional diversion to the bench and was a staunch Friday night regular. His PTSD was still a recurrent problem but since he'd been involved with the team it seemed to have eased. He had even begun to open up about some of his issues, usually to Henry who turned out to be a good listener. Maybe some of his own traumatic experiences as a lifeboatman helped.

* * *

The party was a smart affair. Long evening dresses, black ties and full highland dress for Bob. The restaurant's usual warm and cosy atmosphere had been augmented with some creative decoration by Diego. The staff were all from the Bennett family dressed neatly in black outfits. The menu was firmly based on Norfolk produce and the surrounding sea. Ken's jazz recordings played softly in the background. Before the main course arrived, Henry, who had somehow obtained a gavel, called the assembly to order. "Ladies and Gentlemen, the time has come to honour one of our number who sadly cannot be with us. He is remembered by those who knew him with love and affection, and we all miss him. Please raise your glasses. To Ken." Then there was a moment of quiet before the hubbub revived.

As coffee was served, and with much Old Time Music Hall gusto, Henry banged his gavel again and declared loudly and with a very slight slur, "Ladies and gentlemen may I have your attention. I would like to introduce Commander Robert Henderson from the illustrious Metropolitan Police Force."

There were claps and cheers as Bob stood up. "Firstly, may I thank you for your invitation to this lovely event. I'm not so sure we deserve it. After all, you did all the planning, secured the ransom and captured the criminals. All we had to do was arrest them. I'm sure the three of them will rue the day they crossed your path. I have a small presentation to make." Dick handed him a framed document. "This is a letter from my boss, the Commissioner of the Metropolitan Police." There were a few Oh's and Ah's. "I'll quote one sentence. 'The actions of your group of concerned citizens in helping bring these people to justice is exemplary and demonstrates cooperation between police and public of which we should all be justly proud'." This was greeted by a round of cheers and clapping. Bob handed the framed letter to Henry.

Still standing, Henry banged his gavel again to quieten the applause. It was plain to see he enjoyed his role as chairman. "Somebody else would like to say a few words. I call on Bernadette Dixon from the Burns Croft Care Home."

Bernadette stood to approbation from round the tables. "Thank you for inviting me. This is wonderful. A few months ago Tony and Harry arrived at my care home with a cock and bull story about elderly abuse. I must have been having a good day because I would normally have slung them out on their ears. But it turned out they were right. Grace, one of our residents, was being abused both financially and psychologically by that scoundrel Enrici."

"I knew you were plotting to get him arrested, but I didn't know it would eventually happen in my care home. I'm not complaining. If you had not made that first approach, we wouldn't have known what was happening and that horrible little man would probably have bankrupted Grace. So I would just like to say a heartfelt thank you from me, but more importantly from Grace and her daughter." Applause once again rang round the restaurant. "There is one final message I must pass on. It's to Tuppence from walking-stick-wielding Eddie. He asked me to say that anytime you're passing he can lay on a good time for you in his room!" There were hoots of laughter and a 'you're in there girl' from Henry.

Henry was about to bang his gavel once more when Harry stood up and said "May I say a few words, Henry?"

"Of course my boy. Off you go."

"I'm well aware of my reputation. Most of it is well deserved. But it's amazing how the kindness and friendship of a few people can get you to take a look inward and soften some of the sharp edges. Those few people are sitting around these tables and I'd like to thank you all for your tolerance. Now when we discovered that the project was a success, I took a photo of the group. You don't know this but I'd rather be an artist than an undertaker and thought it would be good to turn that scene into a painting. So I did and I have it here."

Sofia handed it to Harry. "However, as Henry said earlier, one person was missing. With a bit of help from Wayne's funeral slide show, I got a photograph and managed to incorporate Ken into the picture." He held it up and there were some audible gasps from Harry's audience. "I'd like you to have it Margaret."

Harry walked over and handed her the painting. Margaret, completely dumbstruck, just stared at it. A queue formed to take a look. Ken had been added standing beside Margaret dressed not in his saggy jogging bottoms and red pullover but in jeans and a shirt pulled from one of the holiday photographs. Margaret stood and hugged Harry.

"Thank you so much. This is a real treasure."

And with that Henry banged his gavel for the last time. "On with the entertainment. Trevor!" The party continued until way after midnight with music, entertainment and dancing. While capturing the criminal gang was a service to the wider community, the friendships that had been maturing over the last few months were of immense value to the Sillingham Robins themselves. And there was a new friendship born. Bernadette and Dick Sargent arranged to meet the following week to progress their mutual interest in neoclassical architecture. Or at least that's what he told Bob.

Everyone arriving back at Sillingham House was exhausted. Only Tuppence took up Tony's offer of a nightcap. She politely declined the offer of hot chocolate but did accept another glass of bubbly. It was a clear night and they stood on the terrace gazing over the sea towards the twinkling lights of the windfarm in the distance. They didn't say much. They were both simply content to soak in the view, the echo of a wonderful evening and the warmth of their ever-growing friendship. Willie contentedly sat beside Tuppence. Life had changed for him too. It had all started as he flew tail-first through the balcony door and bounced down from branch to branch until he hit the ground. But he was nothing if not a philosophical cat. That was only one life. He had another eight to go.